Acclaim for

Everywhere
I've Never
Been

"Rich with the romance of Italy and haunted by shadows of the past, Daisy Henkle's *Everywhere I've Never Been* is as unforgettable as its characters. With captivating storytelling that weaves threads of magic with mystery, Peter and Eileen's tale speaks to the heart and reminds us that love and grief are not bound by time. Readers won't want to miss this *bellissimo* novel that is both poignant and powerful."

~ SARA ELLA, award-winning author of the *Unblemished* trilogy and *The Wonderland Trials*

"The perfect summertime read that's full of intrigue, romance, and learning to find yourself. Readers will want to jump back into this sweet, heart-tugging story as soon as they finish!"

~ MORIAH KELLY, author of *At All Costs*

Everywhere I've Never Been

Everywhere I've Never Been

DAISY HENKLE

MAU LOA PUBLISHERS

Everywhere I've Never Been

Copyright © 2025 by Daisy Henkle

MAU LOA PUBLISHERS

ISBN: 979-8-9986804-3-4 (paperback)

Cover Artist: Vivien Reis

FOR ALL EVILS THERE ARE TWO REMEDIES –

TIME AND SILENCE.

~Alexandre Dumas,

The Count of Monte Cristo

PROLOGUE

I never imagined that sweet revenge would taste bitter in my mouth.

My chest is rising and falling. My heart is pounding. Palms sweating. Eyes blurring.

The world is still moving, and yet time has stopped–at least for me. I squeeze the handle of the gun and wince at the weight of it in my shaking hands.

As I stand motionless, images run through my mind like a moving picture. Images that used to be full of warmth and light, but are now tainted by the shadow that fell over my family. The shadow that fell over my life.

The cause of that darkness is not more than ten feet away, and I know that this is my chance. It's like all the great heroes in the books I've read–the ones who do everything they can to avenge those they care about. But I'm not a hero. I never have been. Not to myself, at least. Still, there were once people who believed in me enough to give me that title. They've been gone for a long time,

and I didn't think I'd ever have anyone else. But then . . .
there was her.

She made me believe in myself again. She made me
remember the person I used to be. There was a time when
I had all the confidence in the world–back when I thought
I could fix everything. Back when I thought I could protect
the ones I loved from the evils of this world. Oh, how
wrong I was . . . and how wrong she is.

Time is a strange thing. People say that it's constant,
determined by the planets in the sky–but I don't believe it.
Time is always moving differently, depending on the
person. And now, finally, it is my time. My time to make
things right again–once and for all.

As my thoughts continue racing, the world that once
moved in slow motion now begins to speed up. Colors and
sounds whirl around me as my heart seems to beat out of
my chest.

I hear someone call my name.

I

PETER

VENICE, ITALY
SUMMER, 1938

The salty smell of water. The sound of waves splashing softly. The feel of a light breeze mixed with warm, golden sunlight which plays across my face.

For a few brief seconds, my senses enjoy waking up to these things. I let my hand run over the cool, smooth wood beneath me, damp with morning dew–and just like that, I remember where I am, and who I am.

My eyes opening slowly, I take a moment to stare up at the light blue sky. I'm laying down on my back, the gondola I've been sleeping in rocking back and forth. The motion is so calming that I am tempted to let it lull me back to sleep. I almost don't want to get up–the world seems so much sweeter, and life seems so much easier, as long as I'm in my gondola on the water, just watching and listening to the people passing by. But I can't stay here forever.

Taking a deep breath, I sit up and glance around. I can tell that it's early in the day based on the scarce amount of people walking through the streets and the small number of boats moving on the water. The waves are gentle, barely rocking the gondola, and this makes it easy for me to hop out of the boat and onto the short dock, grabbing my pair of worn shoes as I do so.

Rubbing the sleep out of my eyes, I stand on the dock and look out at the sparkling water–the water of *la mia bella Venezia*, my beautiful Venice. The city is framed against the pale blue sky like a painting, the outlines of buildings reaching up to the heavens. I can almost see activity beginning to ripple throughout the city as everyone wakes up and begins their days–a sign that it's time to begin mine. With that, I turn and run down the nearest alleyway, my bare feet slapping against the wet cobblestones.

As I run, I glance into the windows of the small shops that are tucked away inside the alley. Signs of life are just beginning to appear inside as their owners begin setting up for a day of tourists, women buying groceries, and children looking for something fun to do with their summers.

Hearing some laughter and excited chatter, I look up and see a few women hanging their laundry outside their windows. A mix of dresses and various articles of clothing flutter in the wind like flags. Seeing me, the women stop their conversations to wave and call down in melodic voices, "*Buongiorno*, Peter."

I wave back, squinting from the bright sunlight, and reply, "Good morning." As I walk past their doors, their husbands come out, most headed to work as gondoliers, shop owners, or artists. Each pays me a friendly nod in greeting, and I return it.

It doesn't take long for me to reach my destination, mainly because I know it so well. My feet move quickly, and I feel as if I'm flying. For the most part, I like to run everywhere. There's always so much to see and do that I can't seem to stop moving–unless I'm in my gondola. There, I can observe the world around me without any interruptions.

Before I know it, I'm standing in front of *La Libreria di Maggio*. Maggio's Bookshop is an average-sized brick building, with a window display that stretches all the way across the front. It's my favorite shop in all of Venice, and not just because it's filled to the brim with books. No, what makes the bookstore special is its owner: *Signor* Maggio.

Peering through the window, I see that Signor isn't in sight, so I turn and lean against the clay brick wall, simply waiting and listening to the ever-present sound of water splashing. Crossing my arms and resting my head against the wall, I close my eyelids–but not for long.

My eyes detect a new source of light, and I open them to see Signor walking around inside the building, bringing the bookstore to life. His tall frame moves around in the shadows; even though he must rely on a cane, which reduces the appearance of his true height, he still towers over me. However, he is the type of man whose physical appearance and stature are welcoming rather than intimidating.

After he's turned on all three of his green-and-blue-patterned Venetian glass lamps, he walks over and opens the door, bells jingling. I grin and rush over, bounding right past him and into the store with a hurried, "*Buongiorno*." In my eagerness, I almost knock into some teetering piles of old books, and on instinct, I reach out to make sure they're stable.

"Good morning, Peter," replies Signor Maggio, a warm smile creeping across his olive-colored cheeks and reaching his eyes.

Signor isn't old yet–in fact, he can't be more than forty-five–but he has the face of a man who has seen a lot in his life . . . most of which I'm sure I've never heard about. Although his cane–which he is forced to rely on due to an injury from the Great War–has the effect of tricking strangers into initially thinking he's slightly older, and although his eyes are filled with stories of harsher times, I see Signor Maggio for who he really is. He is a man whose capacity to dream has not been tainted or repressed by the difficulties of his past. "Still as spritely as ever, I see. School did not take much energy out of you?"

I scrunch up my face in distaste. "School? No, no–I don't go often enough."

Even as I'm busy running around the shop, inspecting every detail to see what's changed since last week, I catch a glimpse of disapproval on Signor Maggio's face. I stop moving long enough to return the look with a shake of my head. "You know that's not for me, Signor."

The man shakes his head and sits down in the old wooden chair behind his desk, organizing the stacks of books and papers that sit in front of him. "I *never* know what's 'for you,' Peter. One day, you tell me you like to read–the next, you say you don't go to school! You know, you need school to learn how to read, and write. Besides, what would the good people of this city say when they knew you were taking your education for granted?"

I sigh and begin browsing through one of the many shelves of books. Their titles jump out at me from their leather binding, urging me to succumb to their pages and to let the words swallow me whole. My fingers are itching to reach out and grab one of them, but I use all of my self-control and refrain from doing so. "They *do* know. I'm not sure they care, either. If they did, I bet I'd wake up every morning to find them all standing over me, trying to get me to go back. That's what they did to Matteo Bianchi—and boy, was he mad. His mother let all the crazy women inside, and they were all yelling at him and calling him a *forcellino*, and saying that if he didn't go back to school he would be a no-good, lazy–"

"That's not the *point*, Peter," says Signor Maggio sternly. "You have a very special gift. To be able to remember everything you read, word-for-word, and to remember each detailed conversation you've ever had with anyone—that is something you must treasure. Those people are just trying to help you. And besides . . ." Signor stops talking suddenly and lets his eyes shift back and forth, checking to make sure that we're alone. "You are lucky that you were not recruited years ago." He lowers his voice, a sudden tone of urgency underlying his words. "Recruited by the *Balilla*."

An image flashes through my mind of straight-faced young boys in crisp uniforms and hats. For me, the many years that the *Balilla* was in operation were defined by much running and hiding on my part. I hate when Signor Maggio brings them up; those are years that I'd rather forget. I've never wanted to go to school—but to be recruited for a group that Signor Maggio calls "a Fascist youth organization" always seemed like a fate worse than death. Sometimes, they were so distant . . . and other times, it was like the threat of my recruitment was waiting right at Signor Maggio's front door—often literally.

Shivering, I ignore Signor's comment and circle back to the subject of school. "The people from the school know where I live. They could find me any time." I walk through the store and find myself in front of an old mirror, its golden edges intricately designed. I observe my reflection in it, looking up and down.

Signor Maggio shakes his head and leans forward in his chair. He runs a hand over his head, thin streaks of gray peeking out from under his black hair. "A gondola is not your home, *caruso*. It is not anyone's home, but especially not the home of a thirteen-year-old boy. I only gave it to you to fix up, and to use on the water. I don't know how many times I've told you to stay here, in the shop, but do you listen? No— you say you'd rather sleep in a boat."

A small, crooked smile creeps onto my face as I find traces of my home in my reflection, with smudges of dirt on my face and spots on my old clothes, and I nod firmly. "That's right— and it's my home if I say it is."

Signor Maggio sighs and throws up his hands in surrender, smiling in spite of himself. "*Mi arrendo!* I give up; I cannot reason with you. Now, be a saint and try to clean yourself up before customers arrive."

I grin at his words; Signor likes to tell me to 'be a saint' to remind me that I'm named after St. Peter. He points upwards to motion where I should go, but I already know. Rushing to the back of the store, I find the winding, narrow staircase hidden behind overcrowded shelves. I bound up the stairs two at a time, and reaching Signor's room, which features a mirror and water basin, I do what Signor Maggio said and try to clean myself up.

Grabbing the small comb that's sitting next to the basin, I yank it through my thick hair, which I always allow to grow until Signor makes me trim it. The only time I ever tidy my hair is when I help Signor Maggio, and I wince from the first yank. When it's good enough, I bend over and splash my face with a little water from the basin. I don't bother using much soap, which results in leftover dirt on my face. I don't care; in my mind, it shows that I, Peter Chiappetta, am a true Venetian.

Signor Maggio always says that he wants his shop to make a good impression on others, and he can't achieve this goal if I'm there dripping water and muddying up the place. This is also the reason he makes me wear shoes while I'm with him. Outside of the shop, I never wear shoes; I like the feel of cool, wet cobblestones under my feet. I also like having the freedom not to wear shoes, even if I wanted to. I have more freedom than most kids my age, and I know how to take advantage of it. Today, however, is not one of those days. Still, it's worth it. It's worth it, because I get to be here.

When I'm in the bookshop, it's like stepping into another world—or a thousand other worlds, all wrapped into one. I would not normally go so far as to clean myself up, except for the fact that it allows me to spend my days in the bookshop, and with Signor Maggio. Although I pretty much raised myself, Signor Maggio has always been like a kind of father to me. I respect him, and he respects me. He understands the love I have for books, and he supplies me with as many as I can read. He also gives me a home for whenever the weather turns cold, and I'm forced to move indoors.

Leaning onto the wall to balance myself, I pull on my restrictive black leather shoes one foot at a time. With one last look in the mirror, I bound back down the stairs and stand at attention next to Signor Maggio, just in time for the first customer to step through the doors.

For the next few hours, the store is constantly filled with people, some speaking Italian and most speaking foreign languages. These are mainly tourists, and although I'd like to help them, the only people I'm able to assist are Italian. I can't understand any language but my own, so I let Signor help the tourists. Even though he can only speak broken English and German, and next to no French, it's much more than I can speak.

I watch as Signor Maggio heartily assists each customer, whether it's a woman in a beautiful floral dress or a man in a smart-looking jacket and bow tie. He shows them his personal favorite shelf full of the oldest, most beautiful books, explaining their history in detail. Later, he waves goodbye to them when they leave—usually with a leather-bound book in their hands.

I marvel at the way Signor Maggio knows just how to speak to each customer, and knows precisely what sort of book they'd be interested in. At the same time, it makes sense to me–Signor is a storyteller. He can see the words in a person's soul the second he lays eyes on their face. I wish I could be more like him, content in his little shop, happy to spend day after day with his books. I love books, but I do not want to simply read them. I want to *write* them–and to do this, I need to see new places and do new things. I cannot stay in *Venezia* forever.

2
EILEEN

CHICAGO, ILLINOIS
SUMMER, 1961

Chicago is my favorite place to be on a Saturday afternoon. The bright buildings are sparkling as they reach up to the sky; the tunes of Curtis Lee, whose new song "Pretty Little Angel Eyes," has been playing on every radio station these days, are floating like flower petals on the warm summer breeze.

I've lived in a little town near this city for all of my life. I'm used to it; in fact, some might assume that I'm tired of its charms by now. After all, they might think that with fourteen whole years already lived, I've certainly seen everything there is to see around here. Of course, this is a false assumption . . . but it's not just the allure of Chicago that I enjoy–it's *who* I get to enjoy it with.

Every other Saturday, my cousin Carolyn drives me downtown. Right there, you should realize just how special Carolyn is. If I were seventeen, I probably wouldn't want to spend my Saturdays with my younger cousin–but it's not like that with Carolyn and I. Somehow, she gets me . . . which is something no one else can claim to do.

"Alright." Her melodic and soothing voice reaches out to me through the chaos and noise of the busy road just ten feet away from us. The sun is high in the sky now and reflecting against all the shining glass buildings, casting a glare in my eyes. I look up at my cousin through my sunglasses as she sits down at our table, which is settled outside the best ice cream shop this side of Lake Michigan.

"Here you go," she says, handing me a cone with my favorite flavor: mint chip. With her back to the glaring street, Carolyn takes off her sunglasses. Her blue eyes are sparkling from the summer sunlight that's bouncing off the shop windows, and her cheeks are as rosy as the strawberries that grow in my backyard. Everything about her, from her curly hair to her manicured nails, is perfect–and yet, that's not why I love my cousin. I love her because of who she is–and because of who she's taught me to be.

"How's yours?" I ask, letting the first chocolate chip melt on my tongue.

Carolyn raises her cone of butter pecan ice cream and grins at me. "Great."

I take another bite of mine, and Carolyn says, "You haven't told me how the contest went."

I feel heat rise to my face, and I cast my gaze downwards at the round white table we're sitting at. "Oh, yeah. I haven't."

Carolyn stares at me as we sit in silence for a few moments. Finally, she becomes impatient and exclaims, "Eileen! Tell me! Did you win?"

Slowly, I look back up at my cousin. Then, ever so slightly, I give her a nod. My cousin gasps in excitement and leans forward across the table; her eyes are so large that they look as though they're about to pop. "I told you to tell me as soon as you found out!"

"I wanted to see your reaction," I say, my voice quiet.

Carolyn sighs, shaking her head in disbelief. "I should've known you had something to tell me! You've barely said a word all day."

"Well, you can't read my mind all the time."

"True," laughs Carolyn, leaning back in her chair and folding her thin, pale arms. "So . . . What did you win?"

Hesitantly, I reach into my bag and remove the letter which I've been carrying for the past three days. The envelope, which was previously starched and white, is now a bit crumpled and smudged–but the typed words are still just as clear to me as the first day I read them. "The letter says that . . . that my article will be featured in the magazine . . . and–well, I've already been awarded a check."

"Eileen, that's amazing!" cries Carolyn, bubbling over with excitement.

I blush and shove the envelope back in my bag before taking another bite of my ice cream. The sun is still shining bright, and I'm glad to have the excuse so I can hide behind my sunglasses.

My silence seems to inadvertently send some sort of signal to Carolyn, because her smile seems to fade suddenly. "Eileen, what's the matter?"

"What?" I ask, perking up immediately. "Nothing. Why?"

"You just don't seem as excited as I thought you would be." Carolyn raises her blonde eyebrows expectantly as I search for the right words to say.

It's true that I'm not as thrilled about this accomplishment as I would have liked–and I think that's the problem. I hate that I'm not relishing this moment. It just . . . doesn't seem like as big of a step forward as I might have been able to take. I know that most of this has to do with the subject matter that I chose to write about. It was simple–elementary, even. And yet, it won me first place. It won me a place in a magazine. Maybe that's what I'm so upset about, though. I was given a chance to write about something that matters . . . and I didn't.

Perhaps I was lazy, or embarrassed–or just afraid. I can almost hear myself scoffing in my head. Fear . . . it seems to be my constant adversary. When I read in front of my classmates at school, my heart beats wildly in my chest. My palms begin sweating, and I can hardly breathe. It's a quality I wish I could change about myself. All my life, I've always been able to find the words to say–but I've never had the courage to say them out loud . . . or at least, not when or how I want to say them.

"Other people are writing about . . . *important* things," I begin, choosing my words slowly and carefully. "They're writing about current events–controversial topics. Meanwhile, I'm just writing about this summer's fashion." I fix my eyes on a robin sitting in a nearby tree. It seems to be staring right back at me, fluttering its wings and hopping impatiently on a long, sturdy branch.

"But that's insane!" exclaims Carolyn, her voice piercing the strange stillness of the moment. I watch in disappointment as the robin takes off from the branch, swooping under the leaves of the tree and flying off over the busy streets below.

"You're a talented writer," she continues, "and you have incredible thoughts to share. Just because you're not writing about 'important' things right now doesn't mean that your words don't mean something. Do you think I could write at your age? In fact, I still can't. Essays, sure. The occasional short story–maybe. But you're writing articles, and even getting published. Besides, do you really think other kids your age are getting the 'big' news stories? You're way ahead of most girls your age when it comes to a career. It doesn't matter how big or small a step is–just that you've taken it. I refuse to hear another word downplaying your success."

With this speech concluded, Carolyn turns away dramatically, fluttering her eyelashes in contempt. Seeing a hint of a smile dancing across her lips, I relent and sigh. "Fine, fine. I know you're right."

"Good." Carolyn looks closely at me for a moment, and I watch as all the humor is drained from her expression. "Eileen . . . that's not why you're upset."

I avert my gaze and shrug. "I guess you can read my mind more than I thought."

Carolyn sighs. "Come on. Spill, or I'll be forced to ask someone else."

My head shoots up–and just like that, understanding washes over my cousin's face. "Eileen, did you tell your parents about the article?"

I nod. "Of course I did."

"And?"

"And . . ." I hold back just a moment more before caving. "Well, when I told my mom about it, she was just really distracted–talking to Julie, scolding Tommy . . . you know. It wasn't a big deal."

"What about your dad?"

A knot begins to form in my stomach as I try to articulate what I'm feeling. "He'd had a bad day at work. As usual. So when I told him at dinner, he . . . well, he just didn't acknowledge it." No matter how hard I try, I can't keep bitterness from sneaking into my words.

Carolyn closes her eyes and rubs the bridge of her nose with her pointer finger and thumb. "Eileen . . . you don't have to hide that stuff like a deep, dark secret. It's me, remember? We tell each other everything."

"But maybe I don't want everyone to know everything about my life," I say hurriedly, feeling like a bomb about to explode. I become acutely aware of the many people sitting at tables all around us, and I clamp my mouth shut, embarrassed.

"Eileen." Carolyn stares at me so intensely that I feel forced to look back at her. "I'm sorry. I know that it can be difficult at your house. But I'm always here for you. Don't forget that."

I take a deep, shuddering breath and nod. She's right. Deep down, I always knew it. Still, I think I needed to hear those words out of her own mouth. I needed to know that I'm not alone. "Okay," I whisper.

"Okay," says Carolyn, switching gears with a comforting smile. "Well . . . Are you going to try submitting another article someplace?"

I turn to stare at the cars driving by us down the busy road. The nearest stop light turns red, and the tunes of Del Shannon reach my ears from one of the stationary cars. "I'd like to submit one to the school newspaper this fall."

"Good," says Carolyn again, her voice firm and determined. "I'd expect no less."

"What do you mean?"

"Well," she replies as we stand up from the small, circular table, "you've got curiosity, creativity, and talent all wrapped into one." Carolyn fluffs her pale pink dress, and I imitate her without thinking. "That's like the perfect package for a good journalist. Words come naturally to you."

I hear myself scoff as we walk down the sidewalk and reach Carolyn's bright red 1959 Chevrolet Corvette, which is parked on the side of the street. The sun is glaring aggressively and bouncing off the spotless car, causing me to shield my eyes despite my sunglasses. "And there's my problem. I always know what I want to say, but it's so much easier to write it down instead of saying it out loud. I mean, how am I supposed to become a journalist if I'm not brave enough to talk to my own family, let alone strangers?"

Carolyn sighs as we climb into the car. "You may not feel like it, Eileen, but you are a bold person. Everything about you is bold. Trust me; I know you. You'll go to college one day, and you'll become a journalist."

I wait a moment to reply as Carolyn turns out into the road. A nice breeze ruffles my hair as we drive, and I rest my arm outside the window. "Even though it's not what everyone else does?"

I watch as a mischievous smile creeps across my cousin's dimpled face. "*Especially* because it's not what everyone else does."

"Look, Eileen!"

My head snaps up in response to the excitement in Carolyn's voice. The two of us are standing in front of our favorite music store, a small brick building that's packed from floor to ceiling with people, records, and the tunes of the most famous singers in the world. Today, the store seems to be just as busy as usual. Plenty of colorful albums are being displayed in the store window, but as I follow Carolyn's gaze, I realize that there's a certain one she's looking at.

"Oh!" I exclaim, and the two of us rush over to the window, standing so close to the glass that our noses are practically touching it.

"Come on, let's go in."

The two of us walk inside the shop, the tinkling of a bell announcing our arrival. Quickly, I rush to find the record from the window. Thankfully, there are many left since the album is so new. Picking it up gingerly, I feel my heart rate quicken in excitement as I stare at the handsome, romantic grin of–

"Dean Martin," breathes Carolyn, shaking her head of sun-kissed blonde hair. "He really has no business being this dreamy."

"And breaking young girls' hearts," I add with a half smile, eyeing my own brunette ponytail and petite form in the nearby window's reflection and wishing that I looked more like tall, beautiful Carolyn.

Without hesitation, I walk up to the counter and purchase the record, all the while making myself promise that this will be the only album I buy this month. Both my parents grew up during the 1930s, and I guess they've passed down the gift of saving to me. I can't often condone buying things for myself— unless they're records, of course.

As Carolyn waits for me at the counter, I watch as she gingerly picks up an Elvis record and examines the back. I love coming here with her. Being as quiet as I am, I'm grateful to have someone to talk to. Someone who understands me.

Carolyn has been my best friend since we were kids. We do everything together, and now that I'm starting high school in the fall, we'll get to see each other even more. I'm not a big fan of change, but knowing that Carolyn will be by my side, I'm not worried.

Half-consciously, I find myself imitating Carolyn's movements and characteristics. After I pay the girl at the counter and receive my record in a bag, I smooth my dark blue skirt, straighten my necklace, and fluff my hair. Just as I'm finishing up, Carolyn turns to me with her usual smile, her white teeth practically matching the string of pearls around her neck. "Alright. Ready to go home?"

I nod, and just about five minutes later, the two of us are cruising down the road once again in Carolyn's shiny red Corvette. "Go ahead and pick the music," offers Carolyn, glancing over at me through her cat eye sunglasses.

"Okay." Grinning, I reach forward and change the station a few times before the voice of Elvis Presley fills the car.

"Nice," says Carolyn, approving my choice. Then, she begins singing along to "Hound Dog." A few seconds later, I join in.

Strangely enough, Carolyn and I used to fight when we were kids, back before we became friends. With only a three year age difference between us, and the fact that we were each the oldest children in our respective families, we always seemed to be competing for the top spot in our family. However, all that changed around the time that Carolyn turned eleven. I'm not sure how it happened, but gradually, she became my playmate, my protector, and soon, my best friend. Now, we're fourteen and seventeen, and closer than ever.

A few minutes pass, and eventually, the song ends. We reach a red light, and the car slows to a stop. We've exited the city now, and entered the quiet, idyllic suburbs. I rest my arm on the door and lean out the window, watching all the sights around me. It's a perfect Saturday afternoon, and it seems that everyone in town has come outside. I watch a pig-tailed young girl pull a red Radio Flyer wagon behind her, the little boy sitting inside clapping his hands in excitement. Picturesque little houses sit in long rows, all identical to one another aside from their subtle differences, like flower boxes or pale blue shutters.

The light turns green, and the car begins moving again. I close my eyes and enjoy the warm wind hitting my face and whipping my hair around. This is where I'm happiest–with my best friend, soaking up every moment of summer. All I want is for it to last forever.

3
PETER

VENICE, ITALY
SUMMER, 1938

At five o'clock, I get the nod from Signor Maggio–his signal to let me know that it's time to lock the door and close up. I wait and watch as he waves goodbye to his last customers, a woman and her two small children–all of whom spoke in a foreign language. As soon as they've left, I walk over to the door and lock it with Signor's key. It's a beautiful old copper-colored key with a diamond-shaped crystal at the end. Late afternoon light is pouring through the shop windows, and as it hits the diamond, tiny rainbows appear and dance along the wooden floor. I rub my finger over the key, feeling its smooth, familiar texture.

Turning back around, I walk over to Signor and hand it to him. He's already taken a seat in his old chair. You'd think he was tired, but there's a glow on his face–a glow that would reside there even without the sunlight bathing his face. He gets that way every day, right after closing time, as if all the joy in the world is his, just hovering over him in his little bookshop.

Automatically, I pull up a little wooden stool and sit down on it. Every time that I help Signor Maggio in the shop, he tells me a story afterwards. He always tries to give me a day's wages, but sometimes he comes up short. He can't always afford what he would like to pay me, so his stories have become a form of payment. I know he feels sorry about this, but I don't mind at all. The money he gives me is more than I need to live, and his stories satisfy a hunger inside me far greater than any hunger I have for food.

"Well, what'll it be today, Peter?" he asks, reaching over to his desk to grab his pipe. Lighting it, he looks over at me, waiting for a reply.

I bite my lip in thought. "I don't know. Uh–how about something from the war?"

"Ohh . . . I'm not sure."

"Please, Signor? Something good. It doesn't have to be long."

Even as I say these words, I know the real reason why Signor is hesitant. It's not because he isn't willing to tell a long story. He's a storyteller–that's what he does best. The real reason that he's hesitant is because he doesn't like to talk much about what he saw during the war.

Signor Maggio is a hero. I know that because I've seen his medals. He has them hanging on a wall in the back of the shop, a small reminder of the things he did for his country. The first time I noticed the medals, I asked Signor about them, and he told me a few stories from the war. All were fascinating, but none seemed to make him very happy. Since then, his war stories have been few and far between, and I've been longing to hear another.

"Well–alright," sighs Signor with a smile. "Let me see here."

I wait patiently for a moment, letting him think. Then, I watch as his eyes light up, and he begins.

"Ah, I've got one. It was 1917, and the war was nearly over. Of course, no one knew that yet. Anyways, I'd just fought in the Battle of Caporetto. I told you a bit about that one, didn't I? It was a miracle I survived that battle with everything but my foot intact–and, of course, the single bullet I received in that same leg." He motions to his left leg, which I know has given him a limp ever since.

For the briefest moment, I can see a look of pain flash through his eyes. Knowing that this was certainly brought on by my insistence to hear another story, a knot begins to form in my stomach. I open my mouth to protest, but as if he's reading my thoughts, Signor Maggio shakes his head and continues.

"After that battle, I was sent to a good hospital and told that I couldn't return to war because of my injury. Of course, I didn't take that very well. After all, I felt that my country needed me. But I also knew that I wouldn't be of any use to anyone with my injury. So I stayed in the hospital. Well, there was a young woman there–a nurse. She told me she was from Tuscany. Oh, I wish you could have seen her, Peter. She was beautiful, with her long black hair and sparkling blue eyes. I could almost picture her living there among the vineyards."

I smile and try to imagine this woman. Then, I attempt to conjure an image of Signor Maggio as young. It isn't easy, but with some effort, I can see the two of them in a hospital—him lying in bed, her taking care of him.

I realize that Signor Maggio has paused and is staring out the window, as if in a trance. The only sounds are the far-off splashing of waves and the soft, lulling chatter that travels just outside the shop. I clear my throat, and Signor looks at me with a start.

"Oh, I'm sorry, Peter. I was just thinking. Where was I? Ah, yes—Emilia. That was her name. Emilia Vinci. She took such good care of me that I was on my feet in about a month with a new sense of purpose. And to think, Peter—it was all from her. Isn't it strange how one person can make you realize that life is still worth living?"

I nod, and Signor Maggio continues with a smile and a quick puff on his pipe. A small cloud of smoke sails up through the air, the fading, golden sunlight piercing through it. "I won't mince words here, Peter. I wanted her desperately. Emilia Vinci was my every thought. She was part of every wish or dream I now had for myself. I was determined to marry her as soon as possible."

Although I'm not much for romance, Signor has intrigued me. So I ask, "What happened?"

"Well—it was just my luck. It turned out that she was engaged to another man."

I frown. This wasn't what I was expecting. "Did they get married?"

"Yes, I regret to say that they did."

"But didn't you tell her you loved her?" I exclaim, a strange sense of injustice rising from within me.

Signor nods slowly, and despite his practicality, I can see a darkness hovering just beneath the surface. "Yes. Yes, I did. It was my final day in the hospital, and I wanted her to know how I felt. So I told her that I loved her."

"What did she do?"

Signor lets out a sad sort of laugh. "She looked at me with a regretful little smile, and she gave me a kiss on the cheek. And she said, '*Addio, carissimo*; goodbye, dear one.' And that was it."

I stare at Signor blankly. "That was it?"

He nods. "That was it."

I scratch my head of dark brown hair in confusion. "But you said that you loved her."

"*Sì.*"

"Well, somehow, I always thought that if you loved somebody, you were supposed to track them down, and convince them that they love you too, and never give up until you're married and happy." I cross my arms in a satisfied sort of way, completely secure in my belief.

Signor Maggio shakes his head, the look on his face a mix of amusement and regret. "I would not usually say this, Peter— but you read too much. Or at least, you believe too much of what you read. Love is not the same in real life as it is in most books. If it was, then Emilia and I would have been married that very day, and she would be sitting here with us right now."

I sigh and shrug. "I'm not sure I'm up for that kind of love, then. I mean, if it really works that way, then I may never find someone."

Signor raises his eyebrows and gives me a mischievous grin. "Oh, you just might, Peter. You see, I never married because I never found anyone after Emilia. I've never met anyone quite like her. Oh, of course I considered trying to stop her, and to convince her that she should be with me–but I knew I couldn't interfere in her life, because she was happy . . . and that's all that mattered. But you, Peter–you can find someone to love for your whole life. And when you do, I don't believe you'll let her slip away."

A small smile flicks across my face, and Signor stands up from his chair. "Besides," he says with a teasing glint in his eye, "what woman could resist a man who's named after a saint?"

Shaking my head, I watch as Signor moves over to the bookshelves and begins organizing them. His words linger in my mind and quickly take on a different meaning. A meaning that I want to understand, but can't.

I don't know how Signor Maggio could have let that woman go so easily. He's always taught me to work hard for what I want, and to never give up. So, how could he lose Emilia? And is that what love is really like–letting people go?

4
EILEEN

CHICAGO, ILLINOIS
SUMMER, 1961

Before I know it, Carolyn is pulling the car into my family's driveway. As she does so, a strange mix of emotions washes over me. I love my family . . . but they're complicated. And I'm not at all prepared to leave my cousin on a beautiful, summer day like this one.

"Here we are," sings Carolyn, parking the car and looking expectantly at me.

I force a smile and step out of the car, shutting the shiny red door gingerly behind me and look up at my home, which fits right into our perfect cookie-cutter neighborhood. The roof is slanted symmetrically, and an awning on the side provides covering for our car. Our house is just like all the others—except for the bright red flowers and green vines that overflow from our pristine, white flower boxes.

In a last-ditch attempt to keep the day's fun going a little while longer, I whirl around and ask, "Don't you want to come in?"

Carolyn hesitates and begins tapping the steering wheel. Her blonde hair sways back and forth as she shakes her head. "I don't know. My mother wants me back home in time for dinner."

I sigh and try again. "Come on . . . you don't have to stay for long."

Carolyn waits a moment more before cracking a smile. "Fine, fine–but if my mom is upset with me for being late, I'm going to blame you."

"That's totally fair." I grin and step back as Carolyn climbs out of the car.

The two of us walk around the side of the house and enter the backyard, where we are immediately greeted by the smell of strawberries and freshly mowed grass. Tall, leafy oak trees create a sort of canopy above the yard, allowing streams of sunlight to pour through and spread across the ground like golden pools. My mother takes a lot of pride in her garden. In fact, she takes a lot of pride in our entire house. With my dad at work a lot, my mom spends basically all of her time being a model housewife; she's always cleaning the house and entertaining guests.

Of course, this comes with a price. My younger siblings, Tommy and Julie, are the exact opposite of my personality. They're often energetic to a fault, and they always seem to be craving attention–which is something our parents can't afford to give them.

"Do you want to come in?" I try again, acutely aware of the tiny beads of sweat that are threatening to run down my face.

Carolyn nods. "Sure."

I walk to the back door and hold it open, allowing my cousin to walk in first. Then, I follow.

We end up in my family's kitchen, which is spotless, as usual. "Do you want a snack?" I ask, and Carolyn shakes her head. "No, thanks. Maybe just some water."

I'm about to make my way to the cabinet when a loud noise shatters through the peace and quiet of the house. I cringe and brace myself for the chaos which I know is inevitably coming my way.

"Tommy!" The sound of my mother's voice rings through the house like a high-pitched bell.

Just then, my younger brother comes bursting into the kitchen like a tornado. Right behind him is my mother, who is gripping the hand of my six-year-old sister, Julie. Immediately, I know that something is wrong; Julie's cheeks are wet with tears, and she's sucking her thumb—a habit which she reverts to when she's upset.

My mother's gaze lands on Carolyn and I, and she sucks in a breath. "Hello, girls," she manages. Although my mom takes pride in being put together and organized, my siblings seem to have been born with a natural ability to keep our mother on her toes at all times. Judging by my mom's frazzled appearance, I can tell today hasn't been the most peaceful of days.

Tommy, with his dark brown hair and wide, mischievous eyes, darts over to the back door—but Carolyn, sensing that my mom needs her help, steps in front of the door and blocks Tommy's path.

"Aw, Carolyn," he grumbles as our mom makes her way over to my brother and grabs his arm. Julie, meanwhile, runs to Carolyn's open arms, not really crying anymore but just sniffing pitifully.

"Tommy, give Julie her bear," says my mother firmly.

With a scowl, Tommy sticks out his arm and waits for Julie to retrieve her teddy bear. Hesitantly, Julie reaches out and takes it before clinging to Carolyn again.

"Now, apologize."

Tommy huffs and crosses his arms. "I don't know why I should apologize. I was doing her a favor. She has to toughen up if she wants to be an astronaut."

My mother pushes a strawberry-blonde curl out of her face and shakes her head. "Tommy, there is no reason why Julie can't keep her teddy bear, even if she wants to be an astronaut. Alright? Now, go to your room."

Tommy lets out a low groan before stomping off through the house, slamming his bedroom door behind him.

My mother sighs and forces a smile, composing herself. "I'm very sorry about that, Carolyn. We're, uh . . . not in the best of moods today. Do you girls want anything to eat?"

Carolyn gives my mom a sympathetic smile. "No, thank you."

My mom begins rushing around the kitchen, opening cabinets and rifling through the pantry. "Are you sure? We have, um . . . sandwiches . . . and–"

"Really, it's okay," begins Carolyn, and I try to help.

"We're both fine, Mom. We're just going to hang out in my room for a little while."

My mom turns around and brushes her hands off on her pale blue dress. "Okay. Well, just let me know if you need anything."

"Thanks, Aunt Helen," says Carolyn with a smile.

I'm about to walk out of the kitchen when a question pops into my head, and I stop. "Mom? When will Dad be home?"

My mom picks up a notepad from the kitchen counter, and I watch as her gaze passes down the paper, reading something. "Oh, he's working late again. He won't be home till after dinner."

I take a deep breath and nod. "Okay." With that, Carolyn and I walk out of the kitchen and down the hallway.

When we reach my room, I'm about to shut the door when I realize that Julie has followed us. At six, Julie is the picture of the adorable youngest child, with light pink ribbons wrapped around her bouncing, caramel-colored pigtails. Her pink dress and white Peter Pan collar are spotless, and her smile contagious. However, despite all of these things, I don't feel like surrendering Carolyn's attention just yet.

"Uh, Julie? Do you need something?" I ask.

Julie shakes her head. Then, she steps into my room, wide blue eyes taking it all in. Most details about my room haven't changed in years. My flower-patterned comforter is still tucked neatly under my pillows, and my light pink walls are still littered with posters of my favorite bands. Most importantly, my wooden desk sits in the corner, with hundreds of newspaper clippings and pens scattered all over.

I've never been very good at adapting to change, and I guess that's carried over to how I decorate my room, as well.

I bite my lip and try to refrain from acting rashly. Instead, I allow my little sister to climb up on my bed and lay back on my pillows, giggling at the ceiling. "Eileen! Carrie! Come look."

My cousin and I exchange an amused smile before climbing up on the bed. "What is it?" asks Carolyn.

"You have to lie down."

Obediently, Carolyn and I lie down on either side of Julie and look up at the ceiling. To my surprise, my gaze lands on a thousand tiny rainbows which are dancing across the ceiling and shining in the soft summer glow.

"They're beautiful," says Carolyn quietly.

For just a moment, the three of us stay immobile, watching in awe as the little rainbows play across the ceiling. Then, Julie hops up and bounces off the bed, exclaiming, "Let's play with my baby dolls!"

Carolyn and I sit up, and I give her a look that says, "Never a dull moment in this house." Still, she grins and doesn't seem to mind. Somehow, amidst all the chaos of my life, Carolyn never fails to bring some tranquility and calm to my family. She still manages to make me realize that everything is going to be okay.

After a half hour of entertaining Julie with her baby dolls and stuffed animals, my mom and I are standing on the front step of our house, waving to Carolyn as she drives away.

"Okay," says my mom with a deep breath and a tired half-smile, rubbing my shoulders. "I'm going inside."

"Alright. I'll be out here."

My mom nods and heads inside the house, letting the screen door shut with a soft *whack* behind her. I wait until she's disappeared down the hallway; then, I step down and sit on the edge of our front step.

Holding my head in my hands, I watch the occasional car drive down the street and savor the sounds of birds chirping. I like being by myself, especially outdoors. It's so calm in the summertime. So peaceful.

I love my family . . . but on chaotic days like today, I couldn't be more grateful for my cousin's presence in my life. Carolyn may not know it, but I know she does more good for me than anyone else in my life. She is exceedingly patient, overwhelmingly understanding . . . and she treats me like a sister. There's just something different about her that helps her know how to be there for me like no one else can. If I've had a bad day, Carolyn is the first person I talk to. If I have a test to take, Carolyn is the first one to wish me good luck. She lives her life so differently from everyone else. I can't quite understand it–but it's what I love about her.

I want to be a journalist, which means that I care about the facts. And one thing I know with absolute certainty is, even when my family is busy or distracted, my dreams don't become any less important. Slowly but surely, Carolyn is helping me realize this. For her, I will never give up on my goals. Not ever.

5
PETER

VENICE, ITALY
SUMMER, 1938

After talking with Signor Maggio a few minutes more, we exchange our goodbyes. He hands me a new book, and I promise to share it with as many people as I can. Signor makes me promise this every day. He cares deeply about making sure that everyone has a chance to take advantage of the same privileges and opportunities. Of course, I always keep this promise; after all, without Signor Maggio, I'm not sure I would ever have developed the love for reading that I have now.

With a wave, I exit through the bookshop door, take off my shoes, and go running down the cobblestone streets, book and shoes in hand.

The golden sun is casting its rays over all of Venice, and as I run near the water, I watch the way it glitters and beckons me to go out to it. *Not yet,* I think to myself, quieting the irresistible urge to run and jump into the peaceful blue water of *la Laguna di Venezia*. A gondola ride can wait till later, when it's nice and dark, so no one can see me. I've never been to school to learn how to become a gondolier, which means that I can't technically operate one for profit – but I was practically born on the water. I know how to swim, and thanks to all the books I've read about how to become a gondolier, I consider myself to be one.

After a few more minutes of running, I've reached a much different part of Venice–the part that most Venetians avoid. As soon as I've entered the Venetian Ghetto, I'm transported to a different place–a place that lies very far away from Italy.

There are shops here, and homes, and people just like me– except, they're not like me. I'm Italian. These people are Jewish.

I hear someone call, "Peter! Hello!"

Signor and Signora Finzi smile at me as they step through the front door of their home. Their little son and daughter, Jacob and Miriam, are running around in the street. Five-year-old Jacob kicks his ball towards me, and I kick it gently back with a grin. "Hello!"

I keep on running, waving hello to all the people who see me. Most everyone in the ghetto knows me, and they accept me for who I am, just the way that I accept them for who they are. They don't push me to go to school or wear shoes, and I don't push them to forget that they're Jewish, the way some people in Venice do.

I've known all these people since the day that I first wandered into the ghetto two years ago–although it's existed since the 16th century. One day, on my way to Signor

Maggio's shop, I took a wrong turn. It turned out to be one of the best mistakes of my life. I met lots of people on that cool autumn day . . . but most importantly, I met the Hoffman family. Like Signor Maggio, they've provided a place for me to belong–and that fact has made them as important to me as Signor.

As the sights and sounds around me become much more familiar, I slow down to a brisk walk and don't stop until I've reached a certain wooden door with ivy covering the edges. The faded white house is situated right next to a vast cobblestone courtyard. Behind the house, I can hear the soft splashing of water, and a rush of excitement surges through me once more. Rapping my knuckles on the door, I stand there for a moment, impatiently bouncing on the balls of my bare feet. It doesn't take long before the door swings open, and I'm greeted by a tall, slim woman with dark hair and a baby on her hip. "*Buona sera*, Signora Hoffman," I exclaim.

Signora Hoffman smiles, her brown eyes sparkling softly. "Hello, Peter. What's this? Have you brought us something new from Signor Maggio?"

I nod, and Signora Hoffman opens the door wider to invite me inside. I accept her invitation and take in the room for a moment. The Hoffmans don't live in a place as nice as Signor Maggio. There are no books, no medals hanging on the wall, and no second floor. Well, there is one, but another family lives there. Still, the Hoffmans and Signor Maggio do share something in common: a love of stories.

"He says it's a very good book," I say, words jumping out of my mouth faster than I can think of them. "He says it's called *Oliver Twist*, and it's by Charles Dickens, and it's about a boy who goes to London and falls in with a gang of thieves, and they have all these adventures, and–"

"Peter, Peter," says Signora Hoffman quickly, readjusting the baby girl named Abigail slipping down her hip, "I'm sure it's very exciting. Would you go tell it to Rebekah? She's been waiting all week to hear a new story."

"Oh, sure," I say, still talking a mile a minute. "I haven't read this one yet, but I'll give it to her, and she can give it to me when she's finished. Where is she?"

"She's out back."

"*Grazie*," I reply with a smile. Heading out the door, I turn and walk down the alleyway next to the Hoffmans' home. Exiting it, I turn to the right and find nine-year-old Rebekah. She's sitting against the side of the house, drawing on the cobblestones with a piece of charcoal. Her long, dark brown hair is falling in her face as she focuses on her drawing, biting her lip in concentration.

Leaning around the corner, I knock on the wall and look around, as if unsure where the little girl is. "Hello? Anybody home?"

A grin appears on Rebekah's face, and she hops up to run and give me a hug, the white handkerchief on her head almost flying off. "Oh, Peter! Did you bring me a story?"

"I sure did," I say, blushing from her excited greeting. "Signor Maggio told me he thought you'd like it."

Rebekah raises her eyebrows. "Are you sure he knows what he's talking about? I told you I wanted to read something serious this time."

I frown in mock disappointment. "There you go again, Rebekah–doubting me. And doubting Signor Maggio. What would he think if he knew what you were saying?"

"Really, Peter. Will I like it?"

I hold up my finger and take a moment to open the book and skim quickly through the first chapter. The words dance across the page, float through the air, and land in my brain. As always, I can remember almost every single one.

"Yes," I say confidently. "You'll like it." Closing the book, I hand it over to her. Her brown eyes light up in excitement as she takes the book from me. I smile as she runs one hand over the gold lettering that rests on the spine.

"You're giving it to me?" she asks, a dubious look on her face.

"Sure. But I haven't read it all yet, so when you're done, you need to give it to me right away so I can find out how it ends. I need to know what happens to that baby who–"

"Peter!" exclaims Rebekah, almost dropping the book in an effort to cover her ears with her hands.

Laughing, I shake my head and pat her bony shoulder. "Just kidding. I won't say anything about it. That means you can't say anything, either, when you give it to me. Deal?"

Rebekah nods. "Deal."

I take a deep breath and remain silent for a moment, staring out at the peaceful water below us. Then, with an eager gasp, I cross over to Rebekah's drawing. "And what's this?"

I hear Rebekah begin to protest, but I shake my head and pretend not to hear. "Another drawing from the famous *artista* Rebekah Hoffman? And what is this one a depiction of?"

Rebekah sighs and smiles in spite of herself. Walking over to stand beside me, she looks down at the drawing and says, "It's *Venezia*. Can't you tell?"

Staring down at the drawing, I marvel at the texture in its water and the buildings surrounding it. There's even a little gondola floating on top of the water. "I don't know how you do it, Rebekah," I whisper in sincere admiration.

"It's not that hard," replies Rebekah, her cheeks becoming a light shade of pink.

I raise my eyebrows and give the girl a disapproving look. "Oh–so you're getting boastful now?"

Rebekah's brown eyes widen, and she shakes her head. "No, no–"

Laughing again, I try to ease her worries by stepping away from the drawing. "I'm just kidding, Rebekah."

With a relieved smile, Rebekah sits down and runs her hand over the charcoal, giving it more of a texture. She looks at it so lovingly; it's easy to see that she takes pride in her creation.

"You know," I say, leaning against the wall to stare out at the sparkling blue water, "you should really come to Signor's bookshop sometime. He's got the best, most beautiful books– and they've got lots of drawings in them."

I'm ready to keep talking, but I stop when I see the look on Rebekah's face. Her eyes are wide, and she seems to shrink back into herself. "What?" I ask.

"You know I can't, Peter. I want to–but I can't. Mama wouldn't want me to. She says it's dangerous."

"How dangerous could it be?" I reply, brushing off the comment. "You could–"

"*No*, Peter." Rebekah says this so firmly that I look at her in surprise. "I can't. I just can't." The expression on her face is a mix of sadness and fear. It makes her look years older than she really is . . . and something inside begins to hurt as I realize the burden she's carrying. I don't quite understand it, and I'm not sure I ever will–but I do know that it's too much for a little girl.

I swallow hard and nod slowly, running a hand through my dark, tangled hair. "Okay. Okay, well–I'll keep bringing you books. And–it'll be just like you've been to the bookshop, because I'll make sure you read every book it's got."

A small smile appears on Rebekah's face. "Thanks, Peter."

I smile back at her, and I'm about to say something else when I realize that the sun has finally gone down and only a few moments of golden rays remain. "I've gotta go, Rebekah." I turn and run down the alleyway, calling over my shoulder, "Let me know how you like the book!"

I creep quietly onto my gondola, grabbing the sides of the boat for balance. Leaning over to the dock, I grab the rope tethering the gondola, and I untie it quickly, letting it drop over into the boat. With that, I grab my paddle and stand at the very top of the gondola, quickly achieving the perfect posture. I dip my paddle into the water, and away I go down the quiet canals of Venice.

The only sounds are water splashing, soft, faraway accordion music, and my breathing. I take in the quiet with a deep, contented breath, enjoying every second of solitude and peace. Looking around as the gondola floats through the darkness, I notice the reflection of nearby light poles casting a strange sort of glow on the water.

My favorite time to go out on the water is at night. No one's around to get me in trouble for being a gondolier without a license; no one's around to tell me to go to school, or to tell me how I should act. Most importantly, no one can tell me who I should or shouldn't speak to.

It doesn't take long before I've reached the Rialto Bridge. Usually, I would pass right underneath it, but today I feel like stopping. Paddling up to the dock, I grab the rope from the gondola and tie it up. Then I climb out and rush up the bridge, my feet slapping against the cool steps. Stopping at the very top, I sit down on the edge and let my legs dangle high above the water.

As much as I'd like to see Venice in an untainted way, I can't help reliving my conversation with Rebekah Hoffman from earlier today. I can't stop thinking of the intensity in her innocent, brown eyes and the fear in her voice. She said she couldn't come to the bookshop because it was too dangerous. *Too dangerous.*

I know why, of course. It's obvious. Signor has taught me all about the harsh reality that people like the Hoffmans must live in. I remember one day when I was about eleven years old, and I had just met the Hoffmans and many other people living in the ghetto. Excited to have met some new, interesting people, I ran to tell Signor all about them.

To my surprise, Signor informed me that he'd never been to the ghetto. He also told me that he'd only ever talked to a Jew twice. Then, he proceeded to tell me all about the way Jews were viewed, and the biases against them. I didn't understand him fully, but from the way he talked, I caught on to the basic idea. In Italy, Jews were Jews, and Italians were Italians–and I was supposed to accept that.

Thankfully, Signor also taught me that these biases and stereotypes were wrong. I remember him running a hand over his old, leather-bound Bible and teaching me that the Jews were God's chosen people. He said that he didn't believe in all the biases against them, but it was a fact of life that I had to know about. I was glad not to be ignorant of the topic–but I also wished that the rest of the world saw people like the Hoffmans the way I did.

6
EILEEN

CHICAGO, ILLINOIS
SUMMER, 1965

It's a warm Saturday morning when I wake up to the comforting smell of coffee and bacon. I take my time waking up, studying each intricate detail of the Elvis poster that hangs on my wall. Then, rubbing my eyes, I get out of bed, brush my wild brown hair, and head out to the kitchen.

My mom is standing at the stove and cooking bacon in time to the soft, upbeat music that's playing on the radio. Tommy is sitting at the table–in silence for once, but only because his mouth is full of eggs. Julie's place at the table is empty except for her half-eaten plate of food, and she's now sitting in front of the television set, watching *The Flintstones*, her favorite cartoon.

"Hi, Mom," I say, walking over and letting her plant a kiss on my forehead.

"Hi, honey. Here, fill a plate."

Taking some eggs and bacon over to the kitchen table, I sit down at my place across from Tommy, who has just finally swallowed the gigantic bite of food in his mouth. Unlike me, my brother is fully dressed and appears to be ready for the day, aside from the fact that his uncombed brown hair is sticking out in every direction.

"Okay, I'm done. See ya, Mom," he calls over his shoulder, taking advantage of the fact that our mother's back is turned. He goes running towards the front door just as we hear the sound of a kitchen cabinet slamming shut.

"Tommy, wait!"

My brother freezes and turns around. "What?"

My mother raises her eyebrows and uses one finger to beckon him over. "Where do you think you're going?"

"Bruce's. He's just a couple houses away, Mom."

Our mother sighs and crosses her arms, hesitating for a moment. Eventually, she relents. "Alright. Be back in time for lunch."

"Thanks, Mom. Bye!"

In response to my brother's antics, I let out a sound that resembles a snicker, just as my father walks into the room. "And what are you up to today, Eileen May?"

I smile at the sight of my dad–the only person in my family who calls me by my first *and* middle name. He's tall with dark features, bright eyes, and a teasing smile. In contrast to my mom, he appears to have aged quite a bit since the two of them got married. Quite a few gray hairs on his dark head betray his real age–that, and the constant weathered quality about his face.

I can tell he's in a good mood today. He usually is on the weekends. In fact, so is the rest of my family.

"I don't know. I'll probably read for a little while."

My dad raises his eyebrows and turns from greeting my mom to give me a quizzical look. "It's summer. Don't you want to do something fun?"

"You forget, Matthew. We have a star English student in the family," says my mom with a smile and a wink at me. "Reading *is* fun, especially for her."

"Anyways, Carolyn's busy today, so I'm going to a movie with Sandy in a couple hours," I add, standing up with my now-empty plate and bringing it over to the kitchen counter.

"Oh, got it," replies my dad, nodding. "Be careful."

I give my dad a knowing smile. "I will."

Just then, the phone rings, and my dad reaches over to the wall to answer it. "Hello?" A pause. "Eileen, darling, it's Carolyn for you."

I walk over and take the phone from my dad. "Hey!"

"Hey, Eileen," Carolyn's voice says. "Well–you wanted me to tell you if there were any updates with Randy."

Feeling my eyes widen, I ask, "And? Did he ask you out again?"

"We're going out this afternoon."

I squeal, causing my parents to throw some questioning glances in my direction. Trying to act casual, I clear my throat and reply, "What are you going to do?"

"I think we're going out to eat. Maybe we'll go to the drive-in . . . I'm not sure yet."

"Oh my goodness, okay," I begin babbling, overcome with excitement. "You're going to need to do your hair, and your makeup, and do you have your nails done?"

"You do know I've thought of these things, right?" laughs Carolyn, obviously amused. I can almost see her eyes sparkling as she talks.

"Well, sure . . . but it can't hurt to get a reminder." I wait for my parents to sit down by Julie with their coffee. Then, taking a few steps further from my parents and yanking the phone cord along with me, I ask quietly, "Are you nervous?"

I hear Carolyn sigh. "Yeah. Kind of."

"What for?"

"Oh, I don't know. I mean . . . I've liked him for *so* long. I want everything to go just right."

"It will!"

"But what if it doesn't? Love isn't that easy."

I let out an audible gasp, lean in and lower my voice. "Carolyn . . . Do you really love him?"

"Ohh," moans Carolyn. "I can't. I can't say that."

I laugh as if her statement is ridiculous. "Why not?"

"Because love doesn't happen like that. We've been on two dates. Just because I really like him, that doesn't mean he feels the same way about me. It would be too easy."

"Be positive," I say confidently, enjoying the opportunity to be the giver of advice for once instead of the receiver. "Have fun tonight. It'll be great–you'll see."

"Okay," says Carolyn. I can almost hear the smile in her voice. "And now, about you and Kevin Maxwell . . ."

"No, no," I exclaim, feeling my cheeks go bright red at the mention of my long-time crush. I tell my cousin almost everything . . . but I've never been able to truly express how I feel about Kevin Maxwell. "There's nothing to say about that."

"Are you sure? You've liked him *forever*."

"Yeah, I know–and nothing's happened between us."

"Don't give up hope so soon. After all, I liked Randy for two years before he asked me out. Just give it time."

"How about this, then: You take my advice, and I'll consider yours."

Carolyn laughs. "You've got a deal. Listen, I'd better go get ready. I'll talk to you later, okay?"

"Okay. Bye, Carrie."

"Bye."

It's around one o'clock when I finally sit down at the desk in my bedroom. My fingers run over the wood and breathe in the smell of ink and paper. This whole corner of my room is like a special sanctuary for me–a place that I can go where no one will disturb me. Where I can be fully engrossed in the thing I love best: journalism.

When I was about nine years old, I discovered all the Nancy Drew books. Between the ages of nine and eleven, I absolutely devoured them–but they weren't enough. I didn't want to be a detective, per say; I felt that a profession like that was best left to those a bit braver than I. Instead, I wanted to focus on finding the facts and sharing them with the world. So, about a year ago, my parents decided to give me their camera. It was a bit old-fashioned, but it did its job. That was the most my parents ever did to support my dream—but so far, it's been enough . . . especially considering how distracted they always seem to be.

I stretch out my hands and rest them delicately on my old typewriter. A blank sheet of paper waits there, seeming to call my name. The trouble is, I don't know what to write about.

I take a deep breath and lean back in my chair, retracting my hands. Recalling the conversation I had with Carolyn last weekend, I wonder if she's right. Maybe the story I'm meant to write will just fall into my lap when I least expect it. In the meantime, there's lots of life to be lived while I'm waiting.

"Wasn't that the most adorable movie?" asks my friend Sandy Baker as we exit the movie house. "I never knew Hayley Mills was such a good actress! Oh, and that Brian Keith is a dream. Catch me, Eileen—I'm real gone."

Sandy pretends to faint and falls back, catching herself just in time.

I laugh and shake my head. "He is good looking . . . but he's not as cute as Frankie Avalon. Or Elvis. Or Dean—"

"Martin?" finishes Sandy expectantly. "I'm telling you, Eileen, he's up there."

Throwing up my hands, I surrender. "Okay, okay. Whatever you say."

Sandy gives me a satisfied look and adds a pep in her step, her curly blonde hair bouncing. Walking down the street, I'm glad I wore sunglasses today. The sun is setting now, and the rays are practically blinding.

"Okay. Here's my sister's car," says Sandy, and the two of us climb in, greeting her older sister Mary.

On the way home, Sandy and I keep talking about the movie, with Mary jumping in every once in a while. It's dark by the time we pull into my family's driveway, with just a few strands of pinkish-gold sunlight weaving their way through the blue sky. I wave to the two sisters as I step out of the car. "Bye, Sandy. Thanks for the ride, Mary."

I walk around the back of the house just as the Baker sisters drive away. Letting myself inside, I'm surprised to find that all is silent in the normally-chaotic house.

Suddenly, someone comes walking down the hallway and into the kitchen. I expect my mom to be standing there–but she's not. Instead, it's my dad, and there's a look on his face that's more serious than I've ever seen before. This morning, he looked rested and happy. Now, his face is haggard and worried . . . which isn't uncommon, but certainly unwelcome.

"Eileen, honey," he says, looking almost surprised to see me.

Unsure of what to say, I simply ask, "Dad . . . What's wrong?"

I watch my father's mouth open and close a few times as he searches for words. "Honey," he says again. My dad calls me that a lot–but usually, his voice is sugary sweet, like the name. Now, it's just the only word he can seem to get out of his mouth.

I glance around and down the hallway–and that's when I see her. My mom, sitting at the end of the staircase with her head in her hands. I get an awful feeling in the pit of my stomach.

"Dad," I say, my voice barely above a whisper. "Where are Tommy and Julie?"

"Julie's playing in her room, and Tommy is a few doors down at his friend's house."

I let out a sigh of relief. Obviously, something else is wrong. I'm about to open my mouth to try again when my dad opens his, and the words come rushing out.

"Eileen, Carolyn was in an accident."

I stare up at my dad, my brain unable to comprehend his words. "What–what kind?"

"A car accident. She and her boyfriend . . . It wasn't their fault. The other car went through a red light. Her boyfriend tried to swerve . . ."

I can hear my heart begin pounding in my chest. It's getting louder by the second, and all I want to do is scream and drown it out–but I can't. I'm frozen to the spot, and all I can see is Carolyn's face, smiling at me.

"Is she okay?" I ask, my voice cracking. Embarrassed, I rub my throat and avoid eye contact with my dad.

My dad looks down at me with worried eyes. He wants to reassure me–I can see it in his eyes. But I can see something else there, too. He knows me . . . and he knows he can't lie to me. I can almost see the wheels turning in his brain, and I know what he's going to say before he even opens his mouth. "We don't know yet. Your mother and I are about to leave."

Just then, my mom walks down the hallway, and I finally get a good look at her face. Her eyes are bright red, her brow furrowed. Without saying anything, she steps forward and gives me a hug, and I melt into her.

"Watch after Julie for us, please," says my dad quietly.

I don't want to let go of my mom. I want to stay in her comforting arms forever–but I know that can't be. So, for my parents' sake, I let go and watch as they head out the front door.

My first move is to check on Julie. Poking my head through her bedroom door, I get a glance of my little sister. She's sitting in the furthest corner of her pink-painted bedroom, rocking back and forth with her baby doll in her arms. A pool of soft light from her pink-shaded lamp surrounds her spot on the floor, and I can hear her humming "Twinkle, Twinkle Little Star" very softly. Normally, I would smile at such a peaceful, idyllic scene–but I can't. Not right now.

Knowing that Julie is okay, I retreat to my room and begin pacing. They say the best thing to do in these situations is to keep busy, but all I can think about is Carolyn. Why couldn't I go to the hospital? Why did my parents have to leave me here to worry?

Numbly, I walk over to where my record player is sitting near my window. My new Dean Martin record is already set up, ready to be played. Slowly, I set the needle down on the record and wait for the crackling sound to begin. Then, I collapse on my bed.

Lying on my bed, I let my eyes wander. I'm greeted with the familiar sight of my Elvis poster. Overwhelmed, I close my eyes and try to push away the thoughts, and eventually let myself float off to a dream world: A world with music and laughter, where nothing bad ever happens. Where my best friend is going to be okay.

7
PETER

VENICE, ITALY
SUMMER, 1938

$\mathbb{M}$y first thought is to head straight back the way I came–
but suddenly, I'm struck with an idea. There are certain canals
that I don't use very often, and with nowhere to be in the
morning, tonight is the perfect time to explore. I can take the
long way back to the dock, and then I'll get a good night's
rest.

Content with this new idea, I begin making my way
through the canals. At first, they're familiar, but soon, they
become so narrow and so dark that I don't know where I'm
going. Eventually, I'm faced with the possibility that for the
first time in a long time, I might be lost.

Soon, the walls grow so close together that I'm able to
reach out and rest my hand against them, just in order to keep
my balance. I've never been in such narrow canals before–
and I'm beginning to wonder if I've ever seen these at all. A

thick fog has rolled in as well, making it even more difficult to navigate. I squint and then widen my eyes, trying desperately to make out my surroundings. The waves beneath are dark, murky, and unwelcoming. A shiver runs down my spine as my imagination begins to run wild.

Without warning, a strange jolt sends me tottering on top of the boat, back and forth, until finally, I fall down, hitting the bottom of the gondola.

For a moment, I'm in total shock, unsure of why the water in this particular canal is so rough. The waves seem to be growing by the second, splashing and rocking the gondola. Then, something shiny catches my eye through the fog. Looking forward, I can see a strange sort of sparkling light, so close that if I just climb to the front of the gondola, it will be directly in front of me. Stepping forward and grabbing onto either side of the boat to steady myself, I make my way forward.

Now that I can see the sparkling light clearly, I'm faced with the most unusual sight. To my surprise, I see a large, round door made of stone, with a circle of small diamonds at the top and a diamond-encrusted handle. The door is situated right in the center of the wall, and it stretches all the way across. It's so wide that my entire gondola could fit through it. Above the door is the most interesting part of all: a large clock. It is complete with Roman numerals, and the hands are in perfect, working order. The clock, just like the handle, is surrounded by miniscule, glittering diamonds.

I resist the urge to gasp, and instead move further toward the door, balancing at the edge of the gondola. My first instinct is to grab the handle and begin to pull–but the door won't budge. Then, I try prying the two small, glowing diamonds from the top–but these refuse to be moved.

Confused and frustrated, I sit back in the gondola, watching the door. The diamonds are still glittering without help from the moon, giving off an otherworldly glow.

I am fascinated and confused. Nothing like this door has ever been mentioned–and presumably, never been discovered–in Venice. But if anyone might have a clue as to what the door is, it would be Signor Maggio.

I wake up early the next morning, too excited to have enjoyed any restful sleep. At the first sign of daylight, I begin running to Signor Maggio's, anxious to ask him about the mysterious door that I found last night.

On my way, as I pass under the windows of many women hanging their laundry and see children playing in the streets, I spot my friend Matteo Bianchi as he walks through his front door and stares up at the clear, pale blue sky.

"Matteo!" I exclaim, giving him a wave.

Seeing me, Matteo rushes over–but he holds a finger to his lips. "Come with me."

I take the hint, and the two of us begin running down the street, not stopping until we're far away from his home. Then, I ask, "What's going on?"

Matteo sighs and pushes his dark hair out of his face. He is the image of a perfect Italian–a true Venetian. His olive skin and muscular jaw suggest his genuine lineage and make him look older than he is–although, ironically, I'm quite a few inches taller than him. "I'm dropping out of school, Peter."

I laugh lightly. "So what?"

"Well," begins Matteo, stammering and trying to feign confidence, "you aren't in school, so I wanted to get your opinion on the matter."

I lean against a brick wall and cross my arms. "Matteo, you know that I've never liked school–so I simply don't go."

"But how do you manage that?"

I shrug nonchalantly. "Well, you know. I don't have any parents or family holding me down, forcing me to go. That's just how it is. But you–you have a family who makes you go to school. In fact, it's not just them. It seems like every woman in Venice would like you to go!"

"They'd like you to go, too," says Matteo in a hushed voice. His eyes are darting back and forth as though someone is about to spring upon us from the nearest alleyway. "I've heard them say so. But they can't force you."

"Of course not," I say proudly, allowing arrogance to slip into my tone. "So, you see why I wonder why you're asking me for advice. If you don't want to go to school, you'll have to find a trade pretty quickly–or, you'll have to run away."

Matteo frowns and crosses his arms, obviously not pleased by these options. "I can't do either of those. My father would punish me for sure. He thinks I need to study useless stuff. Matteo snickers and does his best American accent "like other languages." According to Matteo, his father fought in the Great War and amused himself by doing impressions of foreign soldiers–a talent which he passed on to his son.

I smirk and shrug, a wave of superiority washing over me. "There, you see? You can't do anything, because your family is tying you down. I can't help you there."

Matteo groans and looks down the street, observing all the various shops coming to life and opening for the day. "I'm not ready to learn a trade. I can't imagine working every day like my father, and getting home late . . . I just don't think I'm ready for that. Besides, my father wants me to join the military, just as soon as I'm old enough. What use would a trade be to me?"

"Then I guess school is all you've got right now."

Matteo wrings his hands and stares at me for a long second, concern written all over his tan face. Then, he begins stammering, trying to sound confident but utterly failing. "Well . . . I'll, um, have to think about it. You know, make sure I'm doing what's best. After all, I suppose I don't want to let my family down. They're counting on me to finish school."

I smile and begin to reply but then remember I am on a mission to find Signor Maggio. Seeing Matteo's eager, friendly face, I almost want to tell him about the mysterious door . . . but I don't. For now, the door is my secret, and will soon be Signor's, as well.

"Well," I say, "I have to go, Matteo. Signor Maggio is waiting for me."

Matteo nods, the look on his face still uncertain and distraught. "*Ciao*," he says.

I give him a wave and begin running down the street, relishing the familiar feeling of the wet cobblestones under my feet.

Matteo is not be much like me. He always seems to be nervous about something, while I'm confident. He's calm, and I'm energetic. But he and I have known each other for as long as I can remember. He, along with Signor Maggio and the Hoffmans, make up my main circle of friends. It doesn't matter that Matteo and I aren't alike in the slightest; we had a common need, and we found the solution in one another.

Before I know it, I've reached Signor's, and I knock eagerly at the door, surprised to see that the shop hasn't opened yet.

It takes a moment for him to answer. When he does, I rush straight inside the bookshop, leaving Signor to stare at me with a surprised look on his face.

"Signor," I say quickly, "have you ever heard of a secret door in one of the canals?"

Signor Maggio stares at me, processing my words for a moment. Running a hand through his tousled, graying black hair, he asks, "Have you been reading more stories, Peter?"

"No," I exclaim, grabbing onto a table eagerly. "This was *real*! I saw it just last night. I was in my gondola, headed down a narrow canal, when the gondola began shaking. I lost my balance and fell. Then, I found a stone door, built into the wall. It had a circle of diamonds at the top, and a handle with little diamonds all over it. And . . . and there was a clock at the top. It was all glowing, Signor! It was beautiful!"

As I finish speaking, I notice the incredulous look that has appeared on Signor Maggio's face. "You *have* been reading stories, Peter," he says with a laugh. "You just described the ancient door that sits in the hidden canal of Venice. The legend says that the door has been revealed only twice, and for very specific reasons."

I open my mouth to continue, but for some reason, Signor Maggio's words make me falter. He seems so sure that the door is just a story, and nothing more. I wanted to share its secret with him, but he doesn't seem ready for that. In fact, he doesn't even seem willing to believe me. So, I simply stop talking and stare out the window, trying to think of something else to say.

"Would you like some coffee, Peter?" asks Signor.

I nod automatically–but my thoughts are focused on anything but coffee. This is because, now, without intention, I'm thinking about the conversation that I had with Matteo.

His family is one of the oldest in Venice. His great-grandfather was rumored to have been a descendant of royalty, and although no one was ever sure of this, the Bianchi family became well-known and respected in all of Venice–and they still are to this day. I begin to wonder about my own family.

Just as Signor begins to pour my cup of coffee, I ask suddenly, "Signor? What were my parents like?"

Signor Maggio stops pouring abruptly. Then, he looks at me, a mix of confusion and surprise on his face. "What makes you ask that, Peter?"

I sit down on a stool and lean forward. "Well, it's a natural question, isn't it?"

"Yes," mutters Signor, "I suppose it is. You've just never really asked it before, is all."

I wait expectantly in silence, willing Signor Maggio to speak. He finishes pouring my coffee and hands it to me.

Then, sitting down in his old, wooden chair, he begins. "Well, I've told you that your father was Italian, and your mother American."

I nod, and Signor continues. His brow is furrowed, as though he has to use a lot of effort to recall every detail he wants to tell me about. "Your mother was beautiful. Tall, blonde-haired, and blue-eyed, she was a rare beauty. I had never seen the likes of her before. She came to the bookstore often; I suppose she must have enjoyed reading very much. Then, there was your father. He'd spent many years in America, but he was from Rome, and he looked the part. He seemed to be from a rich, noble family; he was handsome and dressed smartly. Let's see . . . he had dark hair, and he was tall–a bit taller than myself. I believe he had blue eyes . . . and he always wore a wide smile. You look quite a bit like him, Peter."

I smile to myself, and I listen eagerly as Signor begins to explain how he met my parents. "The two of them arrived in Venice in 1924. Your father told me that they had been touring Europe for the past year, and they were looking to spend an extended amount of time in *Venezia*. I got to know them fairly well, as they stopped by the bookstore quite often, like I said. And then . . ."

Signor's voice trails off, and I watch as a strange sort of look settles in his eyes. "They disappeared for quite some time. They almost never left their hotel room, and when they were seen in public, it was always very brief. They stopped coming by the shop, and after a while, I began to wonder if they had decided to leave."

"And?" I ask, my heart racing in anticipation. "What happened?"

Signor looks at me, and a soft, gentle look comes over his face. "On June 20th, 1925, just ten days after you were born, you were left here–with me. I don't know who left you, but there was a note. That's how I found out that your parents had died. So I promised myself that I would look after you and make sure you were safe. Being a bachelor myself, I was unprepared to care for an infant. I was advised to pass you off to the local orphanage in order for you to receive proper care as a child, and I did . . . but I kept looking out for you."

I stare at Signor Maggio, dumbfounded. I've asked him a little about my parents before, but he always hesitated to share. I certainly never expected him to tell me this much. And at the same time . . . so little.

"So," I say slowly, "is that all?"

Signor is still looking at me gently. "Yes. Whoever left you with me was gone and apparently wished to remain anonymous. I don't know why they chose me–but they trusted me enough to make sure that you were safe."

I stare out the window for a long time, unsure of what to say. Although this is the most Signor Maggio has ever told me about my parents, I still feel disappointed. There has to be something else he can tell me–something I've never known before. *Anything* to give me a better picture of the people my parents were. Did they enjoy school when they were children, or did they hate it, like me? Did they like writing just as much as they liked to read? When they listened to music, did it carry them off to a thousand different worlds and give them a feeling of exhilaration?

A question slips in soundlessly from the recesses of my mind. Quietly, without looking at Signor, I ask, "Why was I named Peter?"

Signor stares at me in a way that makes me wonder if he's trying to search my thoughts. Then, he says softly, "Your parents named you after St. Peter because your father was from Rome. They spent their honeymoon there. Peter, believe me when I tell you that they cared about you. They wanted you to know you were loved."

I nod, and for a moment, I try hard to picture my parents' faces–but I don't see them. Instead, I see myself as a baby, being held by a woman whose face is a mystery. "I wish I could've met them," I whisper. "I want to know what they were like."

Signor looks at me with a smile, and although this smile seems to be a happy one, I can clearly detect a hint of sadness behind it. "I'm sorry, *caruso*," he says. "I wish I could help you. It is an important thing to know where you're from. But, know this: I will always be here for you."

I sigh, nod, and force a smile. "I know."

8
PETER

VENICE, ITALY
SUMMER, 1938

"I want you to have this, Peter."

Dumbfounded, I stare blankly at the beautiful leather-bound book in Signor Maggio's hands. The book is open as it rests in his hands, and I can see that not a single page has been written on. The emptiness taunts me, almost daring me to spoil the crisp paper with ink.

Signor has always let me borrow his books to read, but he has never given me one to keep–much less one that's never been written in. Now, faced with this gift, I'm not quite sure what to say.

"Oh," I whisper, shifting back and forth from one foot to the other. "Uh–well, thank you, but . . . I wouldn't know what to do with it."

Signor looks up at me from his chair and gives me a knowing look and a smile. "Oh, yes you do, Peter. I know you. You're a storyteller–but you've never put your stories down on paper. It's about time that you tried."

I swallow hard and shake my head, feeling heat rise to my cheeks. "But, Signor . . ."

Signor Maggio must sense my hesitation, because he says gently, "I know that you don't really know how to write. It may not come as naturally for you as reading does–but you will never learn if you do not try."

Still not convinced that I deserve such a precious gift, I walk over to look out of the shop window, admiring the way the golden sun casts its light throughout the streets of Venice. "I don't know what to write about."

Signor Maggio laughs and shakes his head. "Write anything! Write about your life. Write about the lives of the people you meet. Everything and every person has a story. Your job is to find out what that story is, and to share it with the world."

Turning back to Signor, I take a moment to stare at the beautiful book from afar, its pages fresh and open to new opportunities. Then, in a moment of impulse, I rush forward and take the book from his hands. "I'll certainly try."

Signor said to write about my life–but I don't see how I can when I don't even know *how* to write . . . at least, not well.

I stare at my crude imitation of the alphabet that rests on the first previously-blank page of my journal. That page was so beautiful before, and now it's been ruined by my failed attempt at simply writing a few letters down.

Sighing, I carefully rip this page out and crumple it into a ball, tossing it to one end of my gondola. I may not be able to write well—but I can certainly manage to piece a few words together to make a story. I told Signor that I'd try, and I'm not going to let him down now.

On the next page, I bite my lip in concentration and take my time writing out the first sentence. *On June 10th, 1925, a boy was born in Venice.*

I stare at the sentence for a while—and the longer I stare, the more I wish the words would burn in front of my eyes. The letters are jumbled and crooked, and the sentence is simple and plain—but I have to continue, if only for Signor.

I place my pencil back down on the paper, ready to write the next sentence—but my hand doesn't seem to want to move. I let it rest on top of the page for a moment, thinking that perhaps, I simply need time to mull over my next words. After a few exhausting minutes of waiting, though, I know the obvious, frustrating truth. I can't write about my life when I don't know half the story.

In frustration, I slam the book shut and set it down. Then, I lean forward and let my head rest in my hands, shielding my eyes from the glaring sunlight.

My mother was beautiful. My father was noble. I let these words repeat themselves over and over again in my mind. They're the words that Signor Maggio spoke about my parents—but no matter how much I'd like to picture them in my mind, I can't. I just can't see them. They're two faceless figures–silhouettes–blurred and erased from my memory. A mystery I'll never be able to uncover.

Leaning over the gondola, I stare into the murky blue water and whisper, "It's not fair." The water doesn't give me even the slightest ripple or wave in response.

Matteo knows where he comes from. Signor Maggio knows where he comes from. Even Rebekah Hoffman knows where she comes from. They know more about their pasts than I'll ever know about mine–and I hate it. It makes me feel like I'm missing something. It leaves me without anyone to call my family.

My parents may not have lived long enough to raise me, but I know they loved me. I know because of the gentle feeling I get when I think of them. I get the same feeling when I'm out on the water, or watching the sun rise or set. I get it when I see families walking together down the cobblestone roads.

Maybe I have family in America right now. Maybe they regret the fact that they weren't able to meet me, but they don't know where I am. I can just imagine what it would be like if we were reunited. I would meet all my grandparents and aunts, uncles and cousins. I would hug them and love them and do everything I could to please them. I would go to school for them, and we would attend church together, and we would tell stories around the dinner table. They may frustrate me sometimes, and we may disagree–but I would never stay angry at them for long, because I would love them, and they would love me. We would be a family.

Exhausted by these thoughts, I lie down in my gondola and watch as the sky turns dark. A few stars appear just as my eyelids become heavy, and I fall asleep shortly after, finding peace in the familiar sound of water splashing softly.

9
EILEEN

CHICAGO, ILLINOIS
SPRING, 1965

I push my way through the crowded hallways of Kennedy High School, passing by countless people who I've known for years but never really talked to. Girls whose lives are defined by red lipstick and dates; boys who wear leather jackets and speed through town in muscle cars on Saturday nights.

Keeping my head down, I manage to avoid eye contact with everyone I pass as I make my way to the restroom. There, for once, I'm able to find some temporary peace and quiet. I fish through my bag for a brush and take it in my hands before going to stand in front of the mirror.

Reaching up, I begin pulling the brush through my shoulder-length, slightly-mussed brown hair; then, I readjust my pale yellow headband. I'm ready to head to class . . . but that's the last place I want to go. I'd rather not go home, either. If I'm being honest, there's nowhere I can go that will help me. Nowhere that will make me happy.

For some people, high school is a time for creating lifelong memories, making friends, and most importantly, finding yourself. So, when I graduated eighth grade four years ago, I decided to go into it with that mindset. Sure, I was nervous–but I thought high school would be an adventure. Then, everything changed.

I'm not the same person I was before I lost my cousin. Back then, I might have been young and insecure, especially when it came to my looks–but I was also optimistic. I was adventurous. I always had this unfailing, ever-present sense of hope about me. Even when my family couldn't seem to move on from the past. Even when we couldn't seem to communicate. It never really mattered, because I always had Carolyn. Until I didn't.

I thought I'd be starting high school with a familiar face. I thought I'd see my cousin in the hallways every day. When that didn't happen, something changed inside me. The confidence which I would have had with Carolyn present seemed to disappear.

My parents became worried about me, especially my mother . . . but I knew she couldn't take another thing. She has enough to worry about with fourteen-year-old Tommy, who now prefers to go by the more 'mature' name of 'Tom,' although his actions at school and the daily phone calls from the principal would say otherwise. So, for our mother's sake, I tried to put on a happy facade, going through the daily routine of school and working my job at the local drive-in.

Eventually, I disappeared into the background of Kennedy High School, and I never reappeared. I made some friends and attended a couple school events, but as the years went by and I passed by my classmates in the hallways every day, I was sure that very few of them even knew my name. It all felt like a terrible dream that I couldn't control. A world where I wanted to be known, but couldn't. A world where no one seemed to understand me.

These are the thoughts flying through my head as I walk out of the restroom, down the hallway, and into history class on May 14th, 1965. In a few weeks, I will graduate from high school–and the closer I get to that day, the harder it gets to pay attention in class. To make matters worse, I have Kevin Maxwell sitting behind me in history. For the past two years, it's seemed to me that he's spent every minute of that time trying to set me on edge. Some days, he succeeds . . . and today is one of those days.

The bell lets out a shrill ring just as I take my seat, and I watch as my teacher, Miss Stone, steps forward to address the class. With her jet-black, curly hair and pale skin, I've always thought that Miss Stone looks sort of like a real-life version of Snow White. The only difference is, she certainly doesn't act like her.

"Okay, class," she says, and I try not to wince at the sharpness of her tone. "Today, we'll be continuing our lesson on the Great Depression. And if you gentlemen would be so kind as to keep silent, I think the class would prefer it if we got through the lesson faster rather than slower." Miss Stone casts a wary eye on the boys sitting behind me, who begin snickering.

"Can everyone please turn to page 85 in their books?" she says as she crosses over to the blackboard hanging behind her desk.

I busy myself with adjusting my reading glasses and trying to locate this page. As soon as I find it, I hear Miss Stone ask the same question that she's been asking me for the past year: "Eileen, will you please read?"

I open my mouth immediately in preparation to read, but even as I do, I can already feel Kevin's breath on the back of my neck. "Oh, look–today's topic is 'How Eileen became the teacher's pet.' I'm surprised Miss Stone is gonna let you graduate. How's she going to handle things without you?"

Somehow, whether she's pretending or not, Miss Stone doesn't seem to hear Kevin's words–so I follow her lead. Leaning forward and sitting up straighter in my desk, I push my glasses up on my nose and begin reading. "The Great Depression began in 1929."

I can hear a couple other people begin snickering. I don't even need to look around the room to know who they are. Denise Clancy and Clark Thomas–two of the most popular kids in school. When I say popular, this doesn't mean that Denise and Clark are smart. In fact, they're probably two of the worst students in the senior class. They're also dating, which means that they agree on most things . . . including how to best make fun of me.

I keep my eyes focused on the page in front of me, but even as I do, I see Denise out of the corner of my eye, flipping her long, black hair and snapping her gum. To my right, I can see Clark readjusting the collar of his black leather jacket and pulling a comb out of his pocket.

I finish reading, and Miss Stone gives me a nod of approval. "Thank you, Eileen. Now, I'd like you all to continue reading on your own. Then, I'd like you to come up with two things that stood out to you."

The class goes silent for the next ten minutes. After that, we have a conversation which finishes just as the bell rings. Letting out an automatic sigh of relief, I practically throw my reading glasses into my bag and rush out of the classroom without a word to anyone, fleeing from their ignorant whispers and taunts.

I should be used to this by now. I was labeled "teacher's pet" from the first day of freshman year, and it never bothered me very much. For someone who's always wanted to be a journalist, I was glad that I was a good student. By the time my junior year rolled around, I was content hiding behind my schoolwork and flying under the radar. I was especially okay not getting close to other people, even though I knew that deep down, I wanted the relationships that my classmates had. But for some reason, as I near the end of my senior year, I can't help but wonder why nothing has ever changed for me.

I've never been one of the kids who hang out in big groups at the drive-in or get together for parties on Saturday nights. They don't mind the poor grades, but I like being a good student. It gives me a sense of accomplishment. However, sometimes I wish that, just once, *I* would be one of those girls who spend their evenings at loud parties, wearing a lot of makeup and hanging onto the shoulder of some guy with slicked-back hair and a pearly-white smile.

Still . . . I've tried that before. And I can't go back.

Walking through the hallway, I steer towards my friend Sandy's locker. Even before I reach the locker, I can see Sandy standing there, her long, blonde hair cascading down her back in perfect curls.

I lean against the wall and sigh. Sandy shuts her tan locker immediately and looks at me, raising her eyebrows. "What happened?" she asks in an expectant tone.

I shake my head and stare out at the flow of kids passing by. I cringe at the sound of their shoes on the squeaky, white floor. Smoothing my yellow pencil skirt and clutching my books tightly to my chest, I say, "Kevin."

Sandy laughs sheepishly. "Isn't it always? I'm telling you, Eileen, you have to get over him. Just because he's mad at you doesn't mean you did something wrong."

"Oh, no, I didn't do anything wrong," I say a bit sarcastically, making a face and shaking my head firmly. "I just turned him down for the winter dance sophomore year–that's all."

"You forget that you turned him down because of the way the fall dance went," Sandy reminds me as we begin walking slowly down the hallway. "He was a huge jerk, and I don't blame you for ending that relationship quickly."

"I don't blame myself, either–but Kevin's tried to make my life miserable since then." I reach up to twist a strand of my medium-length, light brown hair around my finger. Although my hair isn't curly, I've mastered the popular flip hairstyle so that it does turn up right at the ends, making it naturally wavy and nice to maintain. Still, I've never ceased wishing that my hair were a different color–especially blonde.

"So, what? Make *his* life miserable. Get back at him."

I smile at Sandy and shake my head in disbelief. "Why can't I be bold, like you?"

"Takes practice," says Sandy as we approach the door leading to our French class. "But, anyway . . . Don't worry about Kevin or anyone else. We're graduating, remember?"

"Yeah," I say as we step inside the classroom. "I remember."

10

PETER

VENICE, ITALY
SUMMER, 1938

S ummer has flown by almost completely in all its glory, heat, and freedom–the long, warm days slipping through the fingertips of every Venetian. But it doesn't bother me. I still have all the freedom I've always had. However, to my dismay, I've been unable to rediscover the mysterious door.

Yes, I've spent lots of time trying to find it again–but every time I try, I fail. Many times, I've set out on my gondola and spent hours traveling up and down the canals with nothing to show for my efforts. It's almost as if I was meant to find it when I *wasn't* looking for it.

So, although I'm still intrigued, I've stopped thinking about it. I'm able to look forward to spending time inside the bookshop as cooler autumn weather approaches. But for people like my friend Matteo Bianchi, or even Signor

Maggio, the end of summer comes with a few unwelcome changes.

For Matteo, it means the start of school. For Signor Maggio, it means less business, which means a much slower-paced time of the year is beginning. And then, there's the Hoffmans.

Summer is better for those in the ghetto. It brings more work and more opportunities. But autumn is approaching quickly, and before anyone knows it, winter will be here . . . and with winter comes hardship.

Although I stay with Signor Maggio during the wintertime, it doesn't make it much easier for me to bear the bleakness of the season. Years ago, the Venetian Carnival took place during winter–but that was abolished by Napoleon long before I was born. Now, the only bright spot during the season is December 25th, when I get to spend the day celebrating Christmas with Signor Maggio.

Transporting my thoughts back to the present, I take in the sights of the ghetto around me as I run to the Hoffmans' house. I haven't visited them in about a week, and I'd like to see them one last time before the glorious summer ends.

Reaching the house, I knock on the door, panting and out of breath. I wait outside for a moment, bouncing on the balls of my feet impatiently. A few seconds go by before the door swings open. This time, instead of Signora Hoffman answering, I'm greeted by Rebekah, whose face lights up when she sees me. "Hi, Peter!" she exclaims, reaching up one hand in an effort to calm her wild brown hair. "Come in!"

Walking inside and returning her warm greeting with a smile, my eyes land on Signora Hoffman, who is sitting in a worn rocking chair with an angelic Abigail in her arms. Her brown hair is tied back in a loose bun, and although there seems to be an air of calm about her, she appears to be extremely tired.

"Hello, Peter," she says, her eyes smiling at me. Rebekah goes to sit down at her mother's feet, as I find a chair across from the three Hoffmans.

"So," says Signora Hoffman quietly, rocking back and forth, "school is starting soon, Peter."

I blink in surprise. Of all the things for Signora Hoffman to say, this is the last thing I was expecting to hear. "Yes," I reply. "For everyone else, that is."

Signora Hoffman stares at me for a moment. Her gaze sends a shiver down my spine, giving me the feeling that she can read every thought in my mind. "Why don't you try going to school this year, Peter?"

I sigh and shake my head nonchalantly, glancing out the window and staring absentmindedly at all the people walking by. "Signora Hoffman, I think you know me well enough by now to know that I *have* tried school–and it's not for me. I know everything that I'll ever need to know."

Just then, Abigail wakes up from her peaceful slumber, and her wails prompt Signora Hoffman to pass her little daughter over to Rebekah, who walks to the other side of the room to feed her.

With her two daughters out of earshot, Signora Hoffman leans forward and takes a deep breath, her chocolate-brown eyes filled with emotion. "Peter," she says slowly, running a hand over her forehead and temporarily smoothing her few wrinkles. "You've known my daughters and I for many years.

You are a good boy–kindhearted, loyal, and smart. That is why I feel that it is my duty to say this to you. *Please*, Peter–go back to school, even if it's just for a little while."

I shake my head intensely, taken aback by this request. "I don't understand–"

"I never had any opportunities when I was growing up. Not only was I a Jew in a poor neighborhood, but I was a woman. My only hope was to marry a man with a good trade. Well, I did that–and I loved my husband immensely. But when he died, it became clearer to me than ever that I had no hope of raising my daughters better than I was raised."

Signora Hoffman pauses for a moment as a far-off look comes into her eyes, and she lays a hand on one of her angular cheeks. Then, she continues quietly. "Rebekah and Abigail may never escape from here. They may never know any other life than this. I am not afraid for them, because as long as they are happy, it doesn't matter how rich or poor they are. But let me tell you this, Peter: If my girls had half as many opportunities as you do, like the chance to go to school, I would not rest until they had taken advantage of those opportunities and learned everything they could about the world. Peter . . . I care about you as if you were my own son–and that is why I am telling you this. Do you understand now?"

I take a moment to observe Signora Hoffman's earnest, brown eyes, so full of wisdom and truth. Glancing to my left, I watch Rebekah and Abigail for a moment. Rebekah is bouncing her baby sister up and down and whispering tenderly in her ear. The sight of this causes a pang in my heart. These two sisters will never get the education or the life that

I could have. Their mother wants what's best for them–and she wants what's best for me, too. I am moved by her vulnerability and her words, and I want her to know it.

I nod slowly. "Yes. I think I do."

"Signor," I exclaim, bursting through the front door of the bookshop. "I have some news."

Signor Maggio, who happens to be sitting in his old chair, looks up at me from the book he's reading, a startled expression on his previously tranquil face. "Yes?" he says expectantly.

Taking a deep breath, I let the words spill out of my mouth. "I'm going back to school."

The look that appears on Signor Maggio's face is indescribable. Taking his time to stand up, he gazes at me in awe. "Oh, Peter," he says happily. "What made you change your mind?"

I shrug, trying to act casual even as newfound pride swells through my chest. "Well–Signora Hoffman talked me into it. I figured I could give it one more try."

Signor laughs, and it's the easiest laugh I've ever heard from him. "She must be a very convincing woman if she was able to accomplish such a feat as that."

I nod, and Signor takes a shaky step towards me. Laying a hand on my shoulder, he becomes more serious and says, "I'm so glad you've made this decision, Peter. School will not be difficult for you, thanks to your God-given memory.

You'll learn skills that will help you all throughout your life. You will be able to do anything."

Anything. The word sounds big and daunting to me, but thrilling at the same time. Maybe, Signor Maggio was right all along. Maybe going to school will give me more freedom than I ever had without it. As long as I keep my freedom, I'll be happy.

II

EILEEN

CHICAGO, ILLINOIS
SUMMER, 1965

I smile as the wind whips through my hair. Reaching over to turn up the radio, I listen as "I Feel Fine," by the Beatles begins to play. Pushing my sunglasses up on my nose, I turn the steering wheel of my blue Mustang and pull into my family's driveway. I put the car into park, turn off the engine, and simply sit there, almost in shock. It's June now, and I've finally done it–I've graduated high school. Although there's still the ceremony to attend, my finals are over. I'm eighteen and free, and I've never felt so happy in all my life.

I hear a sound coming from the front of the house, and I look up to see my mom opening the door and walking outside. The familiar picture of my tall, slender mother coming to greet me gives me a sense of comfort and calms me immediately. "Eileen," she exclaims, rushing up to give me a hug. "You did it!"

I laugh and take a deep breath. "I can't really believe it."

My mother stops a moment and stares lovingly at me. "I can. Look at you . . . You're so grown up. Ever since you started high school, I can hardly recognize you! You've grown a whole–"

"Two inches," I say with a smirk, doubtful of my mother's well-meaning words.

My mom laughs and shakes her head knowingly. "Oh, well . . . You've grown into such an amazing young woman. You're beautiful, honey–and so smart."

She takes another moment to gaze at me again, her green eyes seeming to well up with tears. Then, they're gone as quickly as they appeared, and a soft smile appears on my mom's face. "Well, come inside–I made some cookies, and you might want to get some before the kids eat them all. Besides, we can't miss the broadcast."

I nod, knowing all too well how quickly my siblings can eat a batch of cookies. I begin walking up the driveway with my mom at my side, feeling lighter than air.

Just as we enter through the front door, Julie comes running from our living room. "It's on! It's on!"

My mother and I glance at each other in excitement before the three of us rush to the living room and sit down on the couch in front of our TV. I'm not surprised to see that Tommy is already sitting just a few feet from the television set. Next to making trouble at school, learning about space seems to be his favorite pastime. Really, it's only when he's busy doing something related to space–or the military–that he's not getting into mischief and hanging out with his trouble-making friends.

"Gemini 4," he breathes, his big, green eyes bulging with fourteen-year-old fascination. "Gosh, it sounds so tuff."

"It looks groovy," observes Julie, her eyes glued to the TV screen.

"I hope your father is getting to watch this from the office," comments my mother, wringing her hands anxiously as we watch the astronauts board the spacecraft.

"Oh, I told him to," exclaims Tommy, his enthusiasm strangely foreign. "I called him."

"Well, there's no need to worry about Dad missing it–you know he'd be up there on that spaceship right now if he could," I reassure them, brushing off my white pencil skirt and readjusting my blue and yellow floral shell top.

Three. Two. One . . .

"There it goes!" yells Tommy, and Julie lets out an automatic shriek of excitement that only a ten-year-old girl could. My mother grabs my hand in anticipation. There, right on our very own black-and-white TV screen, Gemini 4 launches, sailing up and piercing through the cloud-dotted sky. Even though there's no color, I can almost see the fiery-orange cloud of exhaust that the spaceship leaves in its wake.

Suddenly, the phone rings–but no one hops up to answer it. Usually, my siblings would be fighting to reach the phone, but both of them seem transfixed by the TV screen. Even our mother can't seem to look away, one of her fingers nervously curling around a strand of hair. She waves in the direction of the phone and without looking at me, she says absentmindedly, "Eileen, would you please answer it?"

I'm not keen on leaving my place in front of the TV, but the ringing seems to be growing louder by the second.

Reluctantly, I stand up and walk over to the kitchen, where the phone is hanging on the wall. Picking it up, I say, "Hello?"

"Hey, Eileen May," a familiar voice responds.

I grin at the sound of my dad's voice, taking in his light Chicago accent. "Hi, Dad. Are you watching the broadcast?"

"Of course I am. I wouldn't miss it. I wish I were home with you all. Hey, congratulations on taking your last exam!"

That lighter-than-air feeling washes over me again as I'm reminded of my accomplishment. "Thanks!"

There's a pause on the other end of the line, and then the muffled sounds of talking before it clears up again. "Sorry about that, Eileen May–I've been pretty busy today. Well, I just wanted to check in. Besides, talking to you makes it seem like we're watching the broadcast together."

I smile and stare at the TV, trying to picture my dad fitting into this currently idyllic scene. "Yeah. I'll see you later, Dad. Love you."

"Love you, too, Eileen May."

"Oh, Eileen!"

I look up to see Sandy walking over to me. I'm standing behind the counter at Al's Drive-In, the job I've been working for about a year. It's been two days since graduation, and the way the town is hopping, you can tell that it's summertime. I'm supposed to be focusing on my job, but my mind's been wandering a bit, distracted by all the sights and sounds around me. Blinking and directing my attention towards my friend, I focus my eyes on her eager, freckled face.

"Hey! What's up?"

"First of all, I wanted to know what you're packing for the trip."

I let out a little gasp of excitement. It's been so busy lately that I've barely had time to process the fact that in less than two weeks, Sandy and I are leaving on a graduation trip to Italy with our classmates. It's a new idea–one that's made my parents pretty nervous, on account of the fact that my dad fought in Italy merely twenty years ago. However, my teachers were able to reassure my parents, along with everyone else, that things have changed over there in the past two decades, and we'll all be perfectly safe.

"Oh, gosh . . . I've barely had time to think about it. Just the essentials, I guess."

Sandy sighs and shakes her head, and I automatically know what's coming. "Well . . . I've packed my entire summer wardrobe, sundresses included, and my sun hat, and those really cute sunglasses that you said look like something Audrey Hepburn would wear–"

"Woah, there," I laugh, cutting her off and letting the customer behind her order. Sandy steps to the side and waits. "Hamburger? Yes, that'll be fifteen cents. Okay . . . Yes, you're welcome. Have a nice day."

Once the customer has left, I call to the kitchen over my shoulder. "Taking my break now." Then, after retrieving two root beers, I step out from under the blue-and-white-striped awning of the drive-in. I hand one root beer to Sandy, and we take a seat at a nearby picnic table in front of the restaurant. "Sandy . . . I thought Mrs. Nelson told us to pack *light*."

Sandy laughs and wrinkles her small, freckle-spattered nose, obviously enjoying my reaction. "Okay, maybe she did . . . But we're going to *Italy*. Rome is the fashion capital of the world. Why should I be expected to walk through the gorgeous city streets looking like I do on any regular school day? Everything needs to be special."

I fight the urge to laugh at this comment. Sandy is *always* dressed up, even at school. She's had an interest in fashion for as long as I can remember–something that we've always shared. However, once we started high school, Sandy took it a step further, joining clubs and even making her own clothes. While I used to write articles about fashion, I've since moved on to bigger things–or at least, I've tried.

After suppressing my laughter, I finally register the other part of Sandy's sentence. My breath catches in my chest at the thought of Rome, and a huge grin spreads across my face. I can feel my eyes crinkle as I smile–a trait whose effect is being doubled by the bright sunshine pouring onto my face. I've only ever seen the city in black-and-white photographs or movies, and to think that *I'm* going to be right there, in color and everything . . . Well, it's almost too good to be true.

"We leave in a couple weeks, right?"

"Yep."

"And we'll start in Rome, and move on through the country from there?"

Sandy nods, and I grin, overcome with excitement. "Ohh, gosh. I can't wait." In my eagerness, my elbow bumps into the cup of root beer sending it into a wobble. A couple onlookers hear me gasp and watch me panic, but Sandy simply reaches out to steady the cup.

Laughing, she says, "Me neither. I guess we'd better start learning our Italian, huh?"

I grin and take the cup from her gratefully. As I take a sip, my eyes land on a crowd of people gathered nearby, all leaning against a bright red Mustang. Music is blaring obnoxiously from the car radio, which attracts a few annoyed glances from several passersby. Every person standing by the car seems to be coupled off, and it doesn't take long for me to recognize multiple kids from school–including Kevin, Denise, and Clark.

As usual, my heart rate speeds up a bit, and I cast my gaze downwards, trying to breathe. I remark quietly, "Aren't you glad we won't have to put up with them once the trip is over?"

Following my gaze, Sandy nods, her curly blonde hair bouncing. "Sure. I figure there'll always be difficult people we have to deal with, though–no matter what we do in the future."

I turn back towards her and raise my eyebrows, snapping to attention. "In the future?"

Sandy nods again and adjusts her vibrant blue headband. "Yeah. For me, that'll be a job as a fashion designer–I hope. And for you . . . Don't you want to go to college?"

Swallowing hard, I shrug and feel my face go red. At the mere mention of college, I can almost hear the taunting whispers of my classmates, calling me "teacher's pet" and making something that I love turn into something that I hate. I shouldn't be giving them this much power–but it's difficult when words have such an impact on others, especially myself. I think I still want to be a journalist . . . but I don't know for sure anymore. If the past four years have taught me anything, it's that I'm not the sort of person to come up with the right words when I need them. That fact alone has made me doubt my ability to be a successful journalist one day. So, I've decided that I need some time to find myself–time to experience other things.

That's why I need this trip to Italy. I've never been away from home before, and I've heard that people can find themselves that way. I figure that, if I can just discover what I'm looking for on this trip, then I'll know what I want to do with my future. What I want to do with my *life*.

Sandy shrugs. "Well, you've got some time." She turns back to her own drink, but sensing my unease, she gives me a reassuring smile. "Besides, you shouldn't be thinking about anything right now but the trip. Alright?"

I nod and curl a strand of hair around my finger, giving my friend a grateful smile.

12
EILEEN

CHICAGO, ILLINOIS
SUMMER, 1965

Silence. It hangs in the air as my mother finishes cooking dinner, and my father and I sit at the table. My siblings are in the backyard, supplying the rest of us with some much-appreciated quiet. However, it's such an unfamiliar sensation that my parents and I don't seem to know what to do with it.

"Ooh, that looks good," I exclaim as my mother carries out a roast chicken. She sets it down next to the dark blue bowl of mashed potatoes that's already sitting on our small kitchen table.

"Molly, I'm beginning to think you're spoiling me," laughs my father, giving her arm a squeeze as she sits down next to him.

"I think I'm spoiling myself," replies my mom with a satisfied smile. "I'd like to start eating. Where are Tommy and Julie?"

With a knowing look on his face, my father pushes his chair away from the table, stands up, and walks over to the back door to call out to my siblings. "Come on, kids, you're missing out on some great food! Come and get it before we eat it all."

At this announcement, my siblings come running inside, their shoes scuffling against the linoleum floor. No sooner have they collapsed unceremoniously at the table than our mother raises her eyebrows expectantly and motions towards the kitchen sink. Tommy and Julie hop up and rush over to wash their hands, tripping over each other.

"What were you two doing out there?" asks our mom.

"Nothing," says Tommy in his casual, arrogant way, splashing water over the kitchen counter.

"Nothing?" repeats my mother incredulously.

"We were looking for spaceships!" exclaims Julie, receiving an elbow in the shoulder from Tommy.

"Did you see any?" I ask, a playful smile dancing on my lips.

"No," pouts Julie, glaring at Tommy and letting one of her pigtails whip across his freckled face. "He told me we would! All we saw was a lousy bird."

"Hey, what's that bird ever done to you?" asks our father, sitting back down in his chair and loosening his tie. "I'm sure that if he could travel up to space, he would."

"I wish Tommy would travel up to space," grumbles Julie, sitting back down.

Tommy follows and gives Julie a look that could kill. "It's *Tom*."

"That's enough, you two," interrupts my mother quickly. "Julie, next time Tommy–*Tom*–wants to go spaceship-watching, just know that you'll see a lot more birds than spaceships. Now, I'm hungry; everyone hold hands, and let me say grace."

Everyone bows their heads, and my mother prays. As soon as she finishes, my siblings begin a power struggle for who gets to fill their plates first.

"Hold it!" exclaims our mother, putting the fighting to a stop as quickly as it began. "I'll fill your plates. In the meantime, how about asking your father how his day was?"

"How was your day, Daddy?" asks Julie, quick to obey–mainly out of spite, as her question gets an immediate sour reaction from Tommy.

"It was good, darling," smiles our father. "I barely got a break."

"And that was good?" says Tommy doubtfully, receiving his plate of food and immediately diving into his mashed potatoes.

"Yes, it was–because it was another day I have a job. That's something to be grateful for, isn't it?"

I take a bite of mashed potatoes and wonder how in the world my father can be so positive. I like him best when he's like this: perfectly happy and content.

"Your father's right," says my mother, a smile on her rosy face. "We're very blessed. Eileen? How was your day?"

I look up from my food and answer, "I talked to Sandy today. About the trip."

Although my family is well-aware of my trip, saying these words out loud feels almost surreal. As if this trip which I've been planning these past few months has always been some sort of pipe dream–not something that was really going to happen.

"Oh, honey," gushes my mom, who's been helping me pack and plan, "you must be so excited."

"I am. I mean, I just can't believe it's almost here. To think that our plane is landing in Rome, and we'll stay there for about a week . . ."

"That means you're going to meet Dean Martin!" screams Julie, her eyes bulging. She begins leaning towards me in an effort to hang on to my arm and becomes dangerously close to falling off her chair. "Oh, that's groovy! Eileen, you have to get his autograph, and tell him about me, and tell him that I own all his records and that–"

"Julie, Dean Martin doesn't live in Italy," I say gently, biting my lip to keep from laughing at Julie's innocent eagerness.

I watch as my sister's face falls. "But he's Italian."

"He lives here, though, in America."

Julie stops to consider this; I can almost see the wheels turning in her ten-year-old brain. As she's thinking, Tommy looks up from his plate of food to say, "And that's where pasta was invented?"

I nod slowly, surprised by any form of civil interaction with my brother. I almost expect there to be some sort of interesting follow-up question to this. There isn't, and Tommy goes back to eating with a half-satisfied look on his face.

"Matthew?" says my mother softly. "You haven't said anything."

My father's eyes shift between my mother and I for a moment before finally landing on me. "Oh, that's great, Eileen May," he says with a half-smile. "I'm sorry, I'm just– a little surprised."

"You don't look surprised, Dad. You look shocked," observes Tommy, stating the obvious.

"Uh–just a little bit, I guess," replies our father, rubbing his jaw. "Well–I'm just contemplating all this. I mean, I'm not sure how I feel about Eileen going out of the country, especially when it's for a whole month. And with the war in Vietnam . . . Who knows what could happen in all that time?"

"But Dad, you've always been fine with me traveling," I exclaim, trying desperately not to sound like I'm whining. "I just don't understand. Besides, you already told me I could go. And–well, you've been to Italy before. It's got to be safe if you've been there."

My father stares down at his plate of food to cut his piece of chicken, and I watch as a familiar, glazed look appears in his eyes. "That was for war, Eileen. I didn't go to Italy as a tourist–I went there as a soldier. And may I remind you that Italy is not much safer now than it was then."

Tommy's ears perk up at the mere mention of World War II. "But what was it like, Dad?"

"Tommy," my mother hushes him. I feel myself bristle, my body automatically preparing for the inevitable tension that's bound to come.

"It's okay, Molly," interjects my father, in spite of the fact that we all know he'd rather not talk about this. He turns to Tommy and begins scratching his head of dark hair. "Well–it was hard, Tommy. I knew it was going to be hard, but going to war was tough on me. I was only eighteen, and I was too young. I didn't really know what I was doing."

There's a long moment of silence as Tommy contemplates this. Slowly, he nods, and his eyes drift back down to his plate of food–but he doesn't eat.

No one seems to know what to say next, so our mother decides to jump in. "Ah, well," she says quickly, forcing a half-smile and trying to cover her nerves with a sugary-sweet coating. Taking our father's hand in her own, she finishes, "Thankfully, it's all over now, and you're here. And Eileen will be perfectly safe with Mr. and Mrs. Nelson, and her classmates."

At the sound of these words, our father looks up and nods eagerly, his mood switching in an instant. "Of course she will," he says cheerfully, turning to me. "You be safe over there and stick with your teachers. And write us letters every day." At this last sentence, I let out a silent sigh of relief as he gives me a wink and a smile–proof that his hesitation in allowing me to go was only temporary.

Later, as I sit in bed listening to my Herman's Hermits record spin softly on my record player, I open the Italian-English Dictionary which I bought for myself two weeks ago. I've been trying to learn some Italian before the trip, but so far, I haven't proven to be very skilled at it. I bite my lip in concentration and try to sound out a phrase. "*Lei parla inglese?*" I say softly.

Suddenly, I hear a knock at my door, and I crane my neck to see who it is. "Come in."

I almost expect to see my mother or father coming to say goodnight–but instead, the door opens to reveal my sister, dressed in a pink nightgown and carrying one of her Dean Martin record albums. One that used to be mine. At the mere sight of it, a lump rises in my throat–but I swallow hard and push it down.

"Julie?" I say in a questioning tone. "What're you doing?"

"Well," says Julie, climbing onto my bed, I wanted to speak with you."

I raise my eyebrows and move over to make room for her. "About?"

"About . . . your trip."

I wait patiently for an explanation as Julie takes her time looking around. She's always had a fascination with my room, with all the posters on its walls, a collection of records by Herman's Hermits, the Beatles, and Elvis, and the many books on my shelf. Her big, blue eyes have always seemed a bit too large for her small frame, and when she's excited or curious, their effect is amplified, giving her an appearance of childlike innocence and wonder.

"Well," she says slowly, her eyes glued to my poster of the Beatles, "I wanna know . . . how long you'll be gone."

I shrug, my shoulder-length brown hair bouncing. "A few weeks."

Julie nods, her chestnut pigtails swinging. Then, she asks, "But–what about *after* that?"

I get that familiar, uneasy feeling again. "What do you mean?"

"I mean . . . are you going to college someplace far away? Am I ever going to see you again?"

My heart breaks–but I respond in the only way an older sister can. Laughing, I say, "Of course you're going to see me again! What kind of a question is that? Wherever I go to college–*if* I go–it won't be that far. Besides, I would be done in four years."

Julie nods, but she doesn't look convinced. Still smiling, I take hold of one of her pigtails and twirl it around my finger. Deciding to change the subject, I ask, "What'd you bring your record in here for?"

Remembering the record in her hands, a small smile appears on Julie's face. "Oh, yeah. I wanted to play it for you– so you can remember it and write to me to tell me if it sounds like Italy. Like *real* Italian music. And then, I can play it and feel like I'm right there with you."

I almost cringe at the innocence in her words and tone. How is it that my ten-year-old sister is better at communicating her emotions than I am? I can feel my face going red from a mix of confusion and embarrassment, so I force a light-hearted laugh. "Sure. Go ahead."

Jumping up with newfound energy, Julie bounds over to my record player, where she switches "Can't You Hear My Heartbeat" to "On an Evening in Roma." Then, she returns to my bed, where the two of us sit in comfortable silence, enjoying the peace and calm of the night. Meanwhile, I try not to think about the fact that the very music that I used to find solace in is now the music that my heart can barely stand to hear.

13

PETER

VENICE, ITALY
AUTUMN, 1938

$\mathbb{A}$ slight chill fills the air as I walk down the cobblestone streets of the city. In the summertime, the feel of these cool stones was refreshing under my feet; lately, however, I've felt a need for something I haven't wanted in a long time: shoes.

Of course, the weather isn't the only reason I have for finally wearing shoes. I was also encouraged to wear them to school, by Signor Maggio and my teacher, Signora Rossi.

Signor Maggio gave me an old pair of shoes, plus some suitable clothing, and just like that, I found myself heading off to school–ready or not. The first couple of weeks were difficult, to say the least. The weather was still warm, and all I wanted was to be outside, spending my days as I wished. I hated being cooped up in a stuffy room where I felt that I didn't belong, especially when I discovered mathematics.

However, once my teacher found out how "gifted" I was, it was as if I realized it for the first time, too.

As my teacher taught me about the world, how to improve my reading, and–most importantly–how to write, I realized just how much information I could gather in my mind. According to Signora Rossi, I was different, which is why I was able to skip a whole grade after only one month of school. Not only was I different, but I was "special." And I'd never thought of myself in that way before. I'd heard many people say it, like Signor Maggio and Signora Hoffman, but this was different. This time, I was hearing it from a teacher, of all people.

She wasn't perfect, of course. She was pretty strict in the classroom, and she sure fit the role of stern school teacher, with her brown hair tied back in a tight bun and her eyes slanted all the time. But she treated me well, and I listened to her.

I became well-learned in the next four months, reading as much as I could and memorizing as much information as possible. I spent time with my friends, like Matteo. I continued to visit Signor Maggio and the Hoffmans. Lots stayed the same–but plenty changed, too. *I* changed. Sometimes, I like it–but a lot of the time, I don't. That's why I'm headed to see Signor Maggio right now. Today happens to be one of those days when I'm in need of a friendly face after a long day of hard work.

Reaching the bookshop, I burst inside as I always do, letting the door slam behind me. "Signor!"

Signor Maggio is nowhere to be seen. Shutting the door softly behind me, I take a few cautious steps forward. "Signor?"

Just then, he steps out from behind one of his bookshelves, a smile on his face. "*Ciao*, Peter."

I grin and rush forward, a book in my outstretched hands. "I have something to show you."

Signor Maggio raises his eyebrows and limps over to me, leaning on his cane. "This is the journal I gave you."

I nod. "Yes. I filled it up."

"With what?"

I shrug happily. "Oh, stories. Anything I could think of."

Signor takes the book in his hands and returns to his chair. He then leafs through it slowly and thoroughly. I try to stand still, but I end up shifting back and forth, anxious to know exactly what he thinks. Eventually, after about ten minutes, I can't stand the suspense anymore. "Well?"

Looking up, Signor smiles at me. There's a look on his face that I can't describe. "I knew it, Peter."

I frown and take the book from his hands, examining it as though it holds some secret I'm not yet privy to. "What?"

"That you were born for this. Stories come dancing from your pencil faster and more beautifully than anything I've ever seen before."

I feel my face flush, and I shake my head. My eyes land on the rows of books sitting in the back of the shop, and I motion towards them. "Signor, I'm flattered–but that can't be true. You have all these books to compare it to."

Signor laughs and shakes his head. "But that's just it, Peter. I'm not comparing it. I can't compare it, because it's one of a kind. This collection of stories–this collection of your thoughts–could only be written by you."

I smile and stare down at the well-loved journal in my hands.

"Have you shown your stories to anyone else?" asks Signor.

I look back up at him and nod. "Rebekah Hoffman. I've told you about her, remember? She lives in the ghetto."

Signor nods slowly, recognition coming over his slightly-wrinkled face. "Oh, yes. I remember. She's the girl who's been devouring books even faster than you."

Without acknowledging this last teasing sentence, I reply, "I believe her mother taught her–although neither of them received much schooling."

Signor Maggio nods again–and suddenly, a strange feeling comes over me. It's an urge I can't describe, but it's so big and powerful that I have no other choice but to obey it. "Signor Maggio, why don't you come visit the Hoffmans with me today? I'd like to bring Rebekah some new books– and I'm sure she'd love to meet you."

To my surprise, Signor's mouth drops open slightly, and he begins laughing. "Oh, no, Peter–I'm not sure I could do that."

I shake my head in confusion. "Why not?"

Signor lets out a long, weary sigh. "It could be dangerous for everyone involved. It's not dangerous for you, because you are merely a boy, and no one thinks anything of it. But– well, it would not be proper for me to go."

Laughing, I exclaim, "Of course it would! Why wouldn't it be?"

Signor opens his mouth to reply, but he hesitates. There's something in his eyes that I've never seen before: human weakness.

Suddenly, it hits me. He's afraid. Signor Maggio is afraid. And I don't know whether I should feel sorry for him, or ashamed—or both.

Thinking for a moment, I try to find a new tactic to convince him. "Well—it would mean so much to Rebekah. She doesn't go to school, and she doesn't know very many people. I've told her all about you, and she's always wanted to meet you, but she says it's too dangerous for her to come here. Just think about that, Signor. It's more dangerous for her to come to us than for us to go to her. So why don't you come with me? Just this once."

Signor doesn't say anything for a moment. There's a sort of stunned look on his face, as though he's having a difficult time processing the weight of my words. I'm about to break the silence and give up when he hobbles over to his desk, puts on his hat, and picks up two beautifully-bound books. "Alright. Let's go."

The ghetto seems more somber than ever today. Whenever I visit, there always seems to be a sort of energy and feeling of life throughout the streets—but today is different. Maybe it's because the sky is darkening earlier, or maybe it's because this time, I have Signor Maggio with me. Whatever it is, it gives me a strange, uneasy feeling.

The moment we reach the Hoffmans' house, I glance up at Signor's face. It's void of any emotion now–good or bad. I know that Signor must be incredibly curious to know what these people are like.

Reaching forward, I knock on the door. To my surprise, it swings open almost immediately–but it falters halfway through.

"Who's there?" a small voice asks as the door begins closing slowly.

"Rebekah, it's me," I say quickly. "Peter."

Rebekah's brown eyes shift and land on me. The moment they do, a faint glimmer of happiness shines through them. However, Rebekah doesn't open the door any wider.

"Who's that with you?" she says in a voice barely above a whisper.

"Signor Maggio," I answer. "I've told you all about him. Remember? I bring you books of his all the time."

At this, the door swings open all the way, a loud creaking sound accompanying it, and Rebekah stands before us, examining Signor with wide eyes.

"*Ciao*," says Signor Maggio with a warm smile. At the sight of Rebekah's innocent face, Signor is acting like his old self again.

Rebekah doesn't reply. Instead, she simply continues to stare at Signor Maggio through her long, dark hair.

"Rebekah, let them come in," a voice calls from inside the house.

Still too awestruck to open her mouth, Rebekah silently obeys and lets us step inside her home. It isn't a very well-insulated house, but it still protects all of us from the cold.

As Signor and I take a few more steps inside, Signora Hoffman rounds the corner quickly and ends up standing a mere two feet away from Signor.

"Oh, hello," she stammers, taking a quick step back and readjusting little Abigail in her arms. Reaching up, she tucks a few loose strands of dark hair out of her face in an embarrassed way. "You must be the bookseller that Peter talks so much about, yes?"

Signor Maggio nods in an unusually manic way and uses his cane to steady himself. His normally-calm demeanor has vanished entirely, and he's frozen to the spot as words begin tumbling out of his mouth. "Yes. I mean–I believe so. I'm not sure he knows many other booksellers."

Signora Hoffman manages a faint smile which spreads a pink glow to her cheeks, and she looks down at Abigail, loose strands of hair from her bun falling back over her eyes. "Oh."

As the two stand in the middle of the room, making small talk and awkward introductions, a strange sensation comes over me. For the first time in my life, both Signor Maggio and Signora Hoffman look–well, *young*. Neither one is really that old; Signor is in his early forties, and Signora Hoffman has to be in her mid-thirties. But seeing the two of them together gives me a funny feeling that I've never experienced before. I'm seeing them in a new light–and even as Rebekah and I exit the house to go play in the alleyway, I can't help feeling a sense of comfort leaving Signor Maggio and Signora Hoffman together. For the first time, my two worlds have combined–and it feels good.

14
EILEEN

CHICAGO, ILLINOIS
SUMMER, 1965

My heart quickens as I rush through the airport with Sandy at my side. We're surrounded by well-dressed people in suits and floral dresses, all with a different destination in mind. I know that our teachers, Mr. and Mrs. Nelson, are counting on us to get to our plane on time, judging by the way they're practically running just ahead of us, but this is my first time in an airport–and, frankly, I'm a bit too distracted by my surroundings to walk any quicker than I already am.

The sentiment seems to be shared by our classmates. Lois Jefferson and her best friend Janet Willard have been talking non-stop about Rome, their excitement contagious. Even the presence of Kevin and his friend Davey can't put a damper on the day.

After a few minutes of walking, the ten of us, including our chaperones and our two other classmates, Alan and Jay, reach our boarding area. As we stand in line, I turn my head to look out one of the nearby windows. My eyes widen in awe as they land on a large, white plane rolling slowly by.

"Sandy," I breathe in excitement, tapping my friend's arm. "Look."

Sandy, who's been busy brushing off her blue pencil skirt and making sure her ticket is in hand, looks up quickly. "What?"

I gesture towards the plane with a look of, *Isn't it obvious?* In response, Sandy laughs. "Oh. You mean the plane?"

I nod and blush, suddenly remembering that Sandy has been to the airport many times before.

Mr. and Mrs. Nelson reach the front of the line, and the ten of us present our tickets one at a time. As we board the plane, a gust of wind rushes through the gate, ruffling my hair, and I feel a shiver of anticipation run down my spine.

It doesn't take long for Sandy and I to find our seats. She lets me take the window seat, and I sit down, buckling up immediately. I take a moment to glance around and observe all the well-dressed people sitting near me, and once again, I feel grateful to my mom for advising me to wear a nice outfit for the ride. Then, turning to stare out the window and watching a few other planes roll by, I quickly become lost in my thoughts.

There's a strange feeling inside me that I can't quite put my finger on. All I know is, it must be the feeling that something important–something *bigger*–is finally happening to me. I've always been content with my life, but these past four years have been . . . well, monotonous. I just know that this is the start of something different.

My stomach turns into butterflies as the captain begins speaking. "It's time," whispers Sandy as she buckles into her seat. "Are you ready?"

I grin and nod, preparing myself for the feeling of flying through the air–an exhilarating feeling that I've never known before but always imagined. The plane begins gaining speed, rolling faster and faster, until just like that–

Whoosh. My stomach lurches as the plane turbulently lifts into the air. Before I know it, we are puncturing fluffy white clouds. As we gain altitude, I don't feel any fear–simply astonishment. I can see Gemini 4 in my mind, and I wonder if this is what those astronauts felt like just a few weeks ago as they sailed up into the gorgeous, blue atmosphere.

Leaning towards the window, I try to block out everything and everyone else around me. Focused on nothing but the bright, endless sky, I think of the plane without windows, and I imagine my hair blowing in the wind and the warm sunshine on my face.

I never thought my parents would allow me to go on this trip in the first place. These past few years, I've tried desperately to stick with my role of the quiet, obedient daughter. I've never asked my parents for much of anything.

I thought I was content flying under the radar, going through my life as the peacemaker. The appeaser. It's the role I've been in these past four years, and I'm used to it. Once I heard about this trip, though, something changed inside me. Maybe it's because Sandy begged me to join her, or maybe it's because I couldn't imagine spending an entire summer at home. Whatever the reason, I eventually mustered up enough courage to ask my parents about it.

To my surprise, my normally-hesitant mother couldn't have been more excited about the idea. It got to the point where it didn't matter what my father's opinion was about it; my mother was determined to send me on the trip. I didn't push or beg any further, because I didn't have to. Although my mom has her faults, I think that next to Carolyn, she's the member of my family who's always understood me the best. I think that, even if she doesn't entirely know how difficult things have been for me, this is her way of making it up to me. Whatever it is, I'm suddenly filled with gratitude, and I close my eyes, letting the steady hum of the plane lull me to sleep.

15
EILEEN

ROME, ITALY
SUMMER, 1965

My eyes take a moment to adjust to the bright light that surrounds me, and I can't seem to find any good reason to open them willingly–that is, until I realize that someone is shaking my arm. "Eileen, wake up! We're here!"

Sitting up immediately in my seat, I look wildly around the airplane before letting my eyes land on the window. Leaning forward, I expect to see something–anything– resembling the fashionable city which I've dreamt of for so long. Instead, all I see is a regular airport, just like back home in Chicago.

Turning to Sandy, I raise my eyebrows in a questioning way, and she laughs. "Don't worry. We'll see a lot more once we get outside."

I nod, and sure enough, just about a half an hour later, my classmates and I are stepping through the doors of the airport and out to a few taxis.

At first, nothing I see resembles Rome–but after a while, the endless roads begin to close in on each other, and buildings begin popping up and stretching towards us, until finally, we arrive in the heart of the city.

The taxis pull up to our hotel and the moment I step out the heat is intense. However, I barely give it a second thought, because my mind is preoccupied by the gorgeous, ivy-covered buildings, cobblestone roads, and unfamiliar landscape. Fashionably-dressed people are walking casually down the street, looking relaxed and at ease. Women with shoulder-length, dark hair stroll past, looking more confident than I've ever felt in my life.

Sandy grabs my arm excitedly, turning my attention away from the passersby and towards our hotel. "Come on," she exclaims, "it's beautiful here."

A grin spreads across my face, and I follow Sandy through the front door of the hotel, allowing my hand to run against the cool stone wall of the building.

The concierge checks us in, and just a few minutes later, after Mr. and Mrs. Nelson have given out instructions for sleeping arrangements, Sandy and I are standing inside our hotel room, looking out the window and observing the world moving around us. In the distance, I can see a gigantic, round structure which must be the Colosseum. The mere sight of it makes my heart skip a beat. None of this feels quite real–and I'm okay with that. I like the feeling of living in a dream. It makes everything seem so much more thrilling.

"Here," says Sandy suddenly, causing me to tear my gaze away from the window. "Let's unpack, and then we can get some sleep."

I raise my eyebrows and laugh. "Sleep?" I motion towards the window; the sun hasn't quite set all the way, lighting up the entire room. "It's daytime."

Sandy grins. "I know–but we'll need to sleep so we can adapt to the time change. Trust me, it'll help. And then, tomorrow, we can go get a good meal. Authentic Italian food is the *best*."

I nod, and as Sandy begins to unpack her things, I turn back to the window with new thoughts flooding my mind. Was this what my dad saw when he came here almost two decades ago? Did he walk down the same cobblestone streets and marvel at the old ruins? Did he get a chance to fully appreciate the beauty of the city amidst the horrors of war?

With the war in Vietnam being broadcast right to every television in America, no one has been able to escape the reality of it–not even in their own kitchens or living rooms. And yet, as Sandy and I stand here in the middle of picturesque Rome, I can't begin to imagine how this city must have looked when my father was here . . . or what he experienced.

Unsure of how to answer my own questions, I give up and walk over to my bed, eager to begin unpacking and get some rest.

When I wake up, I take a moment to rub my eyes and adapt to the light that's cast throughout the room. For a second, I feel disoriented, and I wonder why. Then, I turn to look at the clock on the wall, and it hits me: I've been asleep for more than ten hours.

Surprised, I take a deep breath of contentment, realizing how rested I feel. Then, as I turn to look over at Sandy's bed, I realize that she's awake and dressed in a white top and lavender-colored skirt. Her blonde hair is piled up fashionably on top of her head, and her makeup is beautifully done.

She's in the middle of reading a book, but as soon as I turn to look at her, she sees me and grins. "Good, you're up! We slept forever–it's time to explore."

I return the smile, and after climbing out of bed, I get ready for the day with lightning speed. Mr. and Mrs. Nelson meet up with us and our classmates in the hallway, and after that, we all head outside, walking through Rome with an excited energy I've never felt before.

Everything I see causes me to gasp. A street musician playing the accordion, a painter taking in the Colosseum, or a scruffy brown dog–all bring me a sort of pleasure that I can't describe. I feel as though I've stepped into another world–a world teeming with beautiful possibilities–and I can't get enough of it. Even the boys are at a sort of loss for words, not really speaking but simply taking everything in.

As the heat of the day has reached its peak, Sandy squeals and points out a shop just a few feet away, whose sign reads, "*Gelateria.*"

"There," exclaims Sandy, grabbing my arm. "We have to go in there."

"What? What is it?" I ask–but Sandy doesn't respond. Instead, she walks over to our teachers, gets a nod of approval from Mrs. Nelson, and grabs my hand. The two of us begin running, and at the prompting of our teachers, our classmates follow at our heels.

The moment we step inside the brightly-colored shop, a wave of excitement washes over me, because it's clear what kind of shop Sandy and I have just entered. It's like an ice cream shop, except it's not. It's–

"A gelato shop," explains Sandy. Dragging me over to the counter, she points out each flavor and begins describing them to me in detail. "Here, look at this one. They call it '*limone*,' which means 'lemon.' I've had that one once before, when I came with my family three years ago. It was good, but . . . Oh, Eileen! You have to get this one. It's called '*menta*,' or mint chip. Oh–I don't know, they're all so good. You choose."

Encouraged by her enthusiasm, I decide on the same order as her: a cone of mint chip. I struggle to order in Italian, but luckily, the man serving me is very understanding.

Once we receive our cones, we step back outside to wait for Mr. and Mrs. Nelson and our classmates, who are standing in line. Heat begins to overwhelm me again, so I begin eating my gelato. From the first bite, I'm shocked at the freshness and difference between this gelato and the store bought ice cream I've eaten my entire life.

"*Wow*," I breathe, causing a big grin to spread across Sandy's face.

"I know, right?" she says, diving into her own cone.

It takes quite a while for all our classmates to order their own cones, but once we're all standing outside, it doesn't take long for us to finish eating, trying to race against the hot Roman sun that's threatening to melt our gelato.

Once we've finished, Mr. and Mrs. Nelson lead us over to the Colosseum, where I find myself simply standing and staring up at the large structure in awe, picturing it in its original glory. I take a mental picture of the scene in my mind, and I try to remember every detail, never wanting to forget anything about this city. It's more beautiful than I ever could have imagined–and I have a feeling that this trip is going to be even more wonderful with each experience.

16

PETER

VENICE, ITALY
WINTER, 1938

"Hey, Peter!"

I stop in my tracks and turn around to see my friend Matteo. He's standing just outside his front door, waving to me.

Waving back, I walk over to Matteo and greet him. "*Ciao!*"

"What are you doing walking outside?" asks Matteo, rubbing his arms and shivering. "It's freezing out here."

He's right, of course–but I don't reply. I've been so self-sufficient all my life that I don't like to admit it when a little cold bothers me. I shrug off Matteo's words and stand perfectly still, despite the fact that I'd like nothing more than to bounce on my toes and rub my arms to keep warm. "It's not so bad, once you get used to it."

Matteo stares at me, and I can see disbelief flash through his brown eyes. "Peter . . . How about you come inside?"

I open my mouth to refuse, but Matteo begins talking quickly. "My mother's here, and she's cooking dinner. We've got a fire going . . . You could get warm and then head back out. I won't keep you if you don't want to stay."

At first, I hesitate–but the look on Matteo's face is so friendly and welcoming, and the smell of good food is wafting through the front door. Taking a deep breath, I nod and force a smile.

Matteo grins back, and with one hand on my shoulder he leads me inside his house. "Mama, Peter's here."

As we enter the kitchen, my eyes land on Signora Bianchi, who turns from the stove to give me a warm smile. "Hello, Peter."

Signora Bianchi holds a striking resemblance to her son. Although they differ in height and stature, as Signora Bianchi is a few inches taller than her son but a bit plumper, there is no doubt that they are related. The pair share the same light brown eyes, high cheekbones, and a full smile. It's the kind of grin that always makes you feel like they're about to burst out laughing . . . but the good kind of laughter. Teasing, yes, but never unkind. This is one of many reasons why I've always liked the Bianchi family.

"Oh, Peter," says Signora Bianchi, the smile melting from her face. At first, I'm unsure why she looks so concerned–and then, as I follow her gaze, I realize that she's taking in my outfit. With my thin shirt and worn pants, I'm not exactly dressed for the cold weather that we're living in right now. "Come here."

Normally, I would have the same reaction to this concern as I did to Matteo's outside–but, out of respect for Signora Bianchi, I obey.

Immediately, she steps forward and reaches out, rubbing my dirt-covered arms. "You must be freezing. Oh, Matteo, add some wood to the fire."

Without a word, Matteo rushes to obey his mother, leaving me to deal with all her concern.

"Really, I'm alright," I protest even as Signora Bianchi leads me to sit on their plush sofa. With its flower pattern and soft cushions, I find myself sinking into the sofa the moment I sit down. The sound of the fire crackling in front of me is almost too much. If the Bianchis were to leave me alone right now, I would certainly fall asleep immediately.

"Stay here," insists Signora Bianchi, holding both hands out towards me as if I'm about to run past her. "Don't move."

She exits the room in a rush, and Matteo sits down next to me. "You haven't been in here lately, have you?"

I shake my head, and Matteo points up at the mantle. "See that? That's my papa."

I follow his gaze and observe the old framed photograph that I've never seen before. "Wow. He looks young."

"He was. That photograph is from the Great War." Matteo smiles proudly, looking back and forth between me and the picture. "It used to be in my parents' bedroom, but we rearranged some things. After all, why should we hide it? My papa was one of the best soldiers in all of Europe."

I'm about to reply when Signora Bianchi re-enters the room. "Here, Peter."

She hands me a full plate of some sort of stew, and it smells so good that all I can manage is a half-hearted, "Are you sure?"

"Why, of course, I'm sure. Go ahead, Peter. We have more than enough."

"*Grazie*." Without any more hesitation, I dive into my food.

Signora Bianchi smiles, and she's about to leave the room again when the front door swings open, sending a gust of cold air sailing through the house.

"Hello?" a deep voice calls.

"We're in here, Antonio," replies Signora Bianchi.

A moment later, Matteo's father walks into the room. Older now, but certainly still young at heart, Signor Bianchi is easily recognizable compared to his picture. If Matteo and his mother look similar, Matteo and his father look like twins. With his muscular jaws, bright eyes, and proud posture, Matteo could truly pass for his father as a young man.

Signor Bianchi greets his wife and son warmly before walking over to me. "Hello, Peter," he says with a firm handshake. "How have you been, son?"

"Fine, sir. Thank you."

Signor Bianchi grins. "Eating my supper, I see." He winks at me and slaps my shoulder.

Suddenly embarrassed, I hand my plate to Signora Bianchi and force myself to stand up from the comfortable sofa. Something about Signor Bianchi's powerful presence has made me feel uneasy once again. "I was just leaving, sir."

"No, no, my boy," exclaims Signor Bianchi, placing a hand on my back and causing me to sit down again. "Don't feel like you have to leave because of me. We're all glad to have the company."

"That's alright," I croak. "I've gotta be heading out. Signor Maggio is expecting me."

"Oh, come on, Peter," begs Matteo, taking a step towards me. "Stay."

Signora Bianchi lays both hands on her son's shoulders and holds him back. "*Silenzio*, Matteo," she whispers, hushing him. "If Peter must go, he must."

With a grateful smile, I stand up and say goodbye to each member of the Bianchi family. "Goodbye, sir. Thank you, Signora. Bye, Matteo."

The little family stands close together in the doorway of their home and waves to me as I walk down the cobblestone street. Taking one last glance at them over my shoulder, a mental image forms unwanted in my mind. For a moment, I'm standing in Matteo's place–but standing behind me are two figures. A man and a woman whose faces are just a blur.

Blinking away the picture, I watch it disappear in my mind like dust blowing in the wind. Then, I turn the corner, leaving the image behind.

Running up to Signor Maggio's house, keeping warm against the cold, I'm ready to burst through the door as I often do when an unusual sight stops me in my tracks. Walking over from another street is Signora Hoffman and Rebekah. In Signora Hoffman's arms is baby Abigail, who is wrapped tightly in a warm-looking gray blanket.

"Signora Hoffman!" I call out, waving.

Signora Hoffman looks up suddenly, and that's when I see it. There's a strange look in her eyes—a look that resembles fear. However, as her face is mostly hidden under the blanket that's wrapped around her head, her concerned look is gone by the time I've reached her. In its place is a warm smile.

"Hello, Peter."

"What are you all doing out here?" I ask.

Signora Hoffman opens her mouth, and at first, I think she's going to reply. Instead, she seems to suck in her breath and doesn't let it out. At a loss as for what to do next, I look over at Rebekah.

Her head is covered in a thick shawl as well, but her long, brown hair is peeking out from under the material. She pushes it out of her face and peeks over at the bookshop. "Is that it, Peter?"

I glance over at the shop and then back at Rebekah. "Yes. Do you want to go inside?"

Rebekah's eyes light up, and she looks up at her mother for approval. Signora Hoffman nods, and after Rebekah and I share a look of excitement, I grab her hand and pull her into the shop, her laughter bubbling over like the sound of twinkling bells.

The laughter seems to summon Signor Maggio, who appears from the back room of the shop with a warm smile on his face. "Why, hello. Who's this, Peter?"

"Rebekah   Hoffman.   You've   met   once   before, remember?"

"Oh, yes—of course! How could I forget? Welcome, *Signorina*." Leaning on his cane, Signor Maggio manages a bow. This brings out more laughter from Rebekah, who responds with a curtsy.

The three of us seem to be in our own little world for only a few seconds–but not any longer. Because that's when Signor Maggio notices Signora Hoffman. She's been standing near the door, bouncing Abigail up and down.

With his eyes locked on Signora Hoffman, Signor Maggio makes his way over to her and manages what seems to be between a bow and a nod. "*Buona sera*," he says softly.

Signora Hoffman smiles and returns the 'nod.' "Hello," she replies.

"It's, uh . . . a very cold day for you three to be outside," remarks Signor Maggio.

"Oh, we don't mind," says Signora Hoffman quickly. "I mean . . . we wanted to come. It's just . . . Rebekah has been begging me to visit the bookshop, and I felt that since the weather was so cold, it would be . . . harmless. After all, we seemed to be the only people outside."

"Yes," replies Signor Maggio, much too quickly. "That is very wise. I mean . . . I'm glad you could come. And, since it's so cold . . . Would you all like some tea?"

Signora Hoffman hesitates. However, after a slight nod of encouragement from me, she smiles and seems to relax. "Yes. That would be very nice."

I watch Signor Maggio's shoulders finally sink from his ears, and he leads Signora Hoffman to the back room. Rebekah and I dutifully follow, both curious to see how this will play out.

The three of us sit down at Signor Maggio's small, wooden table as he begins moving hurriedly around the room, preparing the tea. By the time he's prepared two cups, one for himself and one for Signora Hoffman, he seems to remember mine and Rebekah's presence and turns to us. "How about you, children? Any tea?"

On an impulse, I stand up and shake my head. "No, *grazie*. I'm going to show Rebekah all the books."

"Oh," says Signor Maggio, a look of surprise in his eyes. "Alright, then. Have fun."

"We will," I reply, taking Rebekah's hand and dragging her out of the room. Once we've reached the other room, I press my ear against the wall and motion to Rebekah, waving dismissively. "Go ahead and look at the books, Rebekah."

"Don't be silly, Peter," she says, shaking her head in disapproval. "Don't you think I want to spy, too?"

I sigh and sheepishly run a hand through my hair. "I'm not spying."

Rebekah rolls her eyes. Her boldness surprises me, but I welcome it anyway. Letting her stand in front of me, the two of us keep our ears pressed to the wall and listen intently.

At first, there's silence. Then, I hear the clinking of a spoon against a teacup—a sign that the two adults are both sitting down now.

The topics of conversation move slowly and awkwardly at first. Signor Maggio asks about Abigail's age, and various other things about her, such as "When is her birthday?" and "Does she know any words yet?" However, as the questions quickly come back and forth, with Signora Hoffman asking about Signor Maggio's job, the pair seem to become more comfortable with one another.

It's been about an hour when the two of them begin talking a bit about their childhoods. At this point, Rebekah has become tired of eavesdropping and has convinced me to sit beside her among the bookshelves as she reads–but I can still hear the light, happy tones of the adults' voices . . . and as I listen, I feel a strange sense of peace and comfort. Like something that's always been meant to be is just now coming together.

Perhaps it was because of the Hoffmans' yellow badges that I never saw it before, or maybe because I never thought my two worlds would intersect. Either way, there's something inside me now that knows the truth. Something that knows that not even a little patch of fabric can keep people apart forever.

17
PETER

VENICE, ITALY
WINTER, 1938

It's late when Signor Maggio and I approach the Hoffman house. The wind is chilling, and the sun's rays are stretched out across the sky, holding on for dear life as they're swallowed up into the darkness. It's December 25th–Christmas Day–but it hardly feels like it. Usually, I spend Christmas in the bookshop with Signor Maggio, eating dinner and reading by the fire afterwards. Although snow is a rare thing, it can still become quite cold here in Venice, and I'm always more than content to stay inside. However, we're doing something very different this year.

Signor Maggio rubs his hands together and blows on them briefly, trying to warm them. Then, he reaches forward and raps on the door three times. I shift my weight back and forth, shivering and tugging at my gray coat. The faint light is disappearing rapidly from the sky, and it makes me even more eager to retreat inside the warmth waiting just behind the door.

Just as the world seems to be enveloped in darkness, the door is thrown open by a beaming Rebekah. Her long, brown hair is combed and tucked behind her ears; her face appears to have been scrubbed so clean that it's shining, and she's wearing what I'm guessing is her nicest dress. Her brown eyes sparkle in excitement as she exclaims, "Hello! Come in, Peter–I want to show you–"

"Rebekah," Signora Hoffman calls from further inside the house. "Let our guests inside before overwhelming them, please."

A begrudging huff escapes from Rebekah's lips, but she steps back to let Signor Maggio and I step into the house. Signora Hoffman steps around the corner, looking just as nice as her daughter and I'm suddenly grateful that Signor Maggio encouraged me to dress up for the event. Her hair, in contrast to Rebekah's, is twisted into a bun which sits on the back of her head. A shawl is draped over her shoulders, and she's wearing a long, simple dress which almost reaches the floor. Even little Abigail is dressed up, and smiling at me from her place on her mother's hip.

I resist the urge to yank at my itchy collar as Signor Maggio and I thank Signora Hoffman for her invitation. She makes her way over to the window and we all gather around. She bows her head, and–to my astonishment–begins speaking in another language. I suppose it shouldn't surprise me very much, knowing that the Hoffmans are Jewish . . . but I had never heard any of them speak in Hebrew until now.

From what I can tell, Signora Hoffman is praying. Her head is bent, along with Rebekah's. Signor Maggio and I exchange a quick, questioning glance before bowing our heads, as well. Signora Hoffman's voice has a wonderful, lilting sound as she speaks in a voice tinged with emotion. Glancing up, I can see this reflected in her expression; her dark brows are furrowed, but a smile plays at her lips, tugging them upwards. She looks so . . . grateful. I don't know what she's saying, but somehow, I understand the sentiment.

Signora Hoffman finishes praying, and we all look up. Then, she turns her attention to the window. A golden object like a candelabra sits there, and I watch in fascination as Signora Hoffman takes a moment to light each of the nine candles.

As if reading my mind, Rebekah takes a step closer to me and begins whispering. "It's called a menorah," she explains, her small voice sounding more reverent than I've ever heard it before. "The eight flames stand for the eight days that the sacred oil lasted, even though there was only enough to burn for one day."

Frowning, I ask quietly, "What was it all for?"

"The Maccabees revolted against the Greeks and succeeded. The Jews were finally free again. The Temple in Jerusalem was rededicated with the sacred oil, and the lighting of the menorah." Rebekah pauses for a moment, gathering her thoughts. I can almost see the wheels turning in her brain and know that she's probably wondering how to sum up the meaning of the holiday in a way I can grasp. Eventually, she says, "It's . . . it's a celebration. To show that light always overcomes darkness."

I smile and nod to show her I understand. Then, I continue watching the orange and red hues which begin to dance and cast shadows over the low ceiling and walls. The warm, golden flickering of light seems to change the atmosphere in the room. It gives me a feeling of protection against the cold, bleak world outside of the house.

Once Signora Hoffman has finished, we all move locations for dinner. The small, wooden table barely fits all five of us, but we manage with Abigail sitting on Signora Hoffman's lap. As everyone becomes situated, I take in the sights around me in awe. In all the years I've known the Hoffman family, their house has never looked this grand. The table is covered in a fresh, white tablecloth, and all different types of exotic foods sit on Signora Hoffman's beautiful china. In the midst of it all are more candles, lighting up the room and illuminating the contented faces which hover around the table.

Rebekah sits down next to me, leaving Signora Hoffman and Signor Maggio to sit across from us. "Here, Peter," she exclaims, passing one of the dishes to me. "You have to try these."

I stare questioningly at the golden, circular shapes sitting before me. "Um . . . What are they?"

"Potato latkes," answers Signora Hoffman with an amused smile. "They're like fried potatoes. You'll like them, Peter."

Nodding, I reach forward and take two. Then, I proceed to take a bite. The comforting taste of potatoes settles on my tongue as the latkes practically melt in my mouth.

"How are they, Peter?" asks Signor Maggio, looking almost hesitant from his side of the table.

I grin. "*Delizioso.*"

After the meal has concluded, Signor Maggio and Signora Hoffman remain at the table and talk with one another while Rebekah and I are excused. Rebekah pulls me into the front room, and I follow obediently.

The menorah is still burning brightly, and Rebekah leads me to a chair sitting near it. I take my seat, and she sits in a chair opposite me. Her small face is flushed from all the excitement of the evening, and the light of the candles is reflected in her brown eyes.

Reaching up towards her neck, Rebekah grabs hold of something and pulls it forward, allowing me to see. She's wearing a necklace which I've never seen on her before; the chain is silver, and it holds a pendant in the shape of a star.

"Mama gave me this. Just this morning," she explains. "It's the Star of David. She used to wear it every Hanukkah. It was passed down from my grandmother–but it's mine now." Rebekah looks as though she's about to burst with pride.

I stare at the silver star. I almost wonder if I already know the answer to my question, thanks to all that Signor Maggio has taught me from the Bible, but I've never seen Rebekah so happy. I doubt she's ever had the chance to share a bit of her culture with an outsider before, and she's clearly enjoying it. For her sake, I ask, "What's it mean?"

"Well, Mama says that the direct translation is 'Shield of David.' It's supposed to represent the covenant between God and Israel–and it means that God is our protector. He has always provided for us, just as we celebrate and remember during Hanukkah."

I can tell that Rebekah's words were passed down by Signora Hoffman–but the way she says them, they are entirely her own. She believes in God with all her heart. Even at such a young age, amidst so much hardship and oppression, it's clear to see that she still believes God will protect her.

Once again reading my mind, Rebekah's face goes dark, and she looks past the menorah and out the window. "We used to celebrate Hanukkah with other families," she says, her voice low and wavering. "Some of them have stopped celebrating altogether."

"Why?"

Not for the first time, Rebekah gives me that look–the look that says I should know exactly what she's talking about. But I don't. I'm not like the Hoffmans, or anyone else who lives in the ghetto. I know that they are forced to face trials of many kinds, but I'm oblivious to what extent. Part of me wants to know, so that I can understand . . . and part of me doesn't. It pains me to see Rebekah this way, so I resort to the best way I know to make her smile.

"Well, you'd better not get cross and kick me out. I've never had such good food in all my life–and I mean that. I'll come back here every year. And . . . It's a great holiday, Rebekah. It really is."

Just as I'd hoped, a smile appears on Rebekah's face like a ray of sunshine, ridding it of any dark clouds. "Thanks, Peter. If you keep bringing me books, I'll bet you Mama will make some extra latkes just for you."

18
EILEEN

CENTRAL ITALY
SUMMER, 1965

"Here we are," says Mrs. Nelson, twisting in the passenger's seat of the taxi to look at all us girls. "Go ahead and get out, and we'll all meet at the front of the bridge."

At first, I'm not sure what she's talking about. Sandy and I slide out one door, eager to stretch our legs, and I immediately reach up to shade my eyes, protecting them from the blinding sun. However, once I've put on my sunglasses and my vision adjusts, I see it: a long concrete bridge, stretching up to what appears to be a hill town. Below us is a vast canyon, picturesque with hues of green and gold.

Walking over to the front to join Mr. Nelson and the rest of my classmates, I hear him say, "This town is called *Civita di Bagnoregio*. The Italian people know it as 'The Dying Town,' because it's been around since medieval times and has a population of less than fifty people. It is also eroding over time, due to the wind and rain."

With that, our group begins the long trek up the bridge with Mrs. Nelson calling out, "Everyone be careful, now!" I understand her concern; the incline is overwhelming, and I have to throw my arms out several times to keep my balance. After about ten minutes, we reach the top of the bridge, and the terrain flattens as we step under a large archway and into the city.

Almost immediately, the road opens up to a beautiful main square. I'm surprised by how busy the square appears to be, especially after hearing Mr. Nelson talk about the city's small population. My eyes land on what appears to be a church, and I stare at it through my sunglasses as our group continues walking.

Next, we move on to a small, narrow back street. The brick walls are covered in ivy, and I finger one of the vines as I pass by.

"This is incredible," whispers Sandy.

I nod back, hesitant to speak. This place seems too mysterious and beautiful to put into words.

Unfortunately, Mr. Nelson seems oblivious to this fact, because he immediately shatters the reverent silence. Turning around in front of the group, he says, "Alright, then–I think this is a pretty good spot for a group picture!"

Sandy and I exchange a knowing smile before lining up for the photograph. I stand in the front row next to Lois, who's only a bit taller than my petite frame, and Sandy stands in the back. Mr. Nelson holds up the camera with Mrs. Nelson standing beside him. We all smile, and he takes the picture.

Now that the silence has been broken, the group begins talking together freely–but I don't feel like it. As my teachers and classmates stand talking with one another, my eyes land on an empty road just a few feet from where I am. Taking the opportunity to break away, I slip down the side street, turning corners until almost all the sounds of my group have been lost, carried off in the summer breeze. I keep walking, and walking–and find myself standing mere feet away from a short, brick wall that allows me a perfect view of the canyon. Walking up to the wall, I rest my elbows on top and stare out at the canyon and the blue sky above. Then, I close my eyes.

With all distractions removed, I pay extra attention to the sun warming my face and the gentle breeze ruffling my hair. Finally, I'm surrounded by total silence–complete calm.

"Eileen, check this out."

I open my eyes and look up to see Sandy, Lois, and Janet standing over me. I'm sitting at the bottom of a hill near a beautiful, vibrant-green vineyard in our latest destination: Tuscany.

We've been in Italy for a little over a week, and tomorrow we're heading to Venice. I've loved every part about Tuscany, from the food to the rolling hills and vineyards lined with rows of tall cypress trees. The colors here are bright and the landscape full of natural beauty. To be honest, it is even more captivating than Rome. It's quiet here, and peaceful–the things I like best about a place.

"What is it?" I ask, looking up at my friends. They're framed against a dark, swirling sky, barely illuminated by the distant glow of the restaurant we're about to eat dinner in.

Sandy bends down and holds out her hand. Resting in her palm is a bunch of grapes, round and shining even in the darkness. "They're called . . . Oh, what was it?" She looks to Lois and Janet for help.

"Um . . ." Janet hesitates and furrows her brow in concentration. "I think they're called *Trebbiano* grapes." She struggles over the Italian pronunciation, her Midwestern accent getting in the way.

"And while we were waiting outside, the waiter gave them to us fresh! Come on," exclaims Sandy, grabbing my hand and pulling me upwards. "Our table's ready."

Part of me wants to stay here in the comforting darkness, staring out at the rolling hills and star-dotted sky–but Sandy is already dragging me along. Besides, I am hungry, and the restaurant is beautiful.

"Okay, okay," I laugh, making the voluntary choice to switch my mindset and to prepare for a fun, relaxing dinner.

The four of us make our way up the lush, green hill and head towards the restaurant. It's situated in a villa-like building, complete with twinkling lights and vines draped over the patio. Even from far away, their effect is alluring and draws me in closer.

The inside of the restaurant appears to be packed, full of tourists and natives alike. However, the patio is almost empty, with only a few tables occupied.

Our teachers and the rest of our classmates are just walking onto the patio as we reach them. The four of us merge into the rest of the group as a formally-dressed waiter leads us to a long, candlelit table. The patio has a perfect view of the picturesque landscape beneath us; its hills seem to stretch out into eternity, almost touching the dark, navy blue sky.

I sit down on one side of the table, and Sandy sits down on the end, which is to my right. Lois and Janet sit down across from me, leaving the chair on my left empty. I expect Mrs. Nelson to take this seat; instead, I feel myself bristle and my mouth goes dry as someone very different sits down next to me.

Kevin Maxwell.

My first instinct is to simply ignore him. I clear my throat awkwardly and try to shift towards Sandy. However, there's nothing more I can do. I'm stuck here.

Immediately, I pick up my menu, positioning it so that Kevin can't get a good look at my face. Then, I busy myself with staring at the words, not really reading them but simply hoping that maybe, just once, Kevin will leave me alone.

It's true that I used to like Kevin. It's true that when I was younger, I always thought he was pretty good-looking–but any appeal in his looks vanished once I got to know him better. I watch out of the corner of my eye as he flips up the collar of his black, short-sleeved shirt. The color makes his skin appear more pasty than usual, and makes his sharp, brown eyes look almost black. I look away quickly, not wanting those eyes to land on me.

Kevin's chair knocks into mine, and I feel myself jump. Still, he says nothing, and I can only assume it was an accident. Peeking at Sandy from around the other side of my menu, I try to make eye contact with her, desperate for some sort of aid. However, she's busy talking to Lois and Janet, looking at her menu and gesturing excitedly with her hands.

A sound and a quick movement to my left catches my eye, and I feel myself jerking away at the feeling of Kevin's breath on my neck. "Whoa, there," he says, his voice smooth and condescending. "What's the matter, Madison?"

Glancing over at my teachers, I realize that the waiter has arrived to take our orders, and everyone is engrossed in their menus. I want to look confident; I want to sit up straighter in my chair. Somehow, though, my body doesn't seem to have the willpower. I feel myself shrinking as Kevin leans in closer, causing my skin to crawl.

"Hey, it's alright, Eileen. I know you're probably feeling kind of guilty, right? Embarrassed? Well, I'm prepared to forget about everything that happened sophomore year. That is, if you are . . ."

"I don't know what you're talking about," I interrupt quickly. My right hand brushes my left palm, which is sweating profusely, and I cringe at the realization. I wipe both my palms on my emerald green pencil skirt and avoid eye contact with Kevin.

"Why, that's perfect," he says, his toothy grin repulsing rather than charming. "We can just forget about it, then—no sweat. But I always knew you'd be cool about it. After all, a real fox like you has every right to want a night with—"

"No," I exclaim, my voice wavering underneath its firm tone. "I told you two years ago, Kevin, and I don't want to say it again. Just leave me alone."

Kevin's smile falters a bit, and he leans back in his seat, running his hands through his slicked-back hair. "Don't flip your wig, Eileen. Sure, you've gotta play it cool–I know that. Most girls do . . . except usually, it's the other way around for me. Girls are practically beating down my door. But lucky for you, I've told them every time: I'm not gonna let Eileen Madison down just yet."

I resist the urge to scream in frustration. If Kevin turned me off before, I completely loathe him now. I wrack my brain for something–*anything*–to say. "Just . . . just shut up, Kevin. I wouldn't go out with you again for anything. You really don't know a thing about me."

At these words, the expression on Kevin's face sours immediately. He shakes his head slowly, and I watch as the teasing, taunting look in his eyes switches to one of menace and total disgust. "Now, that's where you're wrong. I know plenty about you, and your family. Who wouldn't?"

I'm left speechless at this remark. I don't know what Kevin means, and I don't want to. He's obviously just trying to get on my nerves–and I can't let him.

Kevin inches closer, and I can see the nearby candlelight reflected in his eyes, sparking like a raging wildfire. "None of that matters to me, though. Nothing that anyone says about you. It won't have to matter–just as long as you agree . . ."

I stand up at his touch, pushing my chair back from the table. It scrapes loudly against the patio floor, and I wince at the sound. My heart is beating wildly, and my face is hot with embarrassment. Most of all, though, my blood is boiling–and I don't know what to do about it.

The waiter has reached Janet now, and the two of them stop for a brief moment to look curiously at me, along with the rest of the table. I make eye contact with Sandy for a split second; then, I'm rushing into the restaurant, and I don't stop until I've reached the powder room.

Inside the bathroom, I stand in front of the golden-framed mirror and clutch onto the white porcelain sink, taking deep breaths. I'm finally alone–but I don't feel safe. In fact, I feel like I'm in more danger than ever of watching my perfectly-constructed world disintegrate around me.

I'm suffocating. I'm so tired of this life–of this facade that everyone around me seems to live under.

All I've ever wanted is control. Control of my life, control of my emotions, and control over the people around me–all so that I don't get hurt. So that none of us ever get hurt again.

I've tried so hard to fake it. I've been the perfectionist, the good daughter, and the people pleaser. I've even seemed to lose the courage I used to have–the courage I used to harness for my writing. I've sailed under the radar in the hopes that by not stirring the waters, everyone around me would be happy. But then, people like Kevin Maxwell make me wonder if it was all for nothing–and if I'll ever attain that control.

At the thought of Kevin, another chill runs unwanted down my spine, and I force myself to take a few deep breaths. I used to think I'd find my dream man one day. When I was younger, he was sort of like a mix of all my favorite literary heroes and movie stars combined. I wanted my life to be just like a book, with some dashing man who would come sweep me off my feet and save me from the dreariness of my world. Now, all I care about is finding someone who loves me with his whole heart. Someone who loves me for *me*, no matter what I've gone through or what he's gone through. Someone who will take care of me because he loves my soul above all else. Someone genuine.

Of course, I had to learn the hard way. I was one of those unlucky, naive girls who had to have her heart broken just to get some sense knocked into her head. And it's haunted me. *He's* haunted me. Not even Sandy knows to what extent. If only she knew, then she wouldn't have left me stranded just now.

I can still feel the touch of his clammy hand on mine, and another shiver runs down my spine. I begin pacing back and forth, forcing myself to count to ten and back down. *Just . . . don't think about him. Concentrate. You're not in the wrong. You can't listen to him, no matter what he's said or done.*

My experiences these past four years have changed me– I'm the first to admit that. But it's not what I wanted. And it terrifies me to think that one person could alter me so much. It terrifies me to know that I'll never be the same.

19
PETER

VENICE, ITALY
SPRING, 1939

"Signor Maggio?"

I walk cautiously around the outside of the bookshop, searching for any sign of Signor Maggio. To my surprise, he's nowhere to be found. The shop is locked, and all is quiet.

Resolving to come back later, I take a few steps in the direction of my gondola–but a familiar voice stops me. "Peter!"

I whirl around, and my eyes land on Signor Maggio. A silhouette in the golden sunset, he's walking down the cobblestone road behind me, leaning on his cane. He's dressed in one of his nicer suits, wearing a hat on his head and a wide grin on his face. It's the kind of grin that makes him look much younger than his forty-something years–and I wonder what's caused this kind of a smile.

I jog over to help him up to the shop, and he looks gratefully at me. "I'm sorry, *caruso*," he says as we reach the door and he unlocks it. "I should have left a note."

"You're almost never gone," I mention casually, hoping that he'll enlighten me.

"Yes, that's true," is all he says.

The two of us walk into the shop, and Signor Maggio turns on his lamp and takes off his hat. I watch him move around the shop, reorganizing his desk and opening the shop windows to let the warm May breeze in. He does all of this with an absent-minded, blissful expression on his face. Finally, I lose my patience and bound over to him.

"Where were you, Signor Maggio?"

The man gives me a mysterious smile that makes me even more frustrated. "Why do you wish to know, Peter?"

I simply stare at him, one eyebrow cocked expectantly. At this, Signor laughs, his smile reaching his eyes. "Alright, alright. If you must know . . . I was visiting Signora Hoffman."

This, I was hoping to hear–but not expecting. I feel my heart leap excitedly. "Really?" I say, feigning surprise.

"Yes," replies Signor Maggio, sitting down in his wooden chair beside the front counter.

"And . . ."

"And, what?" He gestures towards the wooden stool that stands near him, inviting me to take a seat.

I groan, roll my eyes, and fold my arms over my chest, refusing to oblige. "Signor, I'll be fourteen in a month. You can't act as though I don't know what's going on."

"Well, that is an excellent point, Peter . . . but you do realize that a man and a woman can just be friendly with one another, without being romantically involved. Don't you?"

"Yes," I say, leaning against the wall adjacent to Signor's, "and I also know that you're hiding something. Won't you just tell me?"

Signor Maggio looks at me for a long time, and I can almost see the wheels turning in his brain. He's trying to decide whether to tell me the truth. Eventually, a change takes place in his expression–and I realize that he's decided.

I watch Signor take a deep breath. Then, resolving to tell me, he sits up straighter in his chair and clears his throat. "Well, since I know you won't stop until you find out . . . I have been calling on Signora Hoffman for quite a few months now."

I grin, the ecstatic feeling in my heart overflowing. "I knew it. So, are you going to ask her to marry you?"

"Hold on, Peter," exclaims Signor Maggio, his smile hesitant. "It's not that simple."

"Why not?"

Signor Maggio sighs and rubs the bridge of his nose with his pointer finger and his thumb. "Well, there are so many different factors. For one, there are her daughters–"

"Don't you think they need a father?" I interrupt, already prepared to make my case for this union.

"Maybe," replies Signor Maggio slowly, "but that's not the point. I simply can't be the one to disrupt their lives. Abigail wouldn't be affected, but I'm sure that Rebekah remembers her father. Who knows how she would feel about someone new trying to replace him? And then, there's the issue of . . ."

He trails off, and I watch as his gaze drifts towards the open window. The sun has set entirely now, and the comfort I felt before has gone with it. I allow this silence to go on for about ten seconds before breaking it. "The issue of what?"

Signor Maggio blinks the glazed look out of his eyes before looking over at me. "Ethnicity."

Oh. I'd forgotten about that. After Signor Maggio and Signora Hoffman's initial first meeting, I sort of blocked out the fact that they came from separate worlds. Yes, they could talk; yes, they could be friends. But there was no way that they could ever marry.

Of course, my entire life, Signor Maggio has told me time and time again that origin and ethnicity doesn't matter. "It does not matter if you and I do not have the same blood," he told me once. "So why should it matter for the Jewish people?"

Signor Maggio seems to take my silence as a bad thing, because he lets out a quiet, defeated groan. "I . . . I know, Peter. I told myself I wouldn't let it come to this . . . but sometimes, a person's emotions just get the best of them. Attraction . . . and the result of a close friendship."

I look over at him suddenly. "You mean . . . *amore.*"

Signor Maggio stares back at me. "I . . . I suppose. Yes."

"If it's love, then why should anything stop you?"

Signor Maggio sighs and stands up. He looks very tired now—a complete switch from the way he entered the bookshop just minutes ago. Leaning on his cane, he walks over to the front counter and begins stacking some books.

Desperate to get my point across, I quickly say the next thing that pops into my head.

"Anyway . . . My mother was American, and my father was Italian. They loved each other. So why should something like that stop you?"

Signor Maggio stops moving, his head bent and his back turned to me slightly, just enough so that I can't see his face. He stays like this in silence for a few moments. Then, he nods slowly. "You're right. I do love her."

I smile triumphantly, and Signor looks at me and nods again. "Thank you, Peter. I promise you, I'll think about it. Now, be a saint and help me organize those shelves."

I've never been to a wedding before–but from what I've read about them in books, I'm not sure there's ever been one half as nice as Signor Maggio and Signora Hoffman's.

The weddings I've read about were large and extravagant, very different from the one I'm attending right now–but I think that's what makes this one so special. The only people present are Signor Maggio, Signora Hoffman, Rebekah, Abigail, and myself, plus the priest who is marrying the happy couple.

Thankfully, Signor Maggio's priest is sympathetic to the situation. A long discussion took place between them when everything was arranged. The wedding is completely secret, and the Hoffmans are void of anything that would identify them as Jewish. It's the way they plan to live from here on out. It's true that they will be living an isolated, private life . . . but it will be a life of love–and to them, that's all that matters.

We're all standing inside the church, its stained glass windows sparkling and casting a colorful glow around us. It's been quite a few months since I introduced Signor Maggio and Signora Hoffman to each other, and a lot has changed since then, including the start of a new year–but their love has never faltered. In fact, it's grown stronger, leading us all to this beautiful day.

Standing on the outside of her mother, Rebekah stares at the scene before us with a look of wonder in her eyes. With her brown hair curled and hands clasped together in excitement, she looks as if she can hardly contain her joy.

She's ten years old now–still young, but with a depth that I've never been able to fully understand. It's apparent that she's wise beyond her years, which is something that's given me cause for worry every once in a while. I don't like it when she's anything but innocent; I want her to enjoy her childhood. I have no reason for concern today, though. Rebekah seems perfectly caught up in the romantic event that we get to be a part of.

I'm standing on the outside of Signor Maggio. I was given the task of holding Abigail during the ceremony, so that's what I'm doing. Wearing a pretty little yellow dress, Abigail suddenly looks a lot like her mother and older sister. She's only two, but I can already notice the similarities. I can't help but wonder if, as Abigail grows up with Signor Maggio as her father, she'll adopt some of his traits, too.

Signor Maggio is all spiffed up, and Signora Hoffman looks beautiful in her simple white dress–but the true wonder of the moment is the joy radiating from their faces. I've never seen two people more happy to be together. They're in love– and now that they're becoming man and wife, they'll have each other forever. They'll always be one another's family.

I gulp and readjust Abigail in my arms before loosening my tie a bit. I turned fourteen just a few days ago, and I've grown about two inches in the past few months. This enabled Signor Maggio to lend me an old suit of his to wear for the wedding. Of course, my instinct was to refuse; after all, the only other time I've dressed up in my life is when I attended the Hanukkah celebration at the Hoffmans' house. I bit my tongue, but Signor Maggio seemed to notice my hesitation. He informed me that he understood my apprehension, but he was sure it would mean a lot to Signora Hoffman–so, of course, I had to comply.

In a matter of minutes, vows are exchanged, and a hush falls among us as Signor Maggio and Signora Hoffman kiss, sealing their unbreakable bond. Neither of them say anything. There are no "I love you's" or any other words of endearment exchanged between the couple. The reason for this is plain to see: the words just don't need to be said. Right now, the awed, reverent silence that hangs throughout the church is enough.

I take a deep breath and process the events that have just taken place. Now, Signora Hoffman is Signora Maggio. She has a husband, and Signor Maggio has a wife. The two of them have daughters; Rebekah and Abigail have a father.

The newly-married couple steps towards us and bids a grateful goodbye to the priest. Breaking the silence, I give

Signora Maggio a smile and pass Abigail into her white-clad arms. Signora Maggio gives me a warm smile and proceeds to kiss Abigail's head. Signor embraces his new wife and daughters, and the four of them stand in the beautiful glow of the stained glass, coming together as a family for the first time.

Standing there, watching the happy family, I try to fathom the simplicity of the events that have just taken place. In a matter of minutes, one man, one woman, and two daughters became united–they became a family. It was so simple, and yet I can't understand how it happened. How did they become so lucky to have each other? How did Signor and Signora Maggio earn a second chance at love?

I swallow hard and shift back and forth on my feet. My shirt collar feels even more stifling than before, and I wrench two fingers inside it, trying to give myself room to breathe. I want to contain my emotions–but I know it's impossible. I can't stay here a moment longer. I need to get out of this church.

As the family continues to embrace, perfectly caught up in the moment and seemingly oblivious of my existence, I quietly slip out the door to the church, shutting it softly behind me. Then, I take off down the cobblestone roads, refusing to look back.

My feet lead me down the streets, far away from the church, until eventually, I realize where I am. I've reached my gondola.

With my chest heaving, I take off my jacket and toss it onto the dock before climbing into the gondola and sitting down. For a moment, I simply sit and stare at the water. The last few golden strands of sunlight are disappearing quickly, but they're leaving the water sparkling.

I lie down then, feeling exhausted and overcome by emotions that I can't describe. In the distance, I can hear an accordion playing a familiar Italian folk song. The notes float through the air and dance along the glittering water, making their way to my ears in an effort to drown out the emptiness in my heart.

20
PETER

VENICE, ITALY
SUMMER, 1939

A few days have passed since the wedding.

That event has made something clear to me, and that's this: I am on my own now. I'm on my own, and I need to find out who I am, and where I'm from. It's time for me to head to America.

There's nothing here for me in Venice–this city I once loved so well. It's about time I grew up and tried raising myself right. I want a good, paying job and the chance to make something of myself. The chance to do something with my writing.

I know that America is going through hard times right now, like they have for so many years–but I don't care. Whatever that country is going through, it offers something I don't think I have here. All I've ever known about America is that it brings opportunity. I've also known that it's where my mother was born.

Yes–there's a slight hope inside me. A small voice that keeps urging me, that keeps encouraging me to look for my family. I've always wondered if I could find them in America, and what would happen if I did. Maybe I'd learn that I had grandparents, aunts, uncles and cousins. People who could tell me what my mother was like.

No matter what, even if I'd like to find my family someday, I know I'd have to make something of myself first. I'd have to make sure that when I met my family, they'd be proud of me–so proud that they'd *want* to call me their family. And we'd all be happy.

I haven't told Signor Maggio the news yet. In fact, I haven't seen him since the wedding three days ago. Now that the weather is warm again, I've spent most of my time outside. I've been trying to give the Maggio family some space and time to get used to each other. Besides, I'm not so sure Signor would take the news well. He might try to convince me to stay–although, I don't see why. He doesn't need me, and neither does anyone else. No one's lives will be affected when I leave.

Still, I can't help thinking of all the ways that their lives have affected mine.

I'm sitting against the stone wall of the building next to my gondola, reading one of my favorite books, *A Study in*

Scarlet, when I see a shadow appear next to me. Startled, I leap to my feet, my heart racing–but I relax when I realize that it's only Signor Maggio.

"Oh," I say suddenly, trying to hide my surprise. "Um . . . *buon pomeriggio*. Good afternoon."

Signor doesn't reply. He sighs and looks from me to my gondola, to the sparkling water that stretches out in front of us.

I begin bouncing nervously on the balls of my feet. "Uh–how is Signora Hoff–I mean, Maggio? And Rebekah and Abigail?"

Signor nods slowly and gives me a half-smile. "They're doing well."

There's a far-off look in Signor's eyes that I can't describe. I'm about to continue making awkward conversation when Signor turns to me.

"We haven't seen you around lately, Peter."

"I know. I've been busy." I say this faster than I mean to. Swallowing hard, I turn away and pick up my book which I dropped.

"Busy with what?" asks Signor Maggio curiously, leaning against the stone wall and stuffing one hand into his pocket while the other rests on his cane.

I walk over to my gondola and step inside, my back to Signor. Quickly, I let the words flood out of my mouth. "I'm heading to America."

I don't turn around to see Signor's face. I don't have to. His silence is enough.

Feeling as though I need to explain myself, I begin babbling nervously. "I've been waiting my whole life to go.

I'm going to leave and find my family, and learn something about my parents. I can get a job there–a job writing, just like you said I should."

I turn around and take a look at Signor Maggio's face. It's almost unreadable, but I see emotion in his eyes. Perhaps confusion? Or concern? Above all, I believe there's pain. Somehow, I can tell that it's pain for *me*.

"Peter," says Signor slowly, "it is not a good time to go there right now. Remember, everyone is going through hard times. Perhaps you should wait a few years, and then–"

"No," I say firmly, biting my lip and shaking my head. "Now *is* a good time. It's the *best* time. I've been to school for a while now, which means that I'm well-learned and prepared to find a job. And besides, there's nothing keeping me here."

I notice how my last sentence rushes out of my mouth, and how that must have hurt. I raise my eyes to meet his, and the look on Signor Maggio's weathered face provides me with confirmation.

"I know what you may believe, Peter," he says gently. "If I were in your shoes, I know I would feel the same way. But contrary to what you might think, you *do* have people here who care about you. People who feel as if you are as much a part of their family as anyone blood-related to them."

I cross my arms against my chest and breathe one, single, frustrated word. "*Who?*"

Signor Maggio hobbles over to where I'm standing in the boat, and he reaches out to rest a hand on my shoulder. "Peter, I came here to ask you if you would consider living with Signora Maggio and I."

I open my mouth to interject that this is already a common occurrence, but Signor Maggio shakes his head and finishes, "Permanently. As our son."

Just like that, the world stops. The only sounds left are an accordion in the distance, and water lapping at the gondola. Sounds that I've heard my whole life, but never really appreciated.

Then, the moment ends, and I drop the book into the boat with a *thud* before stepping onto dry land and swallowing the lump rising in my throat.

I can feel a few beads of sweat running down my forehead, and something else running down my cheeks. "Do you really mean it?"

Signor Maggio nods firmly. "I do. I've wanted to ask for a long time, but I wasn't confident I could do the best by you. I am here to ask now and to let you know you deserve to have a proper *famiglia*. A mother, a father, and two sisters. And I know you'd like to find your real family in America, but–"

I rush forward and wrap my arms around Signor Maggio– the father I never had. The father I *would* have from this day on. The father I always wanted.

"*Grazie*, Signor," I whisper, so happy I can barely breathe. "Thank you."

21
EILEEN

VENICE, ITALY
SUMMER, 1965

My classmates and I are on the last phase of our trip: Venice.

The ten of us have been walking through the city for about fifteen minutes, searching in vain for our hotel. Our suitcases which we are carrying grow heavier by the minute as we traverse the city's ancient stones. We wander through dark walkways and over bridges crowded with people.

Mr. and Mrs. Nelson are busy looking for our hotel, and Sandy is doing her best to assist them–but I'm taking in every inch of the city and realizing just how different Venice seems to be from Rome. Everywhere we walk, the smell of the sea drifts up to our nostrils. The splashing of water reaches my ears, and it's the most peaceful sound I've ever heard.

Shops of all kinds line the cobblestone streets. There are glass shops, shops selling decorative Venetian masks, and of course, shops with every flavor of gelato.

On the water-filled streets, gondolas sail by, some with accordion players singing romantic-sounding songs in Italian. As we cross a bridge, I pause to lean over it and watch the water sparkle beneath me.

"Oh, good," a voice says suddenly. "It's just over here."

I turn and realize that my classmates have begun walking towards a nearby building which must be our hotel. With one last look at the glittering water below, I turn and walk briskly after them.

About an hour later, Sandy and I have unpacked. Now that she's gone to wash up before we head out for dinner, I've been exploring the room and have noticed that our window is actually a door which leads out to a balcony.

Eagerly, I step forward and push the glass door, letting it swing open. Stepping outside, a water-scented breeze carries up to me from below. The sun is setting, and although its heat is also fading, there's an excitement tingling within me that warms me.

Staring down at the streets of water below, I realize that the number of gondolas passing by has reduced, at least in this area. Right now, there's only one gondolier paddling by, his haunting whistle bouncing off the ivy-clad walls of the narrow canal. His gondola is sailing smoothly over the bluish-green water, and the sight of it gives me a strange and lonely feeling.

The man standing on top of it is young; I don't think he can be more than twenty. He doesn't wear a traditional striped shirt like the other gondoliers I've seen so far. He's wearing a white-collared shirt with the sleeves rolled up to his elbows.

I'm just about to turn around and head back inside when, suddenly, the young man looks up. His eyes meet mine; even from far away, I can tell what color they are. They're as blue as the water beneath us.

With a small, quiet gasp, I step backwards quickly, embarrassed. I stay hovering inside the doorway for a moment; then, I move slowly forward again. The gondola has continued sailing down the water, taking the man along with it.

The next day, it's almost noon by the time my classmates and I leave our hotel. Hungry and eager to start a long day of sightseeing, we spot a small cafe and step inside. Mr. and Mrs. Nelson, along with the rest of the group, split up and walk away to eat elsewhere, leaving Sandy and I glancing around excitedly.

"*Buongiorno*," says a cheerful-sounding voice.

Sandy and I look up, and we realize that the woman standing at the counter in front of us is the one speaking. A bit hesitant, the two of us reply in the same language. We butcher the pronunciation a bit, but the woman doesn't seem to mind. However, she does smile and say, "You are visiting? From America?"

The two of us nod.

The woman's eyes light up excitedly, and she tucks a stray strand of black hair back into her bun. "Have you ever been to Venice before?"

Sandy and I shake our heads. Eagerly, the woman leans forward. "Well, let me give you a piece of advice. If you want to learn anything about this city–and I mean, *anything*–you'll learn it all here. Everyone who works here is a local, and we can give you every travel tip you'd like."

I grin. "Thanks–we'll remember that."

"Actually," begins Sandy, ever the outspoken and conversational one, "what do you know about gondolas? Which place is best to go?"

The woman taps her long chin in thought. "Hm. Well, most will do the job–but if you take a right out the door and stop at the nearest canal,"–she points out the window–"you'll get a good, scenic ride for a fair price." Seeing the glazed looks on our faces, the woman aids us by removing a map from behind the counter and handing it to us, circling the destination with a pen.

Sandy and I nod in understanding, and the woman goes on. "Besides," she laughs, handing me the map, "maybe you'll even get him to say something."

I raise my eyebrows, immediately intrigued. "'Him'? Who's that?"

The woman smiles and shrugs, raising her bony shoulders almost to her ears. "Well, he's the gondolier . . . but he does not say much. He showed up here almost a year ago. My husband and I welcomed him as I welcome you now, but he is the very definition of 'a man of few words.' We never even discovered his name. Of course, it is not like we are paying him for the pleasure of his company, but it is nice to be able to talk to a person, yes?"

"So . . . he didn't say *anything*?" asks Sandy, a curious look on her face.

"Oh, we exchanged the usual pleasantries, like 'please' and 'thank you,' and I expected him to give us some commentary on the tour–but once he learned that we had grown up in Venice, he didn't say much of anything."

Sandy and I exchange a look with one another. Then, I turn back to the woman and ask, "Do you really think we could get him to talk to us?"

"Oh, I don't know," says the woman, shrugging and turning briefly to hand a glass to the man working beside her. "But, if you can. . . that would certainly be a feat."

22
EILEEN

VENICE, ITALY
SUMMER, 1965

The streets are quieter now, and the sun has begun to set. Sandy and I are headed back to our hotel to freshen up before dinner after a long day of walking around the city. Most people seem to have the same idea, because suddenly, there's a different feeling in the air. It seems more tranquil than before–but more solemn and forlorn, too.

We're just about to turn the corner when the wind picks up, taking my map along with it. A little gasp escapes my mouth, and without thinking, I begin running after the map.

"Eileen!" yells Sandy in protest, but I simply keep chasing the map and reply over my shoulder.

"Wait for me! I need to get it back!"

I'm not sure what's come over me. It would be easy to attain another map . . . but something in me keeps going–keeps urging me to run for as long as it takes. I turn a couple corners, each getting quieter and more foggy by the second. I watch as the map is picked up by another powerful gust of wind, and I take a sharp turn around the next corner.

The next thing I know . . . I'm falling.

A strange feeling enters my stomach as I find myself flying weightlessly through the air. However, it lasts for only a moment, because I immediately hit the cool water below.

I completely submerge, so disoriented that I don't quite know what's happening. All I can do is flail my arms and legs, desperately hoping that I'll be able to propel myself to the surface.

My body feels heavier as I continue flailing, and eventually, I stop altogether. My eyes fight to stay open, but the water is strangely peaceful. There's no one around, and no way to get help. And I'm so tired . . .

"Here!" a voice exclaims. The tone is urgent instead of peaceful, reviving me. My eyes are shut now, but I feel two hands take a firm hold of me. I let myself be lifted up by strong arms, and there I stay, limp and barely aware of my surroundings. All I know is, for once, it feels so good not to think. So I don't.

When my eyes open, the first thing I see are streams of light, breaking through the darkness in my vision. At first, the light creates spots, and I try to resist it. However, as the spots disappear and I come to my senses, I realize how happy I am to be awake. And that's when I realize something. I'm not in bed.

Sitting up in a panic, I find myself lying on a bench near a canal. That's when everything comes flooding back.

Taking a quick glance around, I first realize that this is not the same canal which I fell into. The second thing I notice is that I'm not alone. Standing nearby is someone I've never seen before: a young man with dark hair and tan skin that's much lighter than most Italians I've seen. He's wearing a white collared shirt with the sleeves rolled up, suspenders, and pants to match. A smart-looking, light brown jacket is sitting on the bench beside me, where my head was previously resting.

Still confused and disoriented, I clear my throat and wait for the young man to turn around entirely.

At first, he doesn't seem to hear me. Taking a deep breath, I summon the courage to try again. This time, he reacts.

Whirling around, the young man spots me and takes a few steps over. Now, I can get a better look at his face–and the first thing I see is *blue*. The deepest blue eyes I've ever seen. I take in the rest of his face and quickly realize that he can't be more than twenty years old.

His blue eyes appear to be staring straight through me, and they even look haunted on the surface–although there's something under them that reveals a sort of forgotten joy. It's a strange look, and yet it's familiar to me. I've seen it in the eyes of people I know well–people who are much older than me. I've never seen it on people my age.

"*Bene*," is the first thing he says with a soft smile. "*Sei sveglio.*"

I open my mouth and find it too dry to speak. Swallowing, I reply, "What?"

Immediately, an apologetic look of realization appears on the young man's face, and he begins speaking in fluent English. Although his accent is still present, it's much fainter now as he adopts a more American one. "I'm sorry. I said, 'You're awake.'"

Nodding slowly, I ask, "Who are you? Did you . . . Are you the one who saved me?"

The young man's sapphire eyes lock with mine as he nods.

I smile and try to stand up, but my legs begin wobbling unsteadily. The young man rushes forward in alarm. He first reaches to take me by the arm and waist, but immediately retracts his hands in a self-conscious way and places them in mine instead, helping me over to the wall. Funnily enough, this gesture surprises me. No boy at school would hesitate like that. There's something different about this one.

"Are you alright?" he asks, his voice smooth and quiet. The sound of it is like a gentle stream of water, simple and unsuspecting. His lilting Italian accent has something to do with this, as well. In fact, I'm surprised at the confidence of his English, and the American pronunciation and sound which he seems to have adopted for the purpose of speaking my language.

"Y-yes," I stammer, pushing my damp hair out of my face and suddenly realizing how I must look. "Um . . . Did you see me fall?"

The young man shakes his head, his own dark hair falling over his eyes. He pushes it out of the way and answers, "I was in my gondola when I found you in the water. It's not safe around here. At least, not lately."

I raise my eyebrows and lean against the nearby wall for support, my eyes landing on the beautiful gondola that's tied to the nearby dock. "What do you mean? I thought Venice was one of the safest places in Italy."

"Arguably," replies the young man, folding his arms over his chest. "But . . . There's been some extra flooding as of late. You fell into one of the most flooded areas around."

"That's odd," I observe, taking in the nearby canal warily. "My teachers told me that it only floods here in the wintertime."

"Usually," says the young man, concern flashing briefly through his eyes. "No one was prepared for flooding in the middle of summer. It's alright, though–it isn't anything to worry about as long as you're aware of it. And most tourists aren't."

I smile sheepishly, thinking about the fact that I only fell because I was chasing after a map. With this in mind, my cheeks turn hot, and I gather up my wet hair, letting it fall just over my shoulders. I then wipe my face with my hands, aware that my makeup is probably running. Finally, I pat my soaked skirt and gather up enough dignity to quickly say, "Well– thank you very much for saving me. I wish I hadn't made so much trouble for you–but, well, as you say, I am only a tourist."

The soft smile on the young man's face melts instantly, and he takes a step towards me as I try to make my getaway around the corner. "Wait–I didn't mean it like that."

Now further embarrassed by the roughness in my speech, I stop in my tracks and take a deep breath. Why am I acting so foolish? I'm not usually one to let my emotions run away with me. Awkwardly, I slap my forehead with my palm and try to think of a way to counter my behavior.

"No . . . I'm sure you didn't. I'm sorry," I say, trying to sweeten the bitterness of my previous words. "I shouldn't have snapped. I think I'm just . . ." I grapple for what else to say.

There's an earnest look in the young man's blue eyes, and he shakes his head in a forgiving manner. ". . . In shock," he finishes for me.

I snatch up the words like a lifeline and nod, hoping my face conveys the gratefulness I feel. "Yes, yes—exactly. Well . . . again, I'm so sorry for the inconvenience. I'd better be going, now—I'm sure my friends are looking for me."

The young man nods slowly and hesitantly, as if he's not quite sure whether I hit my head in the fall or if I'm always this awkward. "Alright. I'm glad I could be of service."

I give him my most convincing smile. It's the one that Carolyn used to use. The one that I always called her 'movie star' smile. "Believe me, I'm really grateful."

With that, I step around the corner and walk briskly down the street, trying to ignore the burning on my cheeks and the growing thrill of excitement in my heart.

23

PETER

VENICE, ITALY
SUMMER, 1943

"Have a good day, Signora," I say, giving a wave and a friendly smile to the woman who has just exited Signor Maggio's bookshop. Glancing up at the clock on the wall, I realize that it's finally closing time.

Walking over to the door, I lock it with an eagerness and urgency that I've felt more often than usual lately. Then, I retreat to the back of the shop, where I find a comforting, familiar scene.

Signora Maggio, who I've called "Mama," for the past four years, is sitting in a comfortable chair by the fireplace, knitting a scarf. Near her are two young girls–my sisters–who are busy at the table.

One is drawing an incredible sketch which she's been working on for weeks. This is beautiful Rebekah. She's fourteen now, and more talented and lovely than ever. Her long, dark hair lies in seemingly endless waves all down her back, and her eyes are full of wisdom and knowledge.

Years of living in a bookshop have turned little Abigail into as much of a scholar as her papa. She's only six, but she gobbles up books and stories as if her life depended on them. Whenever she sees me or our father, she begs us to read her a book. Even now, I know she'll see me and ask any minute. Sure enough, she turns around, and her eyes light up.

A smile spreads across Abigail's little face, and she hops down from her chair and comes running to me. "Peter, Peter!"

"Abigail, Abigail," I sing back to her in an exaggerated deep voice, picking her up in my arms and twirling her around the room. Her happy shrieks fill the whole house, causing both our mother and sister to cover their ears.

"Peter, make her be quiet," groans Rebekah, balancing her head with one hand while using the other to sketch. "I'm trying to focus."

"Oh," I say, nodding, and I set Abigail down. She opens her mouth to protest, but I put a finger to my lips. "Let's be good for Rebekah, alright?"

Abigail begins pouting, and I shake my head. "Why don't we go look for a new story?"

This curbs the on-coming tantrum, and I bend down a bit to take my little sister by the hand. Leading her into the shop, I let her look around a moment before she retrieves a book of fairytales. Then, we head back to where our mother and sister are, and I sit down in a chair, setting Abigail in my lap.

I open the book to the first page and begin reading, but Abigail begins to protest. "No, no."

I raise my eyebrows. "What is it?"

"We need to take turns."

"Ohh," I say, smiling in amusement. "Alright. You start then."

Abigail nods. Furrowing her brow in concentration, she begins reading. "Once upon a time . . ."

Just then, there's a sound at the shop door. My head snaps up quickly, and I exchange a wary look with my mother. Setting Abigail down, I walk cautiously out to the shop.

Thankfully, one glance tells me that it's just my father coming back home from shopping for groceries. Turning around, I reassure my family with this fact. "It's just Papa."

Excitedly, Rebekah and our mother both stand up to greet our father, who locks the shop door behind him and enters the cozy little room.

"*Buona sera, mi famiglia*," says our father, patting little Abigail on the back as she wraps her arms around his good leg. After giving Rebekah a hug, our father greets our mother, giving her hand a squeeze. The look on my mother's face is one of relief–but there's great fear hiding behind the joy. I can tell that my father sees this, because he leads her over to the table and sits down.

"It's nice and quiet out there today," he says, his voice as peaceful as the water which laps at the edge of the shop. "It's raining and chilly for June, but it allowed me to get some groceries easily." At this, he hands a paper bag to my mother, who takes it gingerly in her hands.

"Yes . . . Well." My mother clears her throat and nods quickly, suppressing any anxiety she might be feeling with a lighter tone and her usual look of confidence. "That's good. That's very good."

Abigail is playing happily on the floor with her doll, thankfully oblivious to the meaning behind our parents' worried eyes and tightened lips. I wish Rebekah were oblivious, too–but she's fourteen now, and too old not to know what the world is like.

I've known for a long time. Even at a young age, I knew about corruption and hardship. I knew about hate. But now, at eighteen, I sometimes wish I didn't know anything at all. I wish I could be like Abigail, perfectly happy and living in her own little world.

My family has been living almost secretly for the past few years. We haven't been hiding, exactly, but something has shifted in the world. Something that none of us have really been able to put into words. I lay awake in my bed every night, knowing that some unknown threat is lurking just around the corner, waiting to strike.

A few years ago, when the Second World War shattered the peaceful lives of everyone around us, I was naive enough to hope that it would never touch us. That the troubles of other people wouldn't ripple across the country and affect my family. After all, we've been through hard times before–all of us, in different ways. My mother and sisters are most familiar with this; after all, they lived in the ghetto until my mother and father were married. But still, what's going on in the world right now . . . it's different. It's not your everyday discrimination or bias. It's not what we're used to. It's so much bigger than that–and although both German and Italian soldiers march through the streets, and those intimidating Nazi banners hang across our beloved, crumbling buildings, my family has been left unscathed.

My parents never sat me down to have a conversation with me. They never had to explain what was going on. I just . . . *knew*. Rebekah and Abigail, however, were given specific instructions three years ago, when our country first joined with Germany in the war. They were not to go outside without our parents' permission; they were not to interact with the soldiers. Most of all, they were not allowed to speak of their heritage.

This piece hurt my mama the most. She, a woman so proud of her heritage and her faith, was–and still is–being forced to suppress her own origins for the safety of her family. But it has been necessary. So far, it has saved us.

I know how my parents have struggled to keep us all together, living a normal sort of life. I know that our lives have been in jeopardy since the day my mother lied about her heritage and married my father. We're a patchwork family, pieced together in the oddest way possible–but somehow, it's worked out. The Maggios are the only family I've ever had, and I know that I'll do whatever it takes to help us go on, even through the hard times that have stretched on for these past couple of decades.

"Well," says my father, "it's a nice night for some music– don't you all think?"

Rebekah gasps excitedly, and Abigail claps her hands. My mother still looks worried–but the lines in her forehead smooth a bit at the suggestion.

A few minutes later, with our old Victrola playing the suave yet bouncing voice of Alberto Rabagliati, Rebekah and Abigail are up on their feet and twirling around the room.

Laughing, Rebekah takes Abigail's hand and spins her around, leaving Abigail like an uncontrollable top.

"Woahhh," cries Abigail, giggling hysterically. Once she finds her balance, her eyes land on me, and she runs over to where I'm sitting at the table. "Come dance with me, Peter!"

"Oh, Abigail," I start, laughing hesitantly.

"Come on," she begs, grabbing my arm and pulling as hard as she can.

With a grin, I cave and stand up. "Alright."

The two of us begin dancing, and Abigail screams, "Spin me, Peter!" I take her by the hands and lift her up, twirling her so fast that it's as if she's flying.

At this point, my father has stood up and convinced my mother to stand and join all of us. The two begin waltzing a bit slower than the music calls for—but they're happy.

After a moment, I set Abigail back down on her feet, and she and Rebekah resume dancing together. Standing back for a moment to observe the joyful scene before me, I can't help grinning. The world is dark outside, but here in my home with the fire flickering gently and my family dancing, the only thought in my mind is, *Life should always be like this*—sempre e per sempre.

About an hour later, I knock on the door of Rebekah and Abigail's room. When I hear a small voice call, "Come in," I open the door and step inside.

The girls share a little wooden bed, just big enough for the two of them. Walking over to them, I sit down on the bed and pull the girls' patchwork quilt up to Abigail's chin, just the way she likes it.

"Peter," she whispers sleepily, "will you read me a story?"

I push her straight, brown hair out of her face and rub her cheek with my thumb. "Not tonight, *quello piccolo*."

"But you have to," whines Abigail, yawning. "At least sing a song."

I laugh gently and sigh, reminded once again that my little sister may be my greatest weakness. "Alright. One song."

Thinking for a moment, I wait for a song to pop into my head. Then, I begin singing the words to "*Nessun dorma*", the classic love song from the opera *Turandot*–the song that I used to hear echoing from the opera house, *La Fenice*. For some reason, I've been singing it to my younger sisters (particularly Abigail) ever since we were all children. It's traditionally a romantic love song–but the way I sing it reflects all the brotherly love I feel for my two sisters.

My voice rings out deep and full, but I sing the song as a quiet lullaby, hoping to lull my sisters to sleep. The words slip naturally off my tongue, barely requiring me to think. By the time I finish, both girls are half asleep–just as I predicted.

"Goodnight, girls." Standing up, I begin walking towards the door to leave–but a whimper from Abigail stops me in my tracks. "What is it?"

Turning around, I realize that Abigail's eyes are wide and fearful. With a bit of hesitation, she asks suddenly, "Are you going to leave us, Peter?"

I frown and walk slowly back to her. "What makes you ask that?"

I look to Rebekah for help, and she sighs, avoiding my gaze. There's a look in her eyes that I can't describe. "She looked through your journal this morning."

At the mere sound of her words, I flinch. I flinch because I know that it wasn't Abigail who could've discovered my journal, which is hidden high up on a shelf. Besides, she can only read children's books. No–Abigail isn't the one responsible for this.

Rubbing my hand over my face, I sigh in frustration. "Rebekah–"

"I didn't read much. Only the most recent entry."

"And yet, that doesn't make it any better. I've told you a thousand times that–"

"I don't care," exclaims Rebekah, her voice strained. "I know that you always meant to leave us."

"No. No, that's not true." I take a deep breath and sit back down on the bed as I try to formulate an explanation. "Rebekah . . . I've wanted to see the world ever since I was a kid. I never meant to keep it a secret from you. I promise you, I love *Venezia*, and I love you all. You're my family; this is my home. Even if I decide to travel one day, I . . . I wouldn't be leaving you forever. We'll always be together."

Abigail sniffs and moves in closer to me, resting her little head on my shoulder. "Do you promise, Peter?"

I smile and kiss the top of her head. "Of course I do." Turning to look at Rebekah, I give her a comforting look, and she returns my smile. "I promise."

24
EILEEN

VENICE, ITALY
SUMMER, 1965

When I make it back to the hotel, Sandy isn't in our room. I manage to wash up and change into a clean dress before she arrives, breathless and panicked.

"Eileen!" she exclaims, lunging forward to hug me. "Oh, I was so worried. You told me to wait, so I did . . . But you took so long that I went looking for you, and then I couldn't find you, and I saw the map in the water, and . . ."

"I know–I'm really sorry. I promise, I'm alright," I reassure her quickly, pulling out of the hug to finish brushing my now-dry hair. "I got a little lost. But . . ." A smile creeps across my face, unannounced. "Someone helped me."

Sandy raises her blonde eyebrows curiously. "Who?"

I picture the young man's face in my head and it hits me. He's the gondolier who I saw from the balcony the day we arrived in Venice. That's twice that I've seen him now.

"A gondolier," I say, a strange feeling settling in my stomach as I think about him. "I slipped as I was running . . . and he saved me."

The look on Sandy's face resembles the exact expression of my sister Julie when she received a new record for Christmas last year. "You were *rescued*? Eileen, that is the most romantic thing I've ever heard in my life."

I laugh and roll my eyes, acting nonchalant. "It was nothing, really."

"What did he look like?"

"Young, with dark hair and blue eyes," I say immediately.

Sandy lets out a sigh that's full of both frustration and longing. "Oh, Eileen. I wish I'd seen it."

"No, you don't," I say with a smirk, cringing at the thought. "I'm sure I looked ridiculous."

"Did you talk to him afterwards?"

I shrug and avoid eye contact with Sandy, instead staring into the mirror and fastening my pearl necklace around my neck. "A little. I was embarrassed, though. I sort of rushed off."

Sandy groans and grabs me by the shoulders, turning me around. "What?"

"It wasn't a big deal."

"You weren't rude about it, though. Right?"

I shrug again, and Sandy shakes her head, blonde curls flying. "As your best friend, I'm going to give you a piece of advice–and I want you to take it."

"Go ahead," I sigh with a smile, despite knowing what's coming.

"You need to go back there and talk to him."

I step away quickly, picking up my purse and preparing to exit the room. "Please, Sandy–cut me some slack. I was kind of in shock. After all, I'd just fallen."

"Well, it's up to you," says Sandy, stepping away from the door as I press on past her. "I'm just trying to do you a favor, Eileen."

I sigh and pause, looking at my friend. "I know. I just don't know what to think . . . and you know I'm so awkward in situations like this. Just . . . Please don't tell anyone else about this. Okay?"

Sandy gives me a half-smile and nods. "I promise."

The next day, Sandy and I meet up with Janet and Lois in the hotel lobby. Then, we set out to get some food.

We're busy talking when we pass by the canal that the woman from the cafe told us about–and perched right there on top of a gondola is none other than the young man. The man I saw from my balcony–the same young man who rescued me. It occurs to me that he's who the woman at the cafe told us about.

I turn and steal a quick glance at Sandy. We make eye contact, and on impulse, she begins talking to Lois and Janet, distracting them. Usually, I wouldn't be on board with possibly embarrassing myself further like this. Still, I can't stop feeling this urge to do something spontaneous and exciting for once in my life. Besides, there are people all around, so there's no danger of anything happening. I simply need to fulfill this growing promise in my heart–a promise to gain confidence and become the person I used to be. The person I was before I grew up–and before everything went wrong.

While attempting to sneak away, I hear Janet call out, "What's the matter, Eileen?" I turn slowly to see she is staring quizzically at me.

"Oh . . . There's just something I'd like to see. A certain bridge. I just . . . heard it looks good at this time of day. But I know you guys want to get lunch, so don't worry. I'll be fine on my own for a few minutes."

Sandy raises her eyebrows with a smile.

"Be careful."

"Yeah, I'll be fine."

After another moment's hesitation, my friends leave. I wait until they've disappeared around the corner. Then, I begin walking slowly towards the canal where the young man is standing.

The closer I get, the more sure I am that this is the young man who I saw yesterday, and the day before that. He's dressed exactly the same, in clothing that seems more old-fashioned than the typical gondolier uniform.

He's stepping onto the dock as I approach him, and tying the gondola to it. Hesitantly, I hold my hands behind my back and clear my throat softly.

The young man turns around quickly, and I see the hint of a smile playing along his lips. "Hello."

"Hi," I say, my mouth dry again. What was I even planning to say? If my plan was to look ridiculous again, then I'm succeeding.

"Um . . . Thank you again. For helping me yesterday. I'm sorry I rushed off . . . but I was just . . ."

He gives me a kind look and finishes tying up the gondola. However, he doesn't say anything.

Unsure of what to say next, I begin talking quickly. "Do you live around here? It's really beautiful. I always listen to Dean Martin's records and I've always imagined Italy, but it was never this cool in my daydreams, you know?" I suddenly realize that I'm rambling, and I stop and stare down at my shoes.

"It is beautiful."

Looking up, I make eye contact with him. His smile is soft, and his blue eyes are sparkling like the nearby water. If I weren't paying attention, I wouldn't put any stock in his words–but the way he says them gives me a breathless feeling, as though it isn't Venice he's talking about.

"And," he continues, his tone lighter now, "it can be dangerous, especially near the water."

His meaningful tone tells me that he's referring to yesterday's events. I clear my throat and step forward, ready to defend myself. However, at second glance, I see a mischievous look in the young man's eyes, and I relax. Smoothing my pale blue skirt, I say sheepishly, "I'm sorry about that. Really."

The young man shakes his head vigorously. "No, please–I'm just teasing. If I were in your shoes, I'm sure I'd do the same thing. It wasn't your fault. Why, if you ever tell anyone what happened–just blame the water."

I laugh, feeling far more at ease. "Have you ever done that? Slipped and fallen because of the water, I mean."

"Oh, sure. Mostly when I was younger. When you become a gondolier, though, you have to learn how to keep your balance–how not to slip on wet surfaces, and all that."

"Do you like it? Being a gondolier?"

I watch as the young man turns to look up at the sky. It's a thousand different shades now, all different blues and white clouds swirling together to create a beautiful sort of painting.

"Oh, yes. Lots of the time, it's a quiet, solitary career–and I like that. But there's also opportunities to meet strangers and get to know them. I like talking to interesting people. Like you."

The words cause my heart to begin racing. "You think I'm interesting?"

The young man looks back at me and studies me for a moment, wiping sweat from his brow with the back of his hand. Then, he says, "I think so. It is not every day I pull a young lady from a canal. You seem to live an adventurous life."

If only he knew. I feel an embarrassed smile spread across my face, and I begin playing with my hands as I try to think of something new to say. My eyes eventually land on the gondola, and I ask, "Is that yours?"

The young man turns and looks at the gondola. His expression is one of warmth and care, and he rests his hand lovingly on the golden top. "Yes."

The look on his face quickly becomes far-off and almost mournful. Hesitantly, I open my mouth to speak–but just like that the look disappears, and he turns to smile at me. "You're from America, then?"

I nod. "Mhm. I'm visiting with some of my classmates and our teachers."

The young man pushes a few dangling strands of dark hair out of his eyes and nods. Then, he asks, "Have you ever been to Venice before?"

I shake my head. "No, this is my first time. In fact, it's my first time traveling in Europe. We started in Rome. Have you ever been there?"

He nods. "Yes . . . briefly. But I haven't traveled many places . . . just throughout Italy."

"Oh."

The young man turns away. Then, abruptly, he says, "You should visit *Piazza San Marco*–I mean, St. Mark's Square. And the Basilica. They're both beautiful."

I nod slowly and smile warmly. "Alright. I will."

Turning to go, I begin walking away, feeling satisfied by my unusual encounter–but that soft, musical voice stops me again. "I'm something of a tour guide . . . if you'd like me to show you around sometime."

I hesitate. I barely know him . . . but his attitude and manner of speaking are increasingly appealing to me in a way I can't describe. There's something about him that's drawing me in more by the second. Besides, didn't he save my life yesterday? So, I earnestly reply, "Yes. That would be nice."

25
PETER

VENICE, ITALY
SUMMER, 1943

It's dark when I go to open up the shop the next morning. For the past year or so, my papa and I have shared the responsibilities of running the *libreria*. Of course, I was honored when he asked me. I spent practically my entire childhood in this store, reading leather-bound books and taking in their musty yet comforting scent. Little typed words on yellowing pages mean more to me than the average person. My father knows that. He also knows that I don't plan on staying in Venice forever, so I likely will not end up running the shop.

These thoughts seem strange in my mind as I contemplate the conversation I had with my younger sisters last night. I still want to travel the world, and maybe even find my family—but if I've learned anything in the past four years, it's that the Maggios *are* my family, just as much as anyone I may be blood-related to. They're the most important people in my life–and if leaving Venice means leaving my family, then I'm not going anytime soon. Besides, with all that's happening in the world right now . . . I couldn't leave even if I wanted to.

I unlock the shop door and open a couple windows, letting a cool, fresh breeze blow inside. The smell of water accompanies it, and I take a deep breath, savoring the comforting scent. Then, I walk over to the front counter and sit down, opening my copy of *The Three Musketeers* and proceeding to read.

Before I've had the chance to read ten words, the front door opens, allowing a powerful gust of wind to send a nearby stack of papers flying off the counter. In a panic, I rush to fix the mess. Bending down in front of the counter, I pick up a few papers and go to stand–and I find myself face-to-face with a familiar young man.

Raising my eyebrows in surprise, I back up and observe the face for a moment. Then, I stammer, "M-Matteo?"

My old friend laughs–but it's a different laugh. A laugh that causes me to glance around to make sure it belongs to him. There's no one else inside the shop–but there are a few men just outside, talking loudly to each other. All, including Matteo, are wearing a certain uniform with multiple patches on the arms–the uniform worn by the National Fascist Party.

Besides all this, Matteo himself hasn't changed very much. He looks just about the same, although he's grown quite a few inches and now stands at my height. His dark hair is combed back, and his smile shiny . . . but it's the kind of smile that makes me feel unsettled. Besides this, there's a look in his eyes that makes me wonder, once again, if this truly is the same timid boy I used to be friends with when we were children. The boy I knew before we went down our separate paths two years ago–although, when I think about it, we were always going down those paths. It was just never quite as obvious as it is now.

I feel a nervous jolt run through my body, but I do my best to keep a smile on my face. "Um . . . It's been a long time."

"Yes, well." Matteo leans against the counter and watches as I fumble with the stack of books. "And you're still here, I see."

"Uh, yes." I swallow hard and adjust one of my suspenders in order to avoid eye contact with my old friend.

"Perhaps my memory has served me wrong," says Matteo, walking further into the shop and scanning the bookshelves, "but I do recall you mentioning that you wanted to travel."

I force a casual smile and shrug. "Well–Venice is just as good as anywhere else. Anyway, I'd . . . I'd like to continue working here with my father a little while longer."

Matteo nods slowly and removes a red leather-bound book from one of the shelves. Flipping through the pages, he asks quietly, "And to be with your mother and sisters, I suppose."

"Ah, yes. That, as well," I say a little too quickly.

"Haven't you thought," begins Matteo, "that by joining my–well, line of work–you could find access to all the benefits you've always longed for? I mean, financial stability for your family, a chance to travel–have you ever considered its appeal?"

"Oh, yes, of course," I stammer, hoping I look as convincing as I sound. "But, like I said before–"

"You want to stick around a little while longer," interrupts Matteo. Slamming the book shut, he turns and looks at me. His cool gaze seems to pierce right through me, and it takes everything in me not to look away.

Matteo sets the book back onto the shelf and looks around another moment. Then, he makes his way back over to me. His walk is stiff but confident, and I take a deep breath as he approaches. "Peter, I've known you a long time. We practically grew up together. So, know that when I say this, it's because I care about you."

I open my mouth to reply, but there are no words waiting to spring off my tongue. So I simply close my mouth and let Matteo continue.

"You don't want to stick around here forever, do you? You're like a family man at eighteen, surrounded by womenfolk and a bunch of old books. But . . . well. I think you know what's going on in the world. There's much more to life than this. Hell, you were the smartest kid in school. Straight A's and a flawless memory. Our teacher couldn't get enough of your writing. Oh, not a day went by that she didn't say you had a gift."

It takes everything in me to keep staring back at Matteo's harsh, glaring eyes. His words and his tone are biting– menacing. There seems to be nothing left of the insecure, soft-spoken boy I used to play ball with in the street.

"She also said that you needed to go places and do things. You need more experience–to give you more to write about. And that's what we all want, isn't it, Peter? Experience?"

Suddenly, there's a knock at the door, and Matteo and I both turn to look. The three men outside have obviously tired of waiting for their friend. One raises the bottle in his hand, and Matteo nods and holds up one finger. Then, he turns back to me, his gaze dark.

"Don't wait much longer, my friend. The world is changing. The last thing you want is to be left behind." Just like that, Matteo walks out of the shop, joining his uniform-clad friends and leaving me to my thoughts.

It's been a week since Matteo visited the shop, and since then, my family has been extra careful. My mother and sisters have spent most of their time in the back of the shop, staying out of sight. I know that it's especially hard on little Abigail, who's at the age when she'll practically explode if she's forced to keep her energy bottled up–but it's the only option we have to keep her safe.

She is not the only one struggling with this arrangement, though. As the days and weeks go on, even my mother and Rebekah seem to be increasingly on edge.

Meanwhile, Matteo's words haven't stopped running through my mind. I've tried to forget what he said–but I can't. He's known me for too long and too well. He knew me back when I was just a kid. He had the tools to get inside my head– and he used them.

"The world is changing," he told me. Well, I've always known that. I just haven't wanted to believe it. For the past few years, I've thought that if I could simply convince myself that I was content with my life, I would forget about my previous desires. I love my family; I can't abandon them, no matter what any part of me says.

Still, at least once a day, a thought or a whisper will slip unbidden into my mind, begging me to dream again. Begging me to stop putting words on paper about places I've never been. Urging me to *go* to these places and do things before my life ends–or the rest of the world ends. Whichever comes first. Even as Matteo spoke to me, his voice so confident and his words so persuasive, I felt a slight tug on my heart to finally do what I've always wanted.

But I can't. My heart is here, with my adopted family. I learned that about myself long ago. Nothing that Matteo said could convince me otherwise. Sure, it might tempt me–but my family is more important. I'll never leave them, and I know they'd never leave me. Most importantly, I could never agree with what those men stand for. What Matteo stands for.

I'm dusting one of the bookshelves in the shop when I hear hushed voices from the other room. My first urge is to ignore the voices and give my parents their privacy, knowing that something must be very wrong–but I can't do that anymore. I'm not naive.

Quietly, I set down the feather duster and move over to press my ear against the wall. Hiding right by the opening to the other room, I can just make out my parents' words.

"It's not safe, Rachel," whispers my father. "The girls–"

"The girls cannot hide all their lives," exclaims my mother, her voice strained with emotion. "Our people have been hiding for years. Someone has to end this cycle of fear."

"But you are not just their people. You are *mine*, as well.

Is it too much to ask that you decline a wedding invitation? For the sake of your husband?"

I swallow hard. So that's what they've been talking about. Last week, we were all invited to a wedding . . . and not a day has gone by that my parents haven't spent at least an hour discussing it in the quiet of the evening.

"Verona is not as far as you may think. Once we are there, we will be in the company of friends, and we will be able to celebrate my sister–and there will be nothing to worry about."

"No, my dear–you are wrong. There is still plenty to worry about. I will not feel that you and the girls are safe while we are away from home. I know it is a disappointment, but we have to make sacrifices. Believe me, your sister will understand."

I take a deep breath. Although my father's words should comfort me, I know him well enough to be certain that he's caving–and fast. I can't wait any longer. Stepping out of hiding, I find myself face to face with my parents, who are sitting at the table. "I agree with Papa."

My mother sighs and shakes her head. "Peter . . ."

"It's alright," interjects my father, looking almost relieved to see me. "Let him give his opinion."

I scoff in disbelief, striding over to the table. "I don't see how either of you could even consider accepting an invitation–and in Verona, to top it off. Haven't you been paying attention to what's happening in the world?"

My father gives me a disapproving look. "Not a day has gone by that we haven't, Peter. You of all people should know that."

I bite my lip and feel my anger start to melt into shame. "I'm sorry, Papa. But . . . I care about Mama and Rebekah, and Abigail. I–I can't help being afraid for them."

"And that, my son, is just the point," says my mother gently, standing and walking over to me. I'm a few inches taller than her now, but she looks just the same as always–confident and serene. Taking my hands, she rubs them and sighs. "I know that it's easy to get caught up in fear, especially after close calls like the one you had with that young man. Trust me, I understand–and it's human to be afraid. But think of your sisters. What do you want to teach them–to live in fear, or to be courageous?"

I study my mother's face for a moment. Sure, there are lines of worry scattered across her forehead, and a few streaks of gray in her dark hair–but those are barely noticeable when I recognize the bravery that's been inside her all along.

For a brief moment, I remember the first time I saw this side of my mother, back when she was Signora Hoffman. It was when she urged me to go to school, back when I was just a thirteen-year-old kid with big dreams and an impulsive, carefree spirit. She wasn't afraid to see Signor Maggio, and later marry him. She was confident enough to tell a truant Italian kid what to do. She even had the courage to become the mother of that same Italian kid. Yes, my mother was, and is, brave–braver than I will ever be. She knows what she's doing . . . and I have no right to stop her.

"Alright," I say quietly as my mother steps away and joins my father, who's stood up from the table. "It's your decision."

My mother smiles. There's a look in her eyes that makes me feel good, despite my concern. It's a look of loving pride. "Thank you, Peter." She then turns to my father. "Luca?"

My father sighs and rubs his forehead. Leaning on his cane, he suddenly looks extremely tired and defeated. Not for the first time, I realize that he and I are so alike. We're prone to let fear get the best of us, simply because we care so much about the ones we love. We're also prone to cave to those same people.

"I'll go with you, and keep you safe," he relents. "But what of the shop?"

My eyes shift back towards my mother, who makes eye contact with me. "Would you mind staying back to take care of things, Peter?"

I feel all of my worries come flooding back. "Mama, I can't–"

"What? You can't let us go by ourselves? Your father can take care of us perfectly fine, thank you very much. You are still young, Peter. Stop acting as though the weight of the world were always on your shoulders. While we are gone, you should have fun and take some time for yourself."

I cross my arms and stare down at the wooden floor. A thousand comebacks and excuses are flying through my head, such as the fact that there is nothing fun left to do in this tense, war-torn city. But I refrain from this. "Alright."

"You're sure you don't mind?"

I shake my head and try to lighten the tone of my voice. "No. I'll take good care of the shop; I promise."

My mother walks over once more and brings my chin up with her finger. There's a smile on her face that's full of peace, and a mischievous look in her brown eyes. "Just don't go running off on us."

At the sight of her confidence and perfect composure, I feel a slight, natural smile appear on my own face. "I won't."

My papa steps forward and claps me on the shoulder, his warm eyes crinkling as he grins at me. "Be a saint and take care of the shop for me, Peter. I know you'll handle things just fine."

I nod my head earnestly. "I promise I will."

The night before my family is supposed to leave for Verona, I walk into my sisters' room to say goodnight, rubbing my hands to keep warm in the cool September air. To my surprise, Abigail is already asleep.

I look over at Rebekah, who has a book in her hands. Walking to her side of the bed, I pull up a stool and sit down there. "What are you reading?"

Rebekah holds out the book, its pages open to about halfway through the story, and I immediately recognize it as *Oliver Twist*.

A grin spreads across my face. "I gave this to you, didn't I?"

Rebekah nods, shadows caused by the nearby candlelight flickering across her face. "Five years ago."

I let out a low whistle and push a few loose strands of dark hair out of my eyes. "Seems like a long time ago now, doesn't it?"

My sister nods again, her long, brown hair spilling over her shoulders. "It's funny, I barely knew you back then. You were just the boy who came and gave me books, and liked me enough to be my friend. You were so different from me–but you cared about me anyway."

I feel my heart swell at hearing the genuine affection and emotion in my younger sister's words. "Of course I cared about you. You were always like a sister to me."

"And now, I really am," says Rebekah softly, her bright smile reaching her eyes.

I let my hand run over the book's fragile binding and observe my younger sister, who's now watching little Abigail sleep. I can imagine how she must feel–torn between two worlds, separated by blood and distance, history and faith. I've experienced the same thing all my life, living out the Italian half of myself and never knowing the American half. But Rebekah has borne it much better than I. She is as brave as her mother, and even wiser than she used to be when she impressed me as a child. She changed my life–she and Abigail, and both our parents. I can't imagine it any differently.

My eyes land on a colorful drawing that sits on Rebekah's bedside table, and I reach out to grab it. "What's this?"

"Oh, that's for you."

I raise my eyebrows. "Really?" Observing the drawing, I realize that it's a depiction of one of Venice's canals. With gondolas riding on the calm, blue water, and pink flowers hanging in baskets on the brick walls, the image takes me right outside and urges me to get back out on the water–something I haven't done in a long time.

"Rebekah," I breathe, "it's beautiful. More beautiful than anything you've ever made."

Rebekah blushes and lets part of her dark brown hair fall in front of her face, the way she has always done when she is embarrassed or shy. "Do you really mean it?"

"Yes. You're talented, *mia sorella*. You need to share that talent with the world."

Rebekah laughs quietly, but there's a hint of bitterness in it. The sound is foreign on Rebekah's lips, and it makes me wince. "I can't."

"And why not?"

Rebekah raises her eyebrows at me as if to say, "Isn't it obvious?" but I'm undeterred.

"You can make a business out of it, and I'll help you," I say earnestly, excitement bubbling up within me. "When you come back from the wedding, we can get started. I know plenty of people who would love to have a beautiful work of art like yours."

Smiling, Rebekah glances at the drawing. "Truly?"

"Yes. I promise. You'll be the most famous artist in all of Europe–no, in all the *world*."

Rebekah laughs, all the anxiety and doubt disappearing from her eyes. Satisfied, I squeeze her hand as I stand up. Her hand still fits inside my own–but it isn't the hand of a child anymore. My sister is a young woman now. She's a person who can take care of herself. It's true that I still see her as a little girl . . . but it's time for me to face the facts. Rebekah has grown up–and although I'll never stop worrying about her, it's time for me to let her grow up.

With a smile, I open the door and walk out, whispering, "*Buona notte*, Rebekah."

"Goodnight, Peter."

26
PETER

VENICE, ITALY
SUMMER, 1943

These past few days have been strange, but in a nice kind of way. It's been a long time since I had the house all to myself, and it's been even longer since I had extra time to myself.

Every day, after closing up shop, I make my way outside under the cover of night and venture out with my gondola. The sound of water is comforting and familiar to me, and I like to look up at the windows I pass by and observe the warm glow that spills out of each. Sometimes, happiness and laughter come echoing from these windows, and they make me think of my family, out in the world on their way to the wedding.

My sisters have never visited a place outside of Venice, and now, I'm glad that my mother was so persistent. They deserve to live a little. They should be able to see things and do things they've never done before. Still . . . there are so many thoughts swirling around in my mind. Mixed emotions, and wishes. Wishes that I want to forget.

I understand why my mother wanted me to stay back to take care of the shop. She is intent on taking advantage of life, and refusing to live in fear. She wanted me to learn how to let go.

Well, I've done that. My family is off at the wedding, and I'm back here. And yet . . . that's exactly the problem. I've never been out of Venice. I can hardly imagine what Verona is like. When my family returns, I know I'll hear about it from them—but that is all. Matteo's persuasive words creep into my mind in a voice that immediately makes me feel guilty.

Arriving back at the dock near home, I tie up the gondola and lay down flat on my back inside it, staring up at the sky. Tonight, it's absolutely covered in a blanket of stars, glittering in a way that fills me with peace. My family is under that same sky right now—and it won't be long before I see them again. Just a few more days, and we'll be reunited.

The stars are twinkling brightly, and as I stare up at them, I begin to softly sing the words of "*Nessun dorma*".

"Nobody shall sleep!...
Nobody shall sleep!
Even you, oh Princess,
in your cold room,
watch the stars,
that tremble with love and with hope.
But my secret is hidden within me,
my name no one shall know..."

The night sky is the last thing I see before I fall asleep.

There's a chill in the air when I wake up. The sky is dark and cloudy, and at first glance, I assume that it's still nighttime.

Stepping onto the dock and making my way back home, I observe the way the entire city seems frozen in silence. I suppose everyone must still be asleep.

Walking inside the shop, I immediately glance up at the clock on the wall. I see that it's already almost noon.

Keeping the front door unlocked in case of customers, I stagger around sleepily and head to the back room, where my dinner plate is still sitting. I busy myself by cleaning up for a few minutes, straightening up the room just the way my mother would, when I hear the shop door open.

To my surprise, there's a man standing inside the shop— one of the same young men who I saw with Matteo before. The moment we make eye contact, he gives me a curt nod. "Peter Maggio?"

"Chiappetta," I correct him, and he nods.

"Oh, uh, yes. I have a telegram here for you."

I roll up my white sleeves and reach out to receive the telegram. "From who?"

"Not sure," says the young man stiffly. He gives me one last nod before exiting through the door, which slams unceremoniously behind him.

I watch the young man until he's disappeared from view. Then, I sit down in my father's old chair and stare down at the telegram in my hands.

I stare at it unopened for a long time. After a while, my eyes begin to burn, and I blink a few times to end the sensation. I have no reason to be concerned. But still . . . I've also never received mail before. Mail that's addressed to *just* me, and not my family.

My hands are shaking, but I manage to open the telegram. My eyes scan over the words, first quickly and then slower. Then, my hands go limp, and the telegram drops to the floor.

I can't breathe.

I stand up too quickly, take a few steps, and slide down against the wall, my chest heaving.

Images of my family flash through my mind. Faces, voices, and memories. Laughter, heartache, and pain.

Abigail, my sweet little sister, full of life and energy.

Rebekah, the girl who started as a friend and quickly became family, full of beauty and wisdom.

My mama, with her loving nature and constant bravery.

And Signor Maggio–my *papa*. The man who raised me. The man who loved me as his real son. The man who saved me.

The tears come quickly, and I begin choking on them, overwhelmed to the point of insanity.

Lies. All lies. They have to be lies.

A stray book is sitting at my feet, and the moment my eyes land on it, I find myself hating it. I grab it and throw it across the room; it hits a nearby pile of books and sends them all falling like dominoes. Then, in one swift movement, I grab the telegram and rip it in two.

I'm gasping for air. I can't breathe. I can't *live* anymore.

For a moment, I stretch out my hands and imagine that the forms of my family will be magically conjured before me–but there is nothing but air. Reaching up, I take my head in my hands and begin rocking back and forth.

I feel just like a kid again, lost and alone–except this time, the pain is far worse. Back when I was a kid, I couldn't even conjure the image of my biological parents in my mind. That way, it didn't hurt as badly. But now . . .

I squeeze my eyes tightly, allowing the tears to fall. Somehow, the one thing my family has managed to avoid these past many years has come to pass. It seemed so far away . . . so distant. As though it would never touch us. But it has. Death has reached down his cold, unmerciful fingers, and he has stolen from me. I have lost the only people I ever cared about. The only people I ever loved. The only people who ever loved *me*.

I don't know how much time has passed, but eventually I manage to stand up and lock the front door, as though that matters anymore. Somehow, a little voice in my mind is still saying, *Lock the door. Take care of the shop. When Papa gets home, he'll want to know you took care of things while he was gone.*

As if in a dream, I make my way to Rebekah and Abigail's room. I stagger to Rebekah's shelf and pick up her drawings.

I regret it the moment a single tear dampens one of her beautiful works of art, spreading the different hues across the page in an explosion of colors.

Observing Abigail's toys, I take one in particular, a little stuffed bear, in my hands and begin stroking it with my thumb. I see my reflection in its glassy eyes, and I hate the sight of it. I hate that I'm *here*, and not with my family. I should have been with them. No–I should have stopped them from going on that God-forsaken trip in the first place.

I squeeze my eyes shut and feel my heart sink lower in my chest as grief, shame, and hatred creates a storm beginning to brew inside me. Still clutching the bear, I lie down on the bed, my breathing shallow–and I fall asleep.

27
EILEEN

VENICE, ITALY
SUMMER, 1965

The sun has almost entirely set when I return to my hotel. Slipping inside the golden-bathed room, I shut the door softly behind me and look around for Sandy. She's sitting on her bed, and when she looks up and sees me, a curious expression appears on her face.

"Eileen? Are you okay?"

I shrug and sit down on my bed, positioning myself so that Sandy can't see the redness spreading across my cheeks. "Yeah. Why wouldn't I be?"

Sandy raises her eyebrows and smooths her pale yellow dress. She stands up and walks over to me, forcing me to look at her. "Well . . . There's a strange look on your face. And I haven't seen you smile like that in . . . well, I guess *ever*."

I laugh and shake my head, feeling an urge to act casually. "Maybe I'm just happy. Is that so weird?"

"Oh, come on. You know it's because of that guy. Don't keep me in suspense!"

I sigh and recall the young man, his blue eyes still there in my mind. "He offered to show me around the city, since he's lived here all his life."

Sandy gasps, her eyes sparkling in excitement. She practically leaps onto my bed, sitting next to me. "Really? Did you say yes?"

"I did."

"Oh, Eileen!"

"No, no," I exclaim, laughing and feeling strangely giddy. It's a completely foreign feeling . . . one I haven't felt in years. But now that I'm feeling it again, I'm enjoying it–and I'm a bit wary of it.

Nervously, I wipe the smile from my face before standing quickly and making my way over to the mirror nearby. Picking up my brush, I begin pulling it through my light brown hair, slowly and gently, as if I'm in a sort of trance. "Let's not make a big deal out of it. I'll probably end up paying him; after all, it's his job. It's nothing more than that."

Even as I say the words, I know I'm hoping for more. The way he looked at me when he offered to show me around certainly didn't seem to be a business proposition. He wanted to get to know *me*, as a person–not as a customer or a random tourist. The very thought of it makes my heart leap–but I can't let Sandy see. I can't get my hopes up now. Not when life has let me down so many times before. Not when my heart has already been broken.

Knowing it would be best to change the subject, I set down the brush and move over to the closet. Sorting through my dresses, I ask, "Do you know how much longer we're going to stay in Venice?"

"About four more days. Mrs. Nelson told me that's just the right amount of time to see everything."

I nod slowly, keeping my back to Sandy in an effort to conceal the expression that I know has settled on my face. The confused, crestfallen look that reflects what I'm feeling inside. Altogether, not counting the day we arrived, our time in Venice will come out to six days. *Six days.* That used to seem like a lot of time–but now, it doesn't seem like any at all. Now that this endeavor of mine has started, I almost don't want it to stop.

I've never had the courage to be this adventurous, but it's almost as if being in a foreign country has given me the extra push; the strength that I never had to act on while around my family or classmates. It may be stupid of me, but I've never taken risks before. Risks like talking to perfect strangers and exploring a foreign city.

Even though I feel these doubts entering my mind, I do my best to ignore them, and remember my reasons for being so spontaneous. Almost as soon as I get back home, the summer will end, and my whole life will change. I won't be returning to the same old routine that I've lived through these past four years. Everything will be different–and I don't know how to face it.

That night, as I'm lying in bed, I try to sleep–but I can't. I've been tossing and turning for hours, opening and closing my eyes in an effort to become drowsier than I really am. I envy Sandy, who always falls asleep as soon as her head hits her pillow. Still, I'm sure she wouldn't be able to fall asleep so easily if she were experiencing the same thoughts as I am right now.

I roll over in bed again and watch as moonlight seeps in through the balcony door. There's an image that keeps appearing in my mind: the face of the gondolier whose name I still don't know. I feel my eyes widen at the realization. How could I not have asked his name?

He was so kind and considerate. When he smiled, it radiated and lit up his face. It made me feel . . . *thrilled*. It scares me, and it excites me, because it's a familiar sensation–but stronger. So much stronger than anything I've ever felt before.

There was a sort of air about the young man, as well. I can't really describe it, but it hung all about his gentle manners and way of speaking. He made me feel like I had stepped into one of my favorite old movies–the ones made when my parents were my age, or even younger.

Besides all these things, there was something mysterious about him. Maybe it was simply because of the way the woman talked about him–or maybe it's because I never learned his name.

Either way, things are going to be different for me from now on. For one glorious summer, I can escape the monotony and challenges of the real world, and embrace the magic of beautiful Venice.

28
PETER

NORTHERN ITALY
SPRING, 1945

My boots feel heavier with every step through the wet marshlands. Thick grass slows me down, but I continue trudging along, if only to keep up with my fellow soldiers. Mountains surround the area, keeping us temporarily trapped. The gray sky is peppered with gunfire, and all I can hear are the shouts and groans of men. I never imagined that my life would be like this . . . and every day, I realize just how true it is that everything can change in a moment.

I remember when my papa used to read me stories from the Bible. Terrifying at times, calming at others, the stories never failed to excite something deep within me. Some greater longing to experience . . . *more*. I wanted to know what it was like to live back then. I wanted to witness God's greatness for myself.

I recall one night in particular when I first heard the story of Sodom and Gomorrah. The city had sinned, so God punished them accordingly. God rained down fire and brimstone; he wiped out the city because of what they had done. I used to be able to understand that–in fact, I still do– but it's left me confused. The people that God punished in the Bible had done something wrong, every time. In many instances, they *knew* that they had disobeyed the Lord. But in my case, I don't understand. I *can't* understand. Because, as flashes of orange and red flames sear through the air and explosions render me almost deaf, I have to wonder what I've done wrong.

After months of grieving and fighting, I've found myself asking that question again and again. *What did I do? Please, tell me what I did wrong, so I can fix it. What did I do?* Every time, nothing but silence responds–cold, aching silence.

Sometimes, I feel the gravity of loss so much that I'm nauseous. Other times, I don't feel anything . . . and that's the part that worries me. Part of my soul is crying out for help, begging for relief–and the other part seems to have accepted my fate. If I die out here on the battlefield, it will be over. I'll be relieved from my sorrows. And if I don't . . . the pain will return–but so will my thirst for revenge.

My moment of contemplation is suddenly interrupted as a high-pitched whistling sound sails by my ear. I grit my teeth and dodge in the opposite direction of the sound, anticipating the pain I know may come. However, I'm lucky–this time.

The sounds of my fellow soldiers blend together, and with great difficulty, I'm able to pick out certain voices that are more familiar to me. Zanetti, a soldier just a few years older than me, is on my left, shouting something almost unintelligible. I crouch down to avoid another bullet that whizzes by, and I squint at Zanetti, trying to figure out what he's saying.

Reading his lips, I can just barely make out the words, "Go! Go, Chiappetta! Get outta here!"

By the time I've comprehended his warning, I realize I'm rooted to the spot, and don't have a spare second to avoid the flash of orange and red that's flying towards me. I take a deep breath. If this is it . . . then so be it. I have no wish to die–and yet, I have no wish to live. I turn away from Zanetti, not wanting to see his face as I'm blown off the face of the earth. I squeeze my eyes shut–

"NO!" My eyes fly open at the sound of Zanetti's piercing cry, and I watch in shock as he comes barreling towards me, pulling me just out of the way before the explosion takes place. I cover my eyes with my arm, refusing to look. Refusing to witness any more damage than I already have.

"Come on, Chiappetta," hisses Zanetti, grabbing at my arm. "Come on."

I turn wildly to get a look at him. His brown eyes are wide, and urgency is written all over his dirt-smudged face. Thankfully, he appears to be unharmed.

"What are you doing?" he cries, pulling me to my feet.

I'd like to ask him the same thing. Quietly, I reply, "You shouldn't have done that."

Zanetti stares at me for a moment. His face is that of absolute perplexity. "Come on," he says before running across the wet marshland once again. I follow helplessly, still debating which would be better: to die or to live.

"Chiappetta."

I look up from the cigarette in my hand and make eye contact with Zanetti. Despite his short stature, he stares down at me as I sit on a little stool inside my tent. "Yeah?"

"It's Ferraro. He's asking for you."

I hesitate for a split second, dread settling in the pit of my stomach. Then, I nod and stand up, following Zanetti through the darkness until we reach another tent.

The sounds of labored breathing and concerned whispers hit my ears the moment we step into the tent. Zanetti guides me past a few occupied cots until we reach that of Stefano Ferraro. He's older than both Zanetti and I, but still young by the world's standards. I don't know him well, but I do know that he has a wife and two children who he is always talking about.

In a conversation I had with him some weeks ago, he said longingly, "I see their faces every night, when I fall asleep. They are always safe at home, sitting in front of the fire, watching the door and just waiting for me. I promised them, Chiappetta. I said I'd be home, and I intend to be there before my daughter's third birthday."

Something inside me cringes as I take in this current image of Ferraro lying on his cot, obviously nearing the end. It destroys me inside to see so many men whose promises will never be kept. In all my time of fighting thus far, I've come to one simple conclusion: The worst part of life is watching others lose theirs.

I would probably not have to see so much suffering had I made a different decision three weeks ago. A soldier I knew well, Daniel Ricci, was on his deathbed and asked for me. We were both around the same age, and we related to one another. We were both dreadfully homesick, and as soon as we met, we began conveying stories of our lives to each other. After a while, Daniel ran out of stories to tell me. He instead wanted to hear my own stories, claiming that they gave him hope. So, I did. And when Daniel breathed his last, I was at his side, telling him about my papa's bookshop.

"Ferraro?" I ask, sitting down on a stool beside his cot.

The man appears to use every ounce of his strength to turn his head and make eye contact with me. Slowly, he opens his blood-coated mouth and utters in a gravelly voice, "Please, Chiappetta . . . Usher me out."

I clear my throat and nod. Then, I do my best to shut out the world around me. I shut out my itchy uniform and the men dying and the darkness that surrounds the tent. I shut out my memories from the past many years, since the war began and a shadow fell over my family.

I let the words transport me home.

"Venice is beautiful in the summertime. The sunlight hits the crystal blue water and makes it sparkle, and the smell of it sails on the wind. Children run down the cobblestones playing ball, and adults hang laundry on clotheslines that hover over the streets. Sometimes, the air smells like flowers, and other times, it smells like food. And the gondoliers . . . They bring the city to life, traveling down the watery streets and singing songs that fly all the way up to the heavens."

I pause for a moment and watch as Ferraro's lips turn up in a small, resigned smile. "I . . . I see it," he whispers. "T-thank you."

Nodding, I wait and watch as Ferraro closes his eyes for what I know is the last time. For a moment, I wonder if I'm supposed to say a prayer or something like that . . . but I don't know how. All I have are my stories.

Besides . . . even if I did know how to pray, I wouldn't be able to bring myself to do it.

A medic steps forward immediately, and I stand up, exiting as quickly as I can from the tent and allowing myself to be swallowed up in the darkness. Zanetti calls my name, but I don't stop.

You never get used to seeing something like that.

29
PETER

VENICE, ITALY
SUMMER, 1945

"And you're certain that you can't find that name for me?"

"I'm sorry, Private Chiappetta, but that is out of the question." The uniform-clad man stares pointedly at me from across his desk. "I've told you many times before. That information is classified."

I stare down at my hands for a moment, my mind racing. It's true that I've been through this before. I've sat in this wooden chair in this same, drab office a million times in the past six months since the war ended–and I've never gotten anywhere. But I'm driven by a force beyond my own power.

Taking a deep breath, I stand up slowly, my jaw clenched. "Fine."

Sergeant Accardi rises, as well. I tower over the short officer, but right now, the look in his eyes and the confidence of his posture gives me the infuriating feeling that the man is looking down on me. For a moment, satisfaction sweeps over his unconcerned face. "Well, good."

"I'll see you tomorrow," I say quickly, turning to leave.

"Ah, ah, no," exclaims Sergeant Accardi, the relief on his face disappearing. Darting over from behind his desk, he exclaims, "I'm afraid that will be impossible."

I sigh impatiently and cross my arms over my chest, glaring. To think he's my superior is laughable–and I would laugh, if I weren't so frustrated in this moment. "And why is that?"

"Well, it's simple–I won't be here," he says, walking over to the mirror hanging on his wall and observing his reflection in it. He twirls his mustache, and I feel a sudden urge to yank it off his face. "I have some business in Verona. Things have still been pretty messy since the war ended."

I watch stiffly as Sergeant Accardi takes his forest green hat from his coat rack, brushes it off, and places it on his dark, round head. Then, he turns back to me and sighs. "Private, I think it best that you abandon this fruitless search. You'll go mad. I've seen it happen before–men and women desperate for answers and thirsting for justice. Well, it's too soon after the war, and you won't get it."

An unwanted lump forms in my throat, and I shove it back down with a single swallow, staring straight ahead as the man continues his grand little speech. "Believe me, I'm sorry for that. I'm grateful for what you've done these past two years, Chiappetta, and I thank you. Your country thanks you.

Without men like you, *Italia* would have been conquered by our old ally Germany, and left to a fate like theirs. But *per favore*–please, do what I said. Focus on building a new life for yourself, like everyone else. Trust me, Chiappetta. We all want answers. But . . . Well, some just seem to get them faster than others." With a tip of his hat and a slight look of regret in his eyes, Sergeant Accardi ushers for me to exit his office.

I obey and wait as he follows, shutting the door behind him. Then, I watch coldly as the man disappears from view, swallowed up by the large crowd of people passing through the foyer. "I couldn't have said it better myself."

I walk through the fog with my head down, avoiding eye contact with the scarce amount of people I pass by on the cobblestone streets. The air feels damp and humid, and gives more weight to every step that I take. Turning down familiar roads, I push against the heaviness of my walk, knowing that my destination is just ahead. As the old bookshop comes into view, I hope to feel something–something warm and comforting, the way I used to when I was a thirteen-year-old kid coming to visit my friend, Signor Maggio. That bookshop was home for me. It meant everything to me. Now, it's nothing. It's a silent building of echoey dreams and haunting memories. It's the place I'd like to forget, but can't bring myself to abandon. Because I know what that's like.

With hesitation, I open the front door and let it swing open slowly. Then, taking a deep breath, I step inside. The musty smell of ancient books floods my nostrils as they greet me like old friends, but I don't stop to return the greeting. Instead, I head straight to the back room.

The house is haunted by ghosts. No matter how hard I try, I can't seem to escape the memories of my family. They don't hang around simply to torment me—but they do. I know that I will never feel a sliver of peace again until I avenge every single one of them.

Visions of my family run through my mind as I observe the old room sitting silent before me. I used to waltz my little sisters around this room. I used to read stories to Abigail as she sat on my lap, and my parents sat close to the fire as Rebekah painted. And then . . . I would sing my sisters to sleep.

I don't think I've sung once in the past two years.

I haven't written, either—at least, nothing other than letters begging for information. I've not had time for the things I used to love. Not while I've spent the last two years trying to protect the rest of the world from the horrors I've endured.

A shiver runs down my spine, and I exit the room quickly, the floor groaning under my feet. Sometimes, the memories are easier to bear—and other times, they're suffocating. Today, they are crushing. In fact, they seem to get worse as time goes on.

In a few seconds, I've reached my room. Stepping inside, I walk over to my desk and merely stand before it, examining it.

I used to sit at this desk to write stories. I would hand write them, and rewrite and revise until I had refined them. My hand would cramp, but I'd shake it a few times and just keep going. I never stopped until I felt confident that my papa would like the words I wrote. He always did. When they were happy or humorous, he smiled or laughed uproariously. When they were sad–which wasn't often–his face would remain solemn, and afterwards he'd pat me on the back. No matter what, he was always impressed. He was never shy to compliment my writing, just as my mother and sisters would encourage my singing.

Well–doing what you love is for happy people. People who have time to enjoy life. People who don't have to worry about avenging their family. This, of course, is exactly what I've spent the past two years trying to do.

Slowly, I remove my hat and sit down at the desk to open up my journal. It's a new one, the old one having been filled up with nonsensical stories long ago. This one is filled with much more useful information.

Flipping through the pages, I eventually let my finger land on the one I'm looking for: the page full of names. Some are Italian, and some are German–but all are suspects.

My eyes trail up and down, up and down the page. "Romano. Moretti. Becker. Achatz." I whisper the names over and over again, but none ring a bell. After having spent two years collecting these names, and the past six months studying them and investigating them, they've become simply that–just names. Even though I know real people belong to them, I have never seen their faces and know little about them, other than their involvement in war crimes. Still, there is a chance that any one of them could have been responsible for the deaths of my family.

Eventually, my eyes grow tired from staring at the endless list of names, and I shut the journal with a small *thud*. Today doesn't seem to be my day for investigating. I don't want to take a break, but I know that I need to, for my own sake. Because tomorrow, I'm going to get my answers.

With a heavy heart, I stand and exit my room, holding my hat in one hand and rubbing the bridge of my nose in exhaustion with the other. I've made it barely five steps out of my room when my eyes land on my parents' bedroom. I haven't been inside in a long time.

Hesitantly, I walk through the doorway and enter the bedroom. A thick layer of dust has settled over my papa's desk. Walking over to it, I lay a hand on the top and breathe deeply, letting the memories of the house transfer from the wood and into my heart. As the memories swirl through my mind, I feel unwanted emotions begin bubbling over, and silent, unheard screams flood my ears. A familiar, raging passion runs through me, and I find myself slamming my fist down onto the surface of the desk, leaving a wide crack.

A pang of regret shoots through my heart, but I barely have time to feel remorse for my actions before I notice something in the place where I hit the desk, except I shouldn't as there's no drawer there. Now, I can see something through the crack. I see a book.

Reaching down slowly, I take hold of the small, leather-bound book and pull it out. For just a moment, I have the urge to look over my shoulder. I feel a sense of shame, as if I'm trespassing on the privacy of my father. But I can't let this opportunity go to waste–this opportunity to find out more about the man who raised me.

Curiosity gets the better of me, and I sit down at the desk to open the book. From the first yellowed page, I can recognize my papa's handwriting, all scrawled out in black ink. I've always felt that handwriting says a lot about who someone is; my papa was no exception. Even now, as I look at his swirling, large print, I can see his personality leaping off the pages . . . and it causes my breath to catch in my chest. Quickly, I force the feeling away and proceed to read.

The first entry is dated, "May 12th, 1920." This causes my heart to skip a beat. If this journal is that old, then perhaps there's something about me inside its pages. There could be some sort of clue as to my papa's past—and my own.

Barely registering the first half of the journal, I skim until I've reached the date I'm looking for. The date where my life changed forever. June 20th, 1925.

With shaking hands, I pick up the journal and hold it closer to my face, practically inhaling the words.

Marion and Leonardo Chiappetta have had a child. A child, who will inherit the powers that his parents have so terribly abused.

They were not able to handle this great gift. Not many could—and it's my job to keep the rest of the world safe from their mistakes. From the mistakes of others. But there is hope for their son. That is why I look after him. Not only must I protect him from the world, but I must protect the world from him.

The door is hidden, and I have ensured he will never find it. And yet . . . his father found the portal, as his ancestors did before him. Somehow, it has a way of revealing itself. If I fail again, the results could be disastrous.

I drop the book. It hits the wooden floor with an almost soundless *thud*.

Of all the things I was expecting to read in the journal, this was never one of them. I wipe my sweating palms on my pants and lean forward, letting my head rest in my hands. My heart is pounding so loudly, it's all I can hear.

I can't quite comprehend the words right now, but there are a few truths that stand out among the rest. They are so glaringly obvious that it hurts my heart to even think of them.

All I know is, my father knew my parents much better than he ever let on. Not only that, but he *lied* to me. If I'm correct, the door that he wrote about in the journal is the same one that I discovered when I was thirteen. And somehow . . . Signor Maggio–*my papa*–was involved.

Slowly, I bend down and pick up the journal with shaking hands. I don't really know what all this means . . . but whatever it is, I have to know more.

I turn the pages cautiously, as though the words will jump out at me and come to life. The entries become less and less, until finally, I reach the very last page. And that is when I see it. *My name.*

As if in a daze, I lift up the journal and begin to read.

Dear Peter,

If you are reading this, it means that I have most likely failed you. I was meant to protect you . . . but I could not. Therefore, it is imperative that you read what I am about to say.

You possess a gift which many people envy. A gift which, for all of my life, I have been instructed to control. But it is impossible to control destiny. That, I figured out as soon as you came to me at the age of thirteen, asking questions about the door that revealed itself to you in the canal.

More often than not, Peter, everyone we meet has a motive. Trust no one, my son. You mustn't let anyone into your mind. Not family or stranger, friend or foe.

I don't know what reason I will have for failing you. I don't know whether the circumstances will arise because of my wife and daughters, or because someone knows my connections to you . . . But I highly suspect it will be for the latter reason. Even if you are told otherwise, there is much you don't know. Trust no one, Peter. Protect your gift–but do not use it for your own gain. That is the most important thing: Never abuse your gift.

I love you, mi caruso. *I have no doubt that you are feeling confused, and believe me, I understand–but I need you to know that I have always cared about you. Always remember, Peter.*

~ Papa

I stare at the words for so long that they begin to blur in front of my eyes. According to this letter, I have some sort of gift–a gift that my family was threatened by. A gift that people want. People who could have been responsible for killing my father.

That's when it hits me.

Perhaps my mother and sisters were killed for being Jewish. Perhaps their deaths were not so strange in light of the circumstances. But . . . My father? He wasn't Jewish.

It's true that he may have been killed for his marriage to my mother. It's true that there are many reasons those monsters may have fabricated in order to wipe out another meaningful life. And yet, as I stare at this letter from my papa, something doesn't seem to add up. Perhaps, as my papa wrote, I have been lied to. Maybe, he was taken from me for a very different reason than I was led to believe.

I loved my family. I will always love them—and that is why I am going to get revenge. I am going to avenge their deaths, and nothing is going to stand in my way. But this journal complicates everything. To know that my father lied to me gives me a feeling of . . . Well, I don't know what. Something between confusion and betrayal, all wrapped into one.

With a heavy sigh, I stand up from the desk, my mind racing. Whatever happens, I must find the door again. It may be the only way for me to discover what happened to my biological parents twenty years ago—and I know that until I find that out, I will never know who I truly am.

The next day, just around half past noon, I find myself back at the familiar, stone building where I spoke to Sergeant Accardi. The difference today, however, is that I won't be speaking to him.

Silently, I enter the building and act as casual as I can, looking distractedly about and trying not to make eye contact with any passersby. Although I'm grateful for the way my old green hat helps shield my face, I feel oddly stiff and uncomfortable wearing my uniform once again; it's only been six months since I last wore it, but the mere action of putting it on brought back a thousand memories I wish to forget. Still, I know it's my best chance at blending in around here while trying to get the information I need.

At the first chance I get, I disappear down a dimly-lit hallway and slip into Sergeant Accardi's office.

The man has refused to give me any information for the past four months. Before him, it was Sergeant Barone, who was transferred to Rome mere months after I began searching for answers. Back then, I was just a kid–desperate and afraid. Well, things are different now. Time has granted me many gifts, such as a persuasive attitude and determination, to name a couple. I need both to achieve success. However, these traits of mine haven't been as useful with Signor Accardi as I would like–so it's time for me to take matters into my own hands.

Throwing a few paranoid glances over my shoulder every once in a while, I rush around the office, grabbing every file and record I can and flipping through them. The floorboards creak under my feet, and the sterile walls seem to be closing in on me–but I don't care. Nothing is going to stop me from getting what I want.

It doesn't take long for me to realize that the files are organized by date, and I look wildly for the day my family was killed. "September," I whisper, pulling out the first file with that date. Opening it up, my eyes widen when they spot the year. "1943."

Skimming vindictively through the file, I let my eyes pick up on the most important words. "Verona . . . Jews . . . mission led by . . ."

I stop suddenly. I squint and read the words again. Then, in a panic, I stuff the file in my jacket and slip out of the office, walking casually back the way I came.

Just as I'm about to exit the building, a shrill voice interrupts the thoughts flying through my head. I stop walking and turn around to see the woman who has acknowledged me. This is the secretary who I've seen working at the front of the building every day that I've come here. With her jet-black hair and sharp brown eyes, the mere look of her has always unnerved me–especially since she has a clear dislike for my very existence.

"*Buon pomeriggio*, Signora Colombo," I say with a half-genuine smile. I don't walk towards her or give her any further acknowledgement; hopefully, she'll let me go without another thought.

"Sergeant Accardi is not here today," she informs me, her brown eyes seeming to pierce right through me over her pointed spectacles.

"Yes, I know," I say, clearing my throat nervously. "I met with his associate."

The look on Signora Colombo's face sends a chill down my spine as I realize how phony this excuse may seem. "His associate? Which one?"

I feel my heart begin to race as I try to conjure a familiar name. "Signor . . . Signor Coppola."

The woman stares me down, and I try not to flinch at the sound of her long nails tapping the wooden counter in front of her. "I thought Signor Coppola was on his lunch break. He has never liked being interrupted."

Taking a deep breath, I decide it's essential that I change tactics–and fast. Painting an awkward, sheepish look on my face, I clear my throat again and shake my head. "Well . . . the truth is, Signora Colombo . . . I simply forgot my hat in Sergeant Accardi's office yesterday. My mind is unforgivingly forgetful, and it pains me to admit when I've forgotten something as ridiculous as my hat. Please forgive the intrusion."

Before Signora Colombo can reply, or question me as to why I'm back in uniform, I give her my warmest smile and bow slightly, tipping my hat. "Good day." Then, I turn on my heel and walk out the door.

As soon as I exit the building and turn the corner, I take off in a mad dash–and I don't stop until I reach the bookshop.

By the time I reach the shop, I'm sweating and almost delirious from the heat. Entering, I shut the door quickly behind me and lock it. Then I pull down the shades, walk over to the bookshelves, and sit down among them, entirely hidden from view.

I take off my jacket and roll up my sleeves, trying desperately to breathe normally. I glance up at the shelves around me, wishing I could take comfort from the books and the characters in them the way I used to. As a child, I could turn to my old friends like Oliver Twist or Edmond Dantès, and I'd find solace in their stories when I was scared or alone.

The thing is, I was never really alone. Not until I lost everyone I had left.

Pulling out the file, I open it again with shaking hands. This time, I have to whisper the words out loud to convince myself that they're true. "Jews in Verona were led out of the city and eliminated by the squad who took their orders from Officer Matteo Bianchi."

I read the words a few times more. Then, I let the file drop to the floor, and I shake my head slowly. "Matteo?" I say, first in disbelief.

The words sink in more fully a few moments later. I feel a new emotion boiling up inside of me. I can feel my fists clench and unclench as I breathe a few quiet, shaky words into the air. "So, it was you, then?" I close my eyes, and all I can see is Matteo's face, unforgiving and cold. "You were right–the world *is* changing. And it's about to change for you, as well."

30
PETER

VENICE, ITALY
SUMMER, 1945

I 've never been able to clear my head without a nice, long ride out on the water. I haven't ridden my gondola in a long time, but when I walk outside, it's still there, waiting for me. A lot has changed in the past seven years or so, but when I get out on the water, I almost feel like a kid again–*almost*.

It's dark as I begin sailing down the watery streets. There are no accordions being played tonight, and no hushed voices dancing on the wind. It's just me tonight–alone.

As my arms begin pushing the gondola across the water, the wheels in my brain begin turning. Even more importantly, I begin to observe my familiar surroundings and realize that in another world, my family could be with me right now. Emotions begin stirring within me, forcing me to come to terms with one simple fact: Whatever I decide to do to avenge my family is entirely justified.

Underneath this swell of determination, I feel myself wince involuntarily. My family . . . They can't help what I discovered today. My mother and sisters were never guilty of hiding things from me; that much is clear. But my father . . . Well, that's another matter entirely.

My heart aches as I think back to all the times he and I talked. Every time I asked him about my parents through the years, however few, he acted as though he knew almost nothing about them. It was as if whatever information he gave me about my parents was made-up; sentimental nonsense meant to curb my desire for something more tangible.

Based on the entry in his journal, my father knew my parents much better than he ever let on. In fact, judging by the tone of his words, he not only seemed to dislike them, but he also thought they were dangerous. And not just them . . . but *me*, as well. He said something that's been echoing in my mind ever since I read it–something about protecting the world from me. A shiver runs down my spine. What could he possibly have been talking about?

I shake my head quickly, as if all my thoughts will go flying out of my mind and disappear. *Focus,* I hiss internally at myself. Of course, I want to learn more about my papa, and my birth parents, and my past–but there's no way I'm going to give up on the task at hand. Among all the confusion and thoughts running through my mind, one thing remains clear: My family didn't deserve to die.

My stomach begins tying itself into knots, and I focus on transforming my pain into anger–just as I have been for the past two years. When I was on the battlefield, watching men die around me, I forced myself to keep fighting for their sakes. When I was injured, I gritted my teeth and bore it as best I could, holding on just so that I could inflict that pain on someone else. I took my pain, and I converted it to hatred. It's all I've been able to do. It's how I've survived. And it's how I will find Matteo Bianchi, and give him the justice he deserves.

As I begin to pass a dark canal, the current in the water changes dramatically. No matter how hard I begin paddling, the water causes me to turn sharply. It takes me down the canal, but I don't really mind. I don't have any place I need to be.

Resolving to sit down and let the water control my journey, I enjoy simply observing the peaceful waves around me. However, it isn't long before an uneasy feeling takes hold. It's both familiar and foreboding–but enticing, as well. Without notice, the waves seem to pick up, rocking the boat back and forth until it's as if I've found myself right in the middle of a storm. And that's when I see it.

The ancient door.

The one that I found when I was a boy.

The one that eluded me for so long that I stopped searching.

It's back, sitting resolutely just a few feet away, as though it had never left–and to me, that can only mean one thing. I was meant to find the door today.

I hesitate for just a moment as I observe the unearthly glow that reflects off the chaotic waves between the door and myself. Then, I dip my paddle in the water to bring my gondola closer, take a deep breath, and reach forward to take hold of the diamond-encrusted handle.

I pull hard, and–

A wave sends the gondola sailing backwards. I feel my head whack the side of the boat as I lose my balance and fall to the bottom.

Gasping for air, I try to reorient myself until the world stops spinning. Then, I sit up–and that's when I realize that the door is open, and the current is pulling my gondola through.

For a moment, I feel as though I've stepped into a dream. Then, I remind myself that this is all very real–which makes it even more unbelievable.

My gondola moves through the water as I enter a brick tunnel. The current is strong enough to pull the gondola along without any help from me, and I watch as the door closes slowly behind me with a heavy, eerie sound.

Before I know it, my gondola reaches dry land, and I'm able to step out, my eyes wide in disbelief.

I'm in a sort of cavernous room. The floor is made of cobblestones, and the walls are solid brick. Somehow, the ceiling appears to be sparkling like the star-studded night sky . . . though I don't quite know how. There's an old bed in the corner, and as I approach it, I notice that although the sheets are pulled up around it, the bedframe is caked with a thick layer of dust. So is the nightstand that sits nearby. No one's been here in a long time.

Slowly, I walk over to the nightstand and reach out to open the drawer. I expect to find only dust; instead, I'm surprised when my eyes land on two ancient books.

The first book appears to be at least one hundred years old, judging by the ornate cover and the yellowing pages. I hold it up to get a better look. The cover is a deep blue, like water, and the binding is lined with gold. Opening it carefully, I begin to scan the first thin, aging page. The large words are printed clearly, and my eyes widen as they take them in.

Time is a precious thing. Not to be wasted, and not to be tampered with—only to be observed by those who are chosen. If you are one of those select few, pray that time is on your side. Most of all, beware: The time is yours but once a year.

That's all. I flip to the next page, hungry for more words—but there are none to be found. Disappointed, I set the book down and pick up the next one in anticipation.

To my surprise, the second book is much less worn than the first. Opening it, I realize that several pages have been ripped out. Only one has any writing. So, I begin to read.

June 20th, 1925

People make mistakes. That's just how life works. But I'm sorry for the mistakes I've made. You may think that, with the ability to travel through time, I would simply be able to go back and fix my mistakes—but that's not true. Some things are irreversible. Some things can never be fixed. That's because I won't be around to fix them.

To the other half of my soul: I am so sorry. My darling—please forgive me someday. Forgive me when you come to realize that all I ever wanted was your love. Forgive me for how hard I tried to win that love, every day of my life. Forgive me for when I told you that the only way our love could survive was if we surrendered the closest person to us in the world. I am so sorry, Marion.

To the one I left behind: You may not understand why you were never given a choice–why your future was decided for you. But I am sure of this: You will certainly be a far better person than I, in every way. If you ever see this, know that I am deeply sorry. And always remember this: Love with passion and without regret.

~ L.C.

The words send me reeling, and I try to comprehend what is written. The name Marion . . . It's so familiar. Wasn't that the name of–

My mother.

A cool wind begins blowing through the air, sending a chill down my spine. I look up slowly–and finally, my eyes land on something that has eluded me thus far: a stone arch etched into the wall at the furthest end of the room. Within the arch, a sparkling purple light is swirling, round and round, as if trying to hypnotize me.

My eyes widen, and I cautiously draw closer. I don't stop until I'm just about a foot away from the arch. Then, I lean forward and watch carefully as the light bends, and the words I just read moments ago run repeatedly through my mind. "With the ability to travel through time . . ."

I instinctively back away from the arch and shake my head in disbelief.

This can't be real. Time travel is make-believe; something only to be read about in books.

And yet . . .

What *if* time travel is real? What if, like the journal entry said, I could travel through time? What if–I could change the past?

"This is insane," I mutter to myself, trying desperately to bring myself back to reality. However, the declaration is too late. Images of my family begin sweeping through my mind. Then, the aftermath of their untimely deaths. And the man who destroyed my life.

I feel my fists clench and unclench, and my eyes glaze over briefly, hatred consuming me for a few seconds. Taking a deep breath, I step closer to the archway . . . then closer . . . and I reach out my hand.

The next few moments are a blur. Instantaneously, I'm swept through the archway and find myself gripping my head as it stings with searing pain. Everything becomes foggy, then darkness. Terrified, I squeeze my eyes shut–and the next thing I know, I'm lying on my back in the same room I just left.

Groaning, I sit up slowly and rub the back of my head, trying to soothe the pain. I'm completely confused at the ordeal that I've just been through.

Looking around the room, I try to find any differences– but there are none. Turning to see the archway, I realize that it's disappeared. There's no archway and no swirling light. Standing up, I begin shaking my head again, and a relieved sort of sigh escapes from my lips.

Although I know that I must have been seeing things, and that I'm still here, safe and sound, I have a sudden urge to get back to the bookshop as fast as possible. Whatever just happened, I don't feel prepared for it . . . at least, not yet.

Walking quickly over to my gondola, I push it out into the water and hop inside, steering it towards the door. To my surprise, as soon as I near the door, it opens. As soon as my gondola has exited safely and is floating on the water of the canal, the door shuts.

I blink a few times, my eyes struggling to adjust to the blinding sunlight. Once I've become acquainted with my surroundings again, I breathe a deep sigh of relief. I am back home. This thought comforts me, but there is still something else that gives me an unsettling feeling. When I first entered through the door just minutes ago, it was pitch black outside. Now, the sun is shining brightly.

Dismissing these thoughts, I resolve to make my way back home, steering my gondola through the now-peaceful waters. When I reach the nearest dock, I tie my gondola to it and start walking through the streets of the city.

Strangely enough, there's a different feeling in the air today. The city seems–*alive*. As if the war had never happened, and tragedy had never befallen this beautiful place. In fact, as I near the heart of the city, I can hear voices. Voices laughing and talking in multiple different languages. This both surprises and confuses me. After all, the war drove away tourists almost indefinitely. The only languages I've heard for the past few years are Italian, German, and more recently, English. Now, I hear French, something I think is Spanish, and many more languages that I can't identify.

After a short while, the towering form of St. Mark's Basilica comes into view, and St. Mark's Square with it. That's when I begin to notice small details–small, but strange.

No one is dressed like me. Practically everyone is dressed colorfully, most of the men in casual short-sleeved shirts and shorts, while the women wear dresses, with a good few of both genders in flashy, flowery prints. They almost look as though they'd emerged from another planet.

I watch from afar as a middle-aged, bearded man lifts up an impossibly small camera. The man smiles at his wife, who is dressed in a short-sleeved red shirt and funny-looking pants made of blue material which flare out at the bottom of her legs. The woman poses in front of the basilica and smiles as the man holds the camera up to his face and clicks it.

Nearby, a small group of boys a few years younger than me chatter as they lean against a brick wall. All are dressed darkly, wearing sunglasses, black leather jackets, and a type of trousers made of the same blue material that I can't seem to identify. Either way, no one standing in the square looks as though they belong here. Unless . . .

A strange feeling begins to sink in, and I back away into the shadows of the city streets. *This can't be right. This can't be my home. Either the world is going crazy . . . or I am. Which is it?*

In a panic, I begin walking quickly through the streets, looking for some sort of clue to tell me what's going on. And that's when it happens. Just as I pass an apartment, with its windows open and sound drifting from inside, I catch a few words.

"*Oggi, 25 luglio 1964 . . .* Today, July 25th, 1964 . . ."

I start at the words, slumping to the ground, and try to breathe deeply. My chest is on fire and the world is spinning. My hands reach out automatically, as if needing the comfort and familiarity of another human being to inform me of the truth–to help me through whatever this is. But I am alone, the shadows of the street concealing me from the rest of the city. I squeeze my eyes shut and try desperately to slow my breathing. *1964?* Is it possible?

When the initial shock finally dissolves, I slowly rise to my feet and summon the courage to learn more. I move closer to the window and peer inside. To my surprise, it's not a person in the house who spoke the words–but someone else entirely. It is not a radio, but rather a box with *moving pictures* on it. I realize that this must be a television set, which I have read of, but never seen before–and certainly never in color.

As I walk through a narrow *calle*, I hear the sound of televisions through open windows–the people inside of the box talking about the weather and how hot it is outside, and how it's been an especially warm summer in Venice . . . during the year 1964.

31
EILEEN

It's early when I wake up and get ready for the day. I was too excited to sleep much, but for some reason, I'm not really tired. I want to see the gondolier as soon as possible.

All night, I struggled in vain, trying to find some reason why I should have politely turned him down. *Don't you remember?* my brain practically screamed. *Don't you remember when Kevin asked you to the dance sophomore year, only to try cornering you all night because you didn't want to–*

Of course I remember. I shiver at the recollection, at the images of myself rushing home alone in the darkness of familiar neighborhoods, my brow dripping with sweat as I ran from the party where Kevin had taken me. Too late, I learned that he didn't want to get to know me as a person; he wanted to use me. He wanted to show me off to his friends.

Yes, it's true that the gondolier might be like Kevin, and I won't let my guard down until I'm sure of his character. That's something I've learned to do over the past few years, and I've become good at it. I don't let anyone in easily. That's how I know that, if I have a good feeling about this man, it isn't just a strange whim.

I grit my teeth at these thoughts. Could I be any more presumptuous? How do I know that he likes me and is as drawn to me as I am to him? He might just be a friendly person, and that's all. Still . . . a friendly acquaintance is better than nothing.

I leave the hotel just a little while after nine o'clock. I spoke to Sandy yesterday about my plan for today, and she was fully supportive of the idea, offering to cover for me if anyone asked questions. Thankfully, everyone seems to be asleep. In fact, it seems that I'm up much earlier than the rest of the city. I just hope that the man will be awake and ready for me when I arrive.

When I turn the corner, this worry increases when I see his gondola sitting stationary on the water–and no sight of its owner. Hesitantly, I step forward and call out timidly, "Hello? Is anyone there?"

Not half a second goes by before I hear the words, "Right here." Looking up, I make eye contact with the young man, who's just stepped out into the early morning sunlight and is smiling kindly at me.

He's wearing a vintage looking jacket today, reminiscent of the 1940s, and although I can tell his dark hair is freshly combed, it still seems to stick out in various places. Walking towards me, he nods at the gondola. "Well. Are you ready to see *Venezia, Signorina* . . . I'm sorry, I forgot your name."

"Eileen," I answer quickly, my heart pounding so loudly that I wonder if he can hear it. "Eileen Madison."

"Eileen," he repeats melodiously, sending a strange sort of tingling racing through my hands and up through my arms. My name seems different on his tongue–as if it's the most sacred word he's ever uttered.

"And–what's your name?" I ask.

The young man seems to hesitate for a split second, and I could swear I see a look of unease flash across his blue eyes. However, as he looks at me, and I at him, he seems to relax. With a smile, he replies. "Peter Chiappetta."

"Well," he says, talking quickly, "shall we? We can go by gondola, if you'd like."

I nod, unsure of what to say. The young man–Peter–holds out a hand to help me onto the gondola, and the next thing I know, we're floating down the watery streets of Venice.

Because of his initial quiet demeanor, I expect Peter to not say much as we ride through the city. However, he seems more passionate to teach me about Venice than anyone I've talked to so far.

In a calm, soothing voice that seems to flow gently like the water beneath us, Peter points out every building that we pass and begins explaining its history. "Just there," he says, nodding his head towards an elegant marble building, "is *La Fenice*. It burned down in 1836, but it was rebuilt; hence its name, which means 'The Phoenix.'"

As we enter further into the heart of Venice, we pass under the famous Rialto Bridge. I expect to hear some historical facts about the bridge, but I don't. Instead, Peter simply stares up at it in silence, a cloudy look in his eyes.

Feeling as though it's my turn to talk, I look over my shoulder and venture, "You seem to know a lot about the city. You said you've lived here your whole life, right?"

The cloudy look on Peter's face seems to disappear as a slight smile breaks through, and his blue eyes lock with my green ones. "Yes."

"And–you've never wanted to go anywhere else?"

Peter begins to nod, and then stops suddenly. Seeing that I'm waiting for some sort of explanation, he furrows his brow. "When I was younger, I wanted to travel. I still do, I suppose. And yet . . . Venice is . . . Well, it kind of gets in your blood. Maybe because I grew up here . . . I mean, it could be different for people who visit. But I truly believe that, even if one wanted to travel elsewhere, once you've been to Venice, it sort of becomes a part of you. You enjoy all of its magic and warmth and familiarity."

"So, you don't feel the need to leave, then?" I ask, nervously straightening my light pink skirt and glancing down at the sparkling blue water.

"I suppose," continues Peter, seeming to stammer and stumble over his words as though he doesn't mean them. As if he's trying to convince himself of their validity. "After all, I'm–I'm only twenty. If I want to travel, I have the time. Besides, I have some . . . business here to take care of first. But still . . . I am anxious for that day to arrive when I get to see some other part of the world."

I let Peter's words trail off, and we ride in silence for a few minutes–him rowing in the back of the gondola, I sitting and taking in the picturesque sights around us. Every canal that we float down is like pure poetry come to life; the water laps peacefully at ancient brick buildings, with green vines and bright red flowers creeping up the walls. I can already understand what Peter was trying to say. Venice has a magical quality to it.

"So," he says, breaking the silence. "Why Italy? I mean–why did you pick Italy to visit?"

"Well, I didn't get to pick, since it's a school trip. I'm here with some of my classmates, in honor of our graduation. The fact that the trip was set to take place in Italy just made me want to join even more. I've seen it in movies, you know, and on television."

"Movies?"

"Yeah. Like . . . like *Roman Holiday*. Do you know that one?"

Peter shakes his head. He looks confused. I suppose it's more of an American movie, so he may have never even heard of it.

"Here," says Peter after a moment, steering the gondola towards a dock and taking out a rope to tie it up. "This is where our walking tour begins."

He helps me up onto the dock, and just like that, the two of us are walking side-by-side through the streets of Venice. It seems that the world has woken up while we were out on the water, because all the store fronts are now open and tourists are filling the streets. As the sun begins to settle in its usual place in the sky, it casts a golden glow over the buildings and causes Peter's blue eyes to sparkle like water.

"So–here are all your usual shops," says Peter softly with his gentle smile. "Restaurants, and . . ."

"Have you been inside all these?" I ask curiously.

No reply. I look over at Peter and realize that he's distracted by something. We're walking by the cafe that Sandy and I ate in not long ago–and standing outside is the woman we spoke to. She seems to have paused in the middle of cleaning tables, and she's now frozen in surprise, staring at–*us*.

I'm relieved when we turn the corner. Peter seems to let out a silent sigh of relief.

"I'm sorry about that," he says, his face red and his quiet voice tainted with regret. "I'm kind of a . . . private person, and this city is pretty tightly-knit. So, lots of people see someone they can't explain, and they . . . sort of jump to conclusions."

"Not for any reason in particular?" I ask hesitantly.

Peter shakes his head and makes direct eye contact with me–and just like that, I know that he's not lying. "No–not at all. See, I've lived here all my life, but my family was always very private. We didn't go out much, so once I started working, most people didn't recognize me. It's just . . . People like to make up stories. Spread rumors. Make false judgements. Do you know what I mean?"

I nod slowly, knowing all too well what he's talking about. "Yeah. I do."

Peter's gentle smile returns–but only for a brief moment. He stops walking, and it takes me a moment to realize why.

We're standing in front of an old, brick building. Faded words stretch across the brick in Italian.

I squint. It looks as if it hasn't been opened in years. "What's this?"

Observing Peter closely, I recognize all the signs of a long sigh being suppressed. Slowly, he says, "This . . . was a much-loved bookshop that I used to live in when I was a boy. The owner was my-my father."

I gaze gently at his deep blue eyes. So full of thought and mystery–and so much sadness. The last thing that I want to do is pry. However, Peter seems to read my mind, for he turns to me and says, "Things didn't work out, and . . . the shop closed down."

"I'm sorry," I reply, my voice barely above a whisper. I tuck a strand of brown hair behind my ear and watch as Peter takes another look at the old, crumbling shop. Then, we continue walking.

Silence hangs in the air as we walk down the street. However, as soon as we turn the corner, Peter's face brightens just slightly, and he begins talking again. "The bookshop was my home," he says. "I wish I had taken care of it, but . . . Well, life just got in the way. Anyway, I'm glad the building's still there with its letters and all. It reminds me of my childhood, and my papa. You learn a lot when you grow up around books."

I'm happy and quite relieved when I notice that a more peaceful look has come over Peter's face. As we continue walking, and he reminisces, I realize something. This tour has gone from a list of historical facts to a personal outpouring of his heart. And although I don't know everything about Peter, it gives me a strange sense of accomplishment and satisfaction to know that he trusts me enough to divulge any part of his past. He, a man who seems so keen on keeping to himself and merely observing the world instead of engaging in it.

"So, where do you live in America?" he asks me as we pause on top of a bridge.

"Near Chicago, Illinois. I've lived there my entire life."

Peter's eyes widen, and I can see excitement sparkle within them. "What's it like there?"

I shrug and lean against the side of the bridge, fidgeting with my skirt. "Well . . . it's nothing special. Nothing like Venice, anyway. It gets really cold in the winter and extremely hot in the summer. Spring doesn't really exist. It's sort of just . . . rainy."

Peter laughs, and the sound of it sends a tingling feeling down my spine. "That sounds interesting."

"Interesting, maybe. Enjoyable, no."

"Maybe not for you . . . but I'd give anything to visit."

Cocking one eyebrow, I look incredulously up at him. "Really?"

Smiling softly, Peter nods. Looking more carefully, I can see a sort of hunger in his eyes. "Yes," he answers. "My mother was from America. I'd like to see where she grew up. Besides that, though . . . I'd give anything to go anywhere."

"Even Chicago?"

"Or New York City, or California, or–well, anywhere. I've only seen a few sections of my home country. When I was a boy, my father told me stories about all the places he'd seen when he was in the military. He told me about Tuscany, and the rolling green hills with little houses dotted throughout the landscape. He told me how the sun reflected the greenery and gave it all a gold tint. And how not even the despair that came from the war could taint the beauty of the landscape. That's the way I want to see the world."

The far-off look in Peter's eyes disappears, and he turns quickly towards me. He clears his throat and continues, bringing the subject back to that of travel. "I assume all the streets in Chicago are paved, correct? I've heard that America is completely different from Italy."

I feel my own curiosity deepen as I realize how different Peter's upbringing must have been from mine. I've traveled to plenty of places before, on road trips when I was younger and now out of the country. He's not been to many places at all, to the point that I'm sure Chicago would seem as foreign to him as Venice is to me.

"That's right."

"And . . . cars?"

"Yes. Cars are everywhere. And motorcycles."

"What's that like?"

I laugh and shake my head. "Loud—especially in the city. It's so different here. So peaceful. I'm not sure I've experienced this much quiet in a long time. I mean, besides all the cars, and television, and radio, there's also my brother and sister."

"What are they like?" asks Peter as we continue walking again. We fall into pace with each other, our footsteps making the same echoing sound on the cobblestones beneath us.

I struggle to find the right words to say. "Well, my brother Tommy is kind of . . . energetic. No . . . rebellious. He's

fourteen and thinks he knows everything. My sister Julie is
ten, and I'd say she's a lot like me, but . . . outgoing and noisy.
What about you? Do you have any siblings?"

The tranquil look on Peter's face disappears, and he turns
his head in the direction of the music that's drifting through
the air. For a moment, silence has returned–but this time, it's
sealed a temporary barrier between us.

Then, quickly, Peter clears his throat and shakes his head,
making eye contact with me once more. "Uh, no."

"Oh." I nod and force a small smile, sensing unease in
Peter's tone. Then, I tactfully change the subject and begin
asking him about his hobbies.

"What do you like to do when you're not working?"

Silence. I stare at him and notice that same, cloudy look
come over his face once again. It's a look that makes me
wonder if he'll ever answer. It's a look that makes me wonder
just what thoughts are running through his mind right now.

"Well . . . I used to like writing," he eventually says. "It's
always come naturally to me, although . . ."

He trails off, and I look up at him expectantly as we sit
down on a nearby bench facing one of the canals. "Yes?"
Peter hesitates before continuing. "Well . . . I've just been too
busy to do much of it lately."

I nod slowly and watch as a few tourists pass by. "Oh."

"I still enjoy it, though," says Peter quickly. "Storytelling
is . . . well, although I haven't done it in a long time . . . it's a
part of what makes me who I am."

I smile brightly at this. "Me too."

Peter looks at me, his eyes full of excitement and curiosity.
"Really?"

"Mhm. I've always wanted to be a journalist. Or, at least, I used to."

Peter raises his eyebrows and pushes some of his wild dark hair from his forehead. "Used to?"

Sighing, I stare out at the sparkling water. "It's . . . complicated. I graduated high school this past spring, and I'm still not sure what I want to do."

As I ask some more basic questions about Peter's life, and he does likewise, I slowly come to realize that he and I are not so different after all. The world doesn't seem to understand us in the way that we'd like. We're both a bit different from everyone else—we both like keeping to ourselves. But I can tell that we also share a craving for adventure. A longing to *do* things, just like everyone else.

Yes, maybe these are characteristics that we dislike about ourselves—but they're also the very things that brought us together. Speaking with him is like talking to an old friend rediscovered, and so much more. He knows Venice like no one else, and the way he speaks of the bookshop, his gondola, and his favorite places in the city—well, I can tell that I've found someone with a zest for life. Someone deep and soulful. Someone who *cares*. Being with him fills me with a deep sense of appreciation for the world around us.

I never want to let go of this feeling. Not ever.

We stop for gelato as the sun begins to set, and I hardly think about the fact that we've spent the entire day together.

With Peter, I feel as though we've known each other for much longer than we have.

The friendly-looking, older man at the counter hands us our order, mint for me and pistachio for Peter. We walk with our cones and talk of books we've read, things we've learned, and people we've met. He talks of his life in Venice, while I talk of mine in Chicago. He is fascinated by life in America, while I pepper him with questions about Italy.

Our cones are finished just as the sun has entirely set, and we find ourselves approaching St. Mark's Square. It's the first time I've been here, and the only word I can think of to describe it is *stunning*. A white tent sits nearby, and its flaps are waving in the warm summer breeze. Inside the tent is an orchestra sending romantic tunes floating over the heads of couples dancing in the square.

For some reason, the two of us seem to know exactly what we're going to do as we step into the lamplight. Peter looks over at me, and with his comforting smile, he offers me his hand. It's an invitation to dance . . . but for me, it's so much more than that. It's the key I need to unlock a piece of my heart that was shut away long ago.

I take it without hesitation–and just like that, we're dancing together. I look up boldly and stare into his eyes, and as I see the warmth and care inside them, I feel an overwhelming sense of peace. I feel at home in his arms–so *safe*.

As we continue dancing, I try to let Peter lead the way. I struggle to hide the fact that I have two left feet, and I expect to feel heat rush to my cheeks–but I don't. Instead, I laugh. It's the kind of laugh that's so carefree and happy that it surprises me. It must be infectious, because Peter laughs, too. Contrary to the darkness I've seen flash through his eyes momentarily, his laugh is as carefree as a waterfall–tumbling and leaping all at once.

And we continue dancing. Me and the gondolier. Me, and the man I just met two days ago. But–*did* I just meet him two days ago? Because now, it seems like we've known each other for years.

32
PETER

VENICE, ITALY
SUMMER, 1964

My feet are flying. I navigate through familiar ancient
streets, barely thinking about where I'm going. I'm looking
for something, anything, to confirm that this isn't real. I don't
care about the people who are probably watching me. I don't
think about how I must appear to them.

I thought I was dreaming—but I wasn't. There must have
truly been a portal, and somehow . . . Well, here I am, in a
time very different from my own. And now, I can't deny that
something extraordinary has happened to me.

No matter how extraordinary this is, though, I don't want
any part in it. I want to get home. I *need* to get home.

As I run, my vision blurs, and I can barely register the
world around me. Vibrant hues of purple and orange jump out
from the clothing that everyone seems to be wearing.

Hundreds of languages reach my ears and blend together, all swirling together in a chaotic mess.

By the time I've reached the door and entered the cavern, I'm sweating and breathing hard–but I barely notice. Frantically, I rush towards the place where the portal was before and throw my fist against the wall. Nothing. Nothing but pain.

Staggering backwards, I collapse on the bed and stare at the wall, feeling the wheels in my brain begin to turn. So . . . I did travel through time. But not to the time I wanted. I would've wanted to go *back* in time. I would've fixed everything. I would have changed history, instead of it changing me. I would have ruined Matteo's life before he ruined mine. Before my family was stolen from me.

Feeling my chest heaving, I stand up and walk over to the drawer with the old books in them. Picking up the journal, I turn around, and my arm moves back, preparing to launch the book across the room. But I stop. Something compels me to sit back down, and I merely hold the journal tightly, afraid to let it go.

I stay up late into the night, staring long and hard at the words written inside the ancient book. Its foreboding tone is more clear to me now than before.

Time is a precious thing. Not to be wasted, and not to be tampered with–only to be observed by those who are chosen. If you are one of those select few, pray that time is on your side. Most of all, beware: The time is yours but once a year.

Scoffing, I let the book drop onto the bed and stare up at the dark ceiling. So . . . that's what happened, then. The portal must open only once a year–and I'm stuck in 1964.

"Imprisoned, is more like it," I whisper to myself, looking warily at my surroundings. That's when it hits me. Inspiration strikes–and suddenly, I know what I need to do.

I'm stuck in a time I've never lived through. A time where Matteo Bianchi may have been living for years, without a care in the world and no repercussions for the crimes he committed. My only choice now is to make sure that Matteo suffers–and I won't be satisfied until he does.

It's still dark when I re-emerge from the cavern. Following the mental map within my brain, I walk without having to think, my mind practically numb from shock and lack of sleep. It doesn't take me long before I've reached my destination.

The bookshop sits dark and quiet, no longer a glowing haven but a graveyard of memories. The painted letters on the front are faded and barely legible. The windows are boarded, and the walls are crumbling.

Two silent tears of anguish creep down my cheeks, and I don't bother wiping them away.

All the people who knew me at the time of my family's deaths used to reassure me. Even as so many were experiencing tragedy, they told me that it was a natural part of life. They told me that two years was enough time to grieve. Still, I always knew they were wrong.

Why should there be a limit to how long one can mourn? I grieved my birth parents all my life, even after the Maggio family adopted me. They never made me feel ashamed or guilty; they let me have questions and doubts. Once they died, all I had were neighbors–neighbors who lived in too much fear to show how sympathetic they truly were. And now that I'm living in the year 1964, I have no one. I'm sure they're all dead and gone, or moved someplace else to escape the aftermath of the war. They've had twenty years to escape the horrific memories.

Well, I haven't been as lucky. No matter where I go or what I do, I'll never be able to escape the guilt that plagues my mind. Guilt over not being able to save them. Guilt over agreeing that they should go. Most of all, guilt that it wasn't me.

33
EILEEN

VENICE, ITALY
SUMMER, 1965

Peter asks me if I'd like to go to dinner tomorrow night. I accept immediately, leaving no room for doubt in my mind. Although I've known him for such a short time, I've quickly begun to notice the way I change when Peter is around. When we're talking, it's like I'm a different person, and the real me is standing on the outside, simply watching. When I'm with him, I'm the person I've always wanted to be. The way I'm drawn to him is inescapable, and I feel as though I'm walking on air as he brings me back to my hotel.

"Alright–here we are," he says, his smile having an even deeper effect on me as time goes by. I feel my heart skip a beat, and I nod.

"What, um . . . What time did you say you'd pick me up tomorrow night?" I ask, clearing my throat to keep my voice from cracking nervously.

"Six."

"Six," I repeat, and I find myself staring up at him, almost in a daze.

I realize how I must look, and I laugh a bit nervously, turning away and walking through the door. "Goodnight," I call over my shoulder, stealing one last look at his soft, comforting smile as I disappear into the hotel.

I run all the way up the stairs as quickly as I can, and I don't stop until I've reached the hallway where my room is waiting. Breathless, I rush to the end of the hallway and stare through the window. Peter is already turning the corner, and in a few seconds, he's disappeared.

I close my eyes for a moment and try to slow my breathing. I've never felt like this in my whole life. I've never met anyone like Peter. He's the definition of a gentleman, and nothing like all the boys I know back home. They wear leather jackets, blast loud music from their souped-up cars, and most have girls hanging all over them. Girls who would put up with anything for a good time. I wanted to be like that, but I never was. Now, I know why. I know what–or *who*–I was waiting for.

When I was a little girl, my dad would always tell me what kind of boy I should look for. I remember one night, when I was about eleven years old and just starting to notice boys, my dad sat down on my bed and gave me a 'talking-to.' It wasn't long; it didn't have to be. I've always been a matter-of-fact person, even as a little girl. I understood the facts that my father gave me, and I tried to weigh them with the desires of my heart.

"Listen, Eileen May. When you start to, uh . . . *like* a boy in that way . . . you need to make sure he's a certain type of person first. Okay?"

I nodded, and my father continued. "He should be a gentleman. He should put your needs before his. He should treat you with love and respect. If he doesn't check all those boxes, my love, then he isn't worth your time."

My dad looked a bit nervous and shifty-eyed while making this speech—but now that I look back on it, I love him for it. He could be a real family man when he wanted to be, committed to making sure I would be taken care of even as a grown woman. That was before . . . When life seemed a little less dark. When I was too young to understand all that my dad had been through.

Whenever I went to the movies as a kid, I observed these traits that my dad named in the dashing heroes of the stories. Their manners were so—*perfect*, and a bit old-fashioned. That's what I grew up knowing, and that's what I found myself loving. And then . . . I stopped believing. But somehow, Peter has single-handedly revived this belief—and he's made me wonder if I've been wrong all this time.

Thankfully, my explanation to Mr. and Mrs. Nelson goes just as planned. Sandy, Lois, Janet and I spent half of the day together before I ended up exploring and met a new friend—that's all anyone needs to know.

I don't feel happy about lying. My teachers and classmates deserve to know the truth. But . . . that's just the problem. In the past, everyone has assumed that they know exactly who I am and what I'm like. They even think that they know what I *want*. To let them in would be disastrous. This has to be my secret, and my choice. I may as well let them go on believing what they want about me, because in the end, what does it matter? As long as I have people like Peter—people who truly understand me—then I'll be alright.

The next day, I spend a few hours sightseeing and eating lunch with my friends, but somehow, the experience is different than a few days ago . . . and I know that it's all because of Peter. In just a short amount of time, he's changed the way that I see Venice. In fact, he's changed the way that I see the world. Everything has more purpose and beauty.

Once my classmates and I head back to the hotel, I wait until they've left for dinner. Then, I change out of my casual pencil skirt and blouse and put on a slightly more formal, white dress.

Peter is waiting for me when I step outside. He's wearing a brown blazer over his white linen collared shirt. His blue eyes are squinted slightly against the golden glow of the sun, but when his gaze lands on me, they widen and sparkle in a way that makes my heart skip a beat. We exchange a smile, and then we begin walking.

"*Sei stupenda*," says Peter softly, looking at me through a few untamed strands of dark hair.

I raise my eyebrows and shake my head in confusion. "What?"

An apologetic look appears on his face, and he repeats himself in English, saying the words slowly and carefully as he looks into my eyes. "You look stunning. You *are* stunning."

My heart begins racing, and I return his smile. I try to say thank you; however, as if he can read my mind, Peter simply smiles and offers me his arm. I take it immediately and stand a little taller, feeling more confident as we walk together.

He seems so calm and collected, which puts me at ease. We find an outdoor table at a restaurant in St. Mark's Square, and he pulls out my chair for me; I sit down, my heart fluttering. Peter takes a seat across from me, and we simply sit there, smiling at each other and looking around for a moment. I enjoy the feeling of being shielded from the night sky by the white awning above us. Everything about this picture feels so . . . *safe*.

I break the silence. "So, what are your parents like?"

Peter looks almost relieved when the waiter walks over to bring us water, interrupting my question. Once he's left, I expect Peter to answer–but he doesn't. He sips his water in silence, avoiding eye contact with me.

After a few more moments, I try a new question, sensing his discomfort. "Um . . . you said you like writing. What sort of things do you like to write?"

At this, Peter's eyes brighten, and he leans forward to meet me in the middle of the table, our faces mere inches away from each other. "All kinds. Novels, short stories . . . Mostly about adventure."

"In Venice?"

"Everywhere." A sparkle appears in Peter's eyes as he repeats the word. "*Everywhere* . . . and anywhere. Everywhere I've never been."

I can feel my eyes widen in anticipation. "Tell me."

A boyish grin spreads across Peter's face–the most genuine I've seen yet. "I write about places like England, France, America . . . and always interesting people. Pirates. Royalty. Always someone planning some sort of evil plot."

I laugh and smile. "All action and adventure?"

Peter's eager grin fades back into a soft smile. "No. I write stories about family, too. Friendship . . . and love."

I nod, a strange wave of comfort passing over me. "That's good."

"My inspiration," continues Peter, suddenly talkative, "has always been authors like Dickens, or Dumas. Have you ever read Oliver Twist?"

I nod, and Peter smiles again. Somehow, I can see his eyes moving as though they're passing over the pages of an invisible book and soaking in the words like sunlight.

"That's one of my favorites. The first time I read it, I was thirteen. And . . ." The excitement leaves Peter's eyes, and a new sort of silence seems to fall over the two of us.

Gently, I urge him to continue. "And . . .?"

He forces a smile, and although the sparkle has come back into his eyes a bit, I can tell that he's suppressing a heavy sigh. "And . . . I haven't read it in a long time," he says finally.

I nod, acting as though I'm content with that answer–but somehow, I can tell that he was going to say something very different before he caught himself. I look at Peter, making eye contact–and he begins talking quickly. "You see . . . I'm *not* an only child."

I can feel my eyes widen slightly in surprise, but I simply nod. "Oh?"

"Well . . . It's complicated. I . . . I used to have two younger sisters. But, uh . . . They both died."

The silence that follows isn't uncomfortable, but thoughtful. I feel my heart sink in a sea of pity, compassion, and sadness as I notice the overwhelming look of despair in Peter's eyes. I realize that it's been there all this time. I just wasn't able to identify *what* it was . . . until now.

"I'm so sorry," is my automatic reply. The phrase feels cold and unfeeling in my mouth, and I hate that even in situations like this, I don't have the right words. I grasp at straws for what to say next, but Peter speaks first.

"Thank you. It was years ago, now . . . but it still hurts."

"I'm sure."

"And . . . that's not all."

I raise my eyebrows and stare hard at Peter from across the table. I can almost see the wheels in his brain turning. "Go on."

I hear a sound coming from under the table, and with a quick glance down, I realize that Peter's foot is tapping uncontrollably. He's stopped looking at me; instead, his gaze is now fixated on the starry sky that stretches above the city.

"My family was a bit . . . complicated. I was adopted, and my parents married when my mother already had two daughters–my adopted sisters. After my parents married, they adopted me. But . . . my parents died when my sisters did."

I swallow hard and feel a tight knot begin to form in my stomach. Peter's grief is so real and raw. Obviously, Peter is on his own, and desperately sad. He's young, but by the look in his eyes, one may take him for years older.

"I'm . . . I'm so sorry, Peter," I whisper. "What . . . What were your sisters' names?"

"Rebekah and Abigail." The mere action of saying his sisters' names out loud seems to provoke a deep feeling of devastation within him, because his eyes close and remain shut for a moment.

I hate myself for being the indirect cause of his pain, so in a brief moment of spontaneity, I decide to be vulnerable in return in hopes of gaining his trust. "I know what it's like to lose someone, too," I stammer, feeling my heart sink in anticipation for the words to come. "It's not the same as you, but . . . I lost my cousin. Her name was Carolyn."

Peter opens his eyes, and we make eye contact again. I feel as though I'm looking into a mirror as I notice the look of pity that's now reflected on his face. "I'm sorry," he replies. "Were you close?"

A lump forms in my throat, and I swallow to shove it back down. I focus my gaze on the flickering candles that sit in the middle of the table, silently willing myself not to cry. The pain wasn't supposed to stick around for this long. I thought I could move on . . . but it never left. "Mhm. She was only a few years older than me. She was one of those people that formed me early in my life–you know? We always watched Henry Fonda movies together, and sometimes she'd take me to the drive-in on Friday nights. She gave me confidence. I think that maybe, if she'd been here while I was in high school, I might be . . . different."

A slight smile creeps into Peter's eyes, and in a master change of subject, he observes, "I guess high school wasn't your favorite time of your life, then?"

I laugh and blink back the familiar, unwanted tears threatening to spill over. "Not even close. How about you?"

Peter leans back in his chair and runs a hand through his dark hair. "Well . . . I'm sure that school was a much different experience for you than it was for me."

Shrugging, I reply, "I guess that's true."

"I enjoyed learning. I had a few friends, and . . . Well, I guess that was it. I spent a lot of time at home."

"That sounds nice."

Peter stares thoughtfully at me for a moment. Then, he says, "Eileen?"

I savor the sound of my name on his lips and look across the table at him. "Yes?"

There's a long pause before he continues. He locks eyes with me, and I see a thousand emotions and thoughts reflected in his deep blue eyes. "I think . . . it's important to remember that your cousin is still looking out for you. Even if she is gone, your memories of her will stay with you—and everything she did for you. You know? There's . . . there's always been something in my mind that's told me that even if my family is gone, I'm a different person because of what they did for me. And that will stay with me forever."

Just like that, something changes inside me. I get the odd feeling that a heavy weight has been lifted and has sailed off like it weighs no more than a feather. No one—and I mean, *no one*–has spoken to me in this way. Not since Carolyn died. It's as if everyone back home felt that I was too fragile and prone to break at any given moment. They hesitated in speaking with me about my cousin when really, that's what I needed to heal.

The lump rising in my throat is that of gratitude instead of sadness, and I try to give Peter a look that reflects all of this. "Thank you."

His smile radiates across his face like a beam of sunlight, and he nods. Behind his smile, I can see more understanding and more kindness than I've ever seen in a person before.

With that, both of our hearts have been opened, revealed, and then locked back up with a key. Anyone who walked by our little table these past few minutes would have been able to peek inside our heads and our hearts.

34
PETER

VENICE, ITALY
SUMMER, 1965

"Where are we going?" laughs Eileen as we run through the cobblestone streets.

"You'll see," is all I say in reply. I steal a quick glance at her and grin. The look on her face is one of breathless excitement–and I can't get enough of it. I love the feeling of her hand in mine. I love everything about her.

It's been a year since I arrived in this timeline–a year since I traveled through the portal–and I thought that, after that surreal experience, I would never be surprised by anything ever again. Three days ago, I was proven wrong. Eileen Madison proved me wrong . . . and I've never been so happy to be surprised.

Maybe I'll regret it. Maybe it's slowing me down. But it's not every day that the mere sight of a person makes your breath catch in your throat. It's not every day that you feel like you've found a missing part of yourself. That's how I feel about her.

My heart is racing excitedly in my chest. I take a deep breath before opening a back door, and the two of us slip inside a large, marble building, almost as familiar to me as the old bookshop.

"Where are we?" whispers Eileen as I shut the door behind us. All is quiet inside the building–for now.

Instead of answering her question, I gesture for her to follow me, and the two of us climb quickly up a flight of stairs. We don't stop until we've reached a dark landing. It's impossible to see, but as instruments begin to tune, I know that I've picked a good spot.

With a grin, I tap my ear. "Hear that?"

Eileen nods, her green eyes wide with curiosity, and as the applause begins, I whisper, "We're in *La Fenice*. The most beautiful opera house in the world."

"And . . . What does *La Fenice* mean, again?"

"The Phoenix."

As the music begins, the look on Eileen's face sends me reeling. The opera seems to excite her further. Music does that to a person–melodies and words intertwining, telling a story and bringing out new emotions. That's what I love about it.

Instead of sitting down, I take Eileen's hand and lead her to peer over the balcony. The sight before us is breathtaking.

I've been inside *La Fenice* lots of times before, back when I was a kid. I liked sneaking in to listen to the music–and mostly the lyrics. I used to sit in the back and let the words wash over me, transporting me to different times and places.

They inspired my stories. They brought me inspiration. And now, to share this place–this *moment*–with someone else makes me realize just how special Eileen is to me.

"Oh," I hear Eileen breathe beside me as we look up at the light blue dome above. The painted angels seem to pop out from the ceiling, as though they're really watching over us and the rest of the opera house. The glittering, golden chandelier casts a glow over the theater, and causes Eileen's wide, green eyes to sparkle.

After a moment, I beckon to Eileen, and we take our seats in the darkness, back where we won't be spotted.

The first song is beautiful. I recognize it as being from the opera *Turandot*, but I can't place the name. I'm too distracted to ponder it over. As my ears take in the sound, my eyes take in the most beautiful part of the room: Eileen.

I met this girl not more than a couple days ago, and yet my heart is telling me that we've known each other all our lives. That, of course, is impossible on many accounts. But what I feel for Eileen is so sudden and unfamiliar that it scares me. However, I don't back down or shy away.

Trying to avoid spiraling in thought, I focus back on Eileen just as the song finishes. The audience is clapping, and she's looking at me with stars in her eyes. Her rosy cheeks are full of excitement, and the way her beautiful, caramel-colored hair is framing her face, all I want to do is reach forward and tuck it gently behind her ear. It would be so simple–such an easy way to convey the tenderness I feel for her. But I can't . . . Not yet.

Looking away quickly, I listen for the next song to begin playing. However, as soon as it does, it has the opposite effect on me than I'm looking for. Instead of calming me, the notes cut into me like shards of glass. I'm immediately transported back to my childhood–back when I still had my family. Back when I sang this song to my sisters every night.

"*Nessun dorma.*"

I can almost feel the lyrics beginning to form on my lips. I can see the little candle-lit room above the bookshop. And I can see their faces.

I stand up, unable to bear this torture anymore. Eileen turns quickly and gives me a concerned look. "Peter? What's the matter?"

I wipe my sweaty palms on the sides of my trousers and shake my head quickly. *Breathe. Breathe.*

"Nothing. I just realized . . . I've got to get back home, and . . . I've kept you out too long, haven't I?"

Eileen shakes her head, obviously confused. I can see disappointment flicker in her eyes, but it vanishes quickly. "No, but . . . if you need to get home . . ."

I nod, mustering a grateful look, and I wait for her to stand before I begin walking to the door, slipping out the way we came in. As the two of us walk down the cobblestone streets and turn the corner, I can hear the song peak, a beautiful mix of words and instruments–and most of all, pain.

I walk alone through the quiet streets. After dropping Eileen off at her hotel, I stood outside for a long time, simply staring up at the warm, golden light that radiated from inside the building. Now, I'm simply walking. I could be walking in circles–heaven knows I'm not walking *to* anyplace in particular–but I don't care.

I take in everything around me with new eyes. The only thing that hasn't really changed about *Venezia* is the city itself. The architecture, the canals, the gondolas–it's all practically the same. It's what's *inside* that's changed. It's the people. The rest of the world moved on and left the city of Venice behind, frozen in time–and then, they came back. They added their technology and their cars and their new clothes . . . but Venice will never really change. It's from the past. Just like me.

These three words echo in my mind as I make my way back home–or at least, what I've learned to *call* home. *Just like me. Just like me.*

How can I go on like this, leading on a girl who has no idea what I really am? Eileen deserves so much more than that. Her innocence, her charm, everything about her deserves to be treasured. I've tried to be honest with her. I've told her almost everything about me–except for the most important part.

There's a lot of reasons for this, the most obvious being that she might not believe me. And why should she? I didn't believe in time travel myself until about one year ago, and even now, I'm having a difficult time wrapping my head around it. Even so, if I told her the plans I have, the thoughts of revenge that run through my mind daily . . . I'd lose her instantly.

Before I know it, I've entered through the secret door and am back in the cavern. Sitting down on my bed, I take off my jacket, lean forward, and try to collect my thoughts.

This is insane. I must be going mad.

Never in my life have I been so enraptured by something as simple as a girl. Even when I was in school, I was so engrossed with my studies and my writing that I never let myself get distracted. So why is it so hard for me to stay focused now?

I guess I always pictured a future for myself as a husband and father. Especially when I was eighteen, and I got the chance to take care of my younger sisters, I could truly see myself in that role. I imagined I would travel for a few years, gather inspiration for my writing, and meet a girl along the way. We would settle down and have lots of kids, and all the while, I would write about my travels . . .

I shake my head quickly and slap my forehead. I have to rid myself of this feeling before it takes hold.

Maybe, in another place or another time, Eileen and I could be together. We could pursue a relationship in which the two of us were both perfectly honest and open. We could do whatever we wanted to. But I made my choice as soon as I decided to track down Matteo. It's true that I've been living a solitary life for a long time now, and I've spent a lot of that time feeling lonely . . . But there's no way I would ever inflict all my pain on someone else. To protect Eileen from everything I've been through, I have to keep her at arm's length. Whatever I do, I can't involve her in my plan–and I can't let her distract me from it.

Still, though . . . The image of Eileen slips into my mind as my heart battles against my head. I can hear her sweet laughter echoing in my ears. I can see the wide grin on her face, and the way her green eyes sparkled when she heard the music begin to play in *La Fenice*. She is everything I've ever dreamt of–kind, gentle, fun, and sincere. But what if that's all she'll ever be–just a dream?

I can't help but wonder . . . if this is what *amore* feels like?

35
EILEEN

VENICE, ITALY
SUMMER, 1965

The smell of water drifts up on a breeze as I lean over the hotel balcony. It's late now, but I've been standing in the same place since I got back from my date with Peter. I simply haven't been able to stop the thoughts that are racing through my mind.

I know that Peter and I haven't been acquainted for very long, and I've never believed in 'love at first sight.' Maybe that exists for other people, but not for me. High school taught me there is no such thing as the perfect guy. I watched my friends date and breakup, date and breakup, while I stayed on the sidelines. While I stayed safe. After my failed stint with Kevin, I made a promise to myself that I was never going to get hurt again. Besides . . . Who would want to be in a relationship with someone carrying as many burdens as I am? It would be unfair of me to make a guy put up with all that.

Leaning over the railing of the balcony, I stare up at the sky, which is dotted with glittering stars. Peter has changed everything for me. I felt closer to him today than ever before–and that's why I was so surprised when his manner turned abrupt and closed-off. We were sharing a moment, and he was the one who broke it off.

As this truth sinks in, my heart begins to hurt. I know I can't jump to conclusions. There has to be more to the story–but what if there isn't? After all, Peter doesn't owe me anything. Just a few days ago, we were strangers. Then, I let myself get carried away. I saw an opportunity to change my course, and I seized it. Now, I can't help but wonder if I was wrong.

Glancing over my shoulder, I realize just how tired I am, and how useless it is to stand here wondering what went wrong. Turning, I take a step towards the open door–and I stop suddenly when I hear my name.

"Eileen!"

I recognize that voice immediately. My heart leaps, and I rush back to the balcony. Looking over it, my eyes land on the one person I've been longing to see.

Peter.

He's standing on his gondola, waving up at me.

Grinning from ear-to-ear, I whisper, "What are you doing?"

"May I come up?"

I nod, and in a few short moments, Peter is making his way over the water and scaling the wall, grasping the vines and bricks for support. Just like that, he's standing in front of me. He pushes his dark hair out of his face, revealing his blue eyes. They're full of a childlike excitement that I've rarely seen in him before. It's innocent and giddy and so many things wrapped into one look–and it's the way every girl wants to be looked at. A look that tells me there's nowhere else he'd rather be than right here, with me.

Reluctantly removing his gaze, he turns and plucks a pink flower from the balcony railing. Tucking it behind my ear, he doesn't say a word. Everything I need to know is reflected in his silence.

"Why are you here?" I breathe.

But I already know the answer.

Our faces are mere inches away from each other now. I can see every detail on his face–every freckle, scar, and imperfection–and I love them all.

"I . . . have never felt this way before. About anyone," replies Peter. There's so much boyish fear in his voice, and warmth, too. "My life has been . . . difficult. But my father always taught me what to look for in a woman. He told me that she would help me through the difficult times–that she would help me learn to hope again. He was right."

We're slightly closer now, and I search Peter's eyes, trying to find any traces of dishonesty or insincerity in his words. I can't. That's when I know that I love him.

Half of me, the rational half, keeps me upright–keeps me from completely melting. The other half, the one that's waited for true love since she was a little girl, holds Peter's hands tightly and happily embraces the kiss that comes. Immediately, electricity seems to burst like fireworks within me, shooting all the way down through my fingers and toes.

I remove my hands from Peter's and instead wrap them around his neck, lingering for a long time.

A whirlwind love story. It's just the right amount of realistic and fantasy, all wrapped up into something beautiful. It's not entirely unbelievable, nor easy to understand. My family certainly wouldn't understand. I'm sure that my old classmates wouldn't believe it, either. After all, people have had me labeled my entire life. They've put me in a box, categorized me, and shipped me off to a future I never wanted. But I've taken matters back into my own hands.

This boy standing in front of me is meant to be mine–I can feel it in my soul. There's no going back now, and I'll never want to. The world may be in constant turbulence around me, but for just one moment, I feel total peace. And that's enough for now.

We break away at the same time, both of us turning to lean over the balcony. We're both smiling and laughing a bit nervously. The two of us are young, and as far as I know, we're both inexperienced when it comes to love . . . but whatever just happened between us, it felt so natural. So *right*. And I didn't feel silly or awkward at all. I felt like . . . *me*.

As we stand side-by-side, Peter's arm slides across the cool railing to simply touch mine. The warmth of his skin sends another shiver of excitement down my spine. "This . . . doesn't feel real," I say almost to myself, playing with the petals of another one of the soft, pink flowers that sit on the balcony.

Peter doesn't reply for a moment. Then, he says gently, "'Two of the fairest stars in all the heaven, having some business, do entreat her eyes to twinkle in their spheres till they return.'"

These words usually have the effect of drawing me back to my sophomore year English class–but this time, they give me quite a different feeling. They transport me back to another time, in a place not far from here, in a situation very much like the one Peter and I are in.

"Do you know where those words were spoken?" says Peter. He points out into the distance. "Just out there."

"But you do know that those words weren't actually spoken, right?" I laugh softly. "It's just a quote from a book."

Peter smiles. It's the kind of smile that makes me wonder if he can see something I can't. "Maybe so . . . but no one can say those words have never been spoken or thought in different ways. No one can say those feelings have never been felt. People fall in love every day."

"But is it true love? Was the story of Romeo and Juliet a display of true love, or just childlike fantasies come true? After all, there's more to love than what they had. They knew each other for, what–an hour? That's when they pledged their love to one another. They never truly got to know each other before they married. Their love was based on a fleeting emotion instead of a partnership."

Even as I speak, I can't believe the words that are coming out of my mouth. I've finally found someone that I truly love and care about, and instead of soaking in this moment, I'm talking to him about all the relationship issues between two of the most iconic characters in literature.

Laughing sheepishly, I feel my face go red, and I shake my head. "Sorry. I think that's the journalist in me. Always focusing on the facts."

I expect Peter's reaction to be embarrassed, or annoyed. However, he doesn't frown or back down. He doesn't even laugh, like most of the guys back home would. Instead, he smiles and looks me in the eye. "Don't apologize. You're completely right. But . . . Well, while facts are important, I think it's just as important to be able to put yourself in the character's shoes, and just imagine what they're going through. Imagine how they're feeling. Besides, I think that even in fiction, we can find truthful bits of knowledge and facts that we can apply to our real lives."

I smile, and Peter continues. "And when it comes to Romeo and Juliet . . . Yes, their choices were irrational and led them to a devastating end—but I think people still act that way. After all, the story is romanticized to no end—so there must be some value and truth to it. People are sometimes reckless when they care about another person that much."

"Like climbing a balcony when you could break your neck?" I hint, bold enough to regain eye contact with him.

Peter grins, continuing to show me this innocent, fun-loving, boyish side of himself that I love so much. "Yes. Were you that worried?"

I press my pointer finger and thumb together, keeping a small amount of space between them. "Just a little bit."

I'm smiling to show that I'm just kidding around, but the grin on Peter's face melts suddenly, and he reaches over to take my hand. He looks at me with deep blue eyes, peering through his wild dark hair, and all I can see in his expression is something overwhelming. Something like . . . love. Deep, reckless, passionate love–for *me*.

"Don't be. Eileen, maybe this is crazy, since we've known each other for such a short time. But . . . I've never met anyone like you before."

I listen and watch silently as Peter tries to gather his thoughts. His right foot is bouncing a little, the way it always seems to when he's overcome by certain emotions. "When I'm around you, it's like . . . like everything is right in the world. And . . . I want to be here for you, too. Whatever *this* is, I want it to last."

I nod slowly, surprised at just how accurate his words are to what I'm feeling at this moment. "Me too. I've never felt this way before about–well, anyone. And . . . no one has ever cared enough about me in return to . . . to try making it something real. After all, a relationship needs to be built on more than just words, right?"

Peter grins, his blue eyes sparkling, and the two of us turn to face one another. We lean forward and embrace once more when a noise from inside the hotel room causes us to break away. "Eileen?" a familiar voice calls softly. "Are you out there?"

"Coming," I reply much too loudly, stumbling towards the door in a panic. However, coming to my senses, I stop and rush back to Peter. I stand up on my tiptoes to kiss him on the cheek, and in one swift movement, I slip the pink flower from behind my ear and hand it to him, tracing my thumb along one of the soft petals as the flower exchanges from my hand to his. Then, I walk back inside the hotel room and shut the door behind me, giving him a smile before he disappears from view and I retreat inside the warm glow of the room.

36
EILEEN

VENICE, ITALY
SUMMER, 1965

"Eileen?"

I look up, snapping back into reality. "What? What's up?" I laugh sheepishly.

Sandy raises her eyebrows and lowers her eyes, drawing my gaze to the fact that my right hand is uncontrollably twirling my spoon in my cup of coffee.

"Oh–" I grimace and set my spoon down on the table. "I guess I'm just tired."

Sandy sets down her own cup of cappuccino and re-ties the bow on her pale yellow dress. "You sure?"

I shrug and turn my head to the right to observe the streets through the window. Venice is busy today, filled with people. Total strangers who I've never met before. But somewhere out there is someone who I *have* met–someone who I can't stop thinking about. And it scares me.

To be a high school graduate is terrifying. It has to be one of the most intimidating things I've ever experienced. But to fall for someone in the midst of all this? I never thought I could do that. I never thought I would *let* myself do that.

I've always been pretty level-headed, and I've never cared much about things like this before. Still . . . I'm different now. Somewhere along the way, something changed. And it's almost like, all this is happening at just the right time, in just the right way. Whatever happens now, how can I question it? What if I was meant to find Peter right about now—or he was meant to find me?

Tucking these thoughts away in a corner of my mind, I focus on talking with Sandy as we finish our coffees. After this, the two of us begin walking back to the hotel with the rest of the group. Sandy and I hang at the back, our teachers about ten feet ahead of us.

"So," whispers Sandy, tucking a blonde curl behind her ear, "what about the guy?"

I feel my heart flutter excitedly and my breath catch in my throat. "Peter? What about him?"

Sandy raises her eyebrows expectantly. "What's going on between you two?"

My cheeks flush, and I shake my head. "Well . . . it's hard to—"

I feel two hands grip my waist, and I turn suddenly, looking around.

"Who are you talking about, Madison?"

I shove his arm off and open my mouth to reply, but Sandy beats me to it. "Mind your own business, Kevin."

Kevin throws his hands up in surrender as he and his friend Davey laugh. Kevin's sharp, brown eyes look like black, burning coals, and I find myself shivering automatically. "That's alright, Miss High-and-Mighty Baker. I think Madison can speak for herself."

I speed up, but Kevin grabs my arm, yanking me backwards. "Come on, tell me. I won't bite." I elbow him in the ribs with my free arm, and the look in his eyes seems to shift. He tightens his grip, and I let out a cry so soft that I'm sure no one can hear it. "Go on, Eileen. I can wait."

I turn in a panic, looking wildly for someone to help us. The other girls and guys are busy chatting up ahead, completely oblivious as to what's happening behind them. As for Mr. and Mrs. Nelson, they're at least twenty feet away, busy navigating and talking together.

Kevin's hand moves back to my waist, pulling me violently towards him. Sandy rushes forward, but Davey steps in front of her. "Kevin!" she yells. Even as I'm busy struggling, I can see fear flash through her eyes. "Cut it out!"

My heart is racing so fast, I can barely breathe. It's like sophomore year all over again–except this time, I'm in a foreign country with no one to turn to.

Yet again, I feel utterly alone.

"Hey!" a new voice exclaims.

Kevin's hands release me immediately, and I stumble backwards into the arms of Peter.

His stance is confident and intimidating, but even underneath that, I can see a look of deep concern in his eyes. "What's going on here?"

Kevin looks Peter up and down. I always thought of him as tall, but compared to Peter, he looks small–not just in height or stature, but in character, as well. Seeing these two next to one another makes it that much clearer to me how I feel about Peter.

Still, Kevin doesn't back down. In fact, he takes a step closer to us. "And just who do you think you are to be asking that?"

I watch in a stunned silence as Peter rushes forward and takes Kevin by the collar of his shirt. His blue eyes, which usually remind me of water, are now like fire. "You stay away from her. From both of them. I swear, if you don't, you'll wish you'd never been born."

Peter holds on a moment longer. "Now, tell me once more. What's going on?"

"N-nothing," stammers Kevin, looking at Davey out of the corner of his eye.

"That's what I thought," replies Peter, his tone firm and warning. He releases Kevin and steps back towards me. "Let's just make sure that 'nothing' never happens again."

Kevin and Davey exchange a glance before stalking away. Sandy looks at me with wide eyes, and I give her a nod of reassurance. She rushes after the group, and once she's gone, Peter places his hand gently on my back and leads me away down a nearby street.

We don't stop until we've reached a bench near the water. Then, Peter helps me sit down and takes his place beside me. "Are you alright?" he asks. His voice is soft and warm, and I notice the way his hand dangles on his knee, resting there in case I want to take it.

I let my fingers gently touch his before they intertwine. "No. Yes. I mean . . . now I am."

Peter stares into my eyes, and I can tell that he doesn't believe me. "Who was that?"

Shaking my head, I tear my gaze away and let it land on Peter's gondola, which is bobbing up and down in the water nearby. "No one important. One of my classmates. He–well, he just . . ."

I take a deep, steadying breath. I never thought I'd be discussing Kevin with Peter. It feels almost . . . *embarrassing*, really. But Peter cares about me. I can't withhold things like this from him.

"He's been–bothering me–ever since sophomore year," I say quietly. "When I found out he was coming on the trip, I guess I thought it would be okay, since we've graduated. I thought he was over all that . . . but it was stupid for me to assume."

Peter shakes his head firmly and squeezes my hand. "No. It wasn't stupid. You like to see the best in people. That's a good thing."

I feel my eyes beginning to well with tears, and I continue avoiding eye contact with Peter. "No . . . it's not. And that's not me. Peter, I'm not trusting. I *don't* see the best in other people. I'm just confused. I don't know who I am . . . and I don't think you do, either. It's just . . . you don't understand. Everyone at home . . . They see me differently. If you knew who I really was, then you wouldn't be saying all this."

Peter reaches out and touches my cheek gently, turning my head so that I'm forced to look at him. "That's where you're wrong. I *do* know you, Eileen–and you know me, too.

We've revealed who we truly are, and not just what other people see. Just because someone perceives you a certain way doesn't make it true."

He hesitates a moment, collecting his thoughts. A sigh escapes from his lips, and it's one of frustration–and desperation. Desperation to convince me of the truth of his words. "Eileen . . . I don't care what anyone else says. I don't care who they think you are, or what they see. I see *you*."

"And . . . What am I?"

Peter's mouth turns up in a small smile. "You are *tesoro*. Treasure, Eileen. Don't let anyone ever tell you otherwise."

I open my mouth, but Peter shakes his head. "I swear to you–I will love you no matter what."

These words finally break through to me like a ray of sun bursting through the clouds. It's the first time he's uttered those words. Deep down, I knew he felt this way–but now, I know for sure. Now, more than ever, I understand that the kiss we shared wasn't for nothing.

I realize I'm smiling, and I let myself relax and lean back into Peter's arms, watching the city move peacefully around us.

I feel Peter make a slight movement, and I lift my head from his shoulder to take a look. "What have you got there?"

Peter glances down and clears his throat. He's holding a small, leather-bound book in his hands and is thumbing through the pages absentmindedly.

"Oh . . . Well–I have a new idea. For a story."

"Really? Can I read it when you're done?"

Peter nods. "No one's read my writing in years . . . in fact, I haven't written in years . . . but then, I haven't been inspired.

So, of course. You would be the first reader. You would always be the first."

Peter doesn't say anything more, but as he stares at my curious, wide-eyed expression, he seems to take the hint and opens the notebook. "I've been writing for so many years, and yet . . . I've never seemed to finish a story entirely. Sure, I've written short stories, and those are alright. And then, there are the scenes that fill my head at night. The ones that I can see in my mind, as if I were a character living through them."

I watch as he flips through the notebook, just slow enough so that I can see the abrupt, cut-off sentences. The notebook seems almost brand-new, so untouched that only a few pages have been entirely filled. Nodding, I stare into Peter's blue eyes and find so much depth and wisdom inside them–so many secrets, and love . . . not to mention heartbreak. But I can't read all that's written on his heart in just a few moments.

"You'll find your story," I say quietly. "I know you will. You have a talent with words."

Peter smiles gently, but he shakes his head. "How can you tell? You've never read anything I've written before."

"Words aren't always written. They're spoken. Every word you've ever spoken to me has meant something–so there's no reason why you can't put them all together and make something out of them. Your words have more power than you may ever know."

37
EILEEN

VENICE, ITALY
SUMMER, 1965

Peter offers me his hand. I take it, and I step into his gondola. A moment later, we're floating down the watery streets.

"Peter," I say suddenly, squinting against the golden sunlight that dances on top of the water. "What do you want?"

A light-hearted laugh comes from the front of the gondola. "Right now? To take you on a gondola ride, I suppose."

"No," I smile, enjoying the rare glimpse of humor. "I mean . . . What do you want in *life*?"

I watch Peter's strong arms push his paddle through the water. For a moment, the only sound I hear is that of my breathing, and the lapping of the water against the gondola. Finally, he replies.

"I want . . . I want to change the world for the better. Maybe not in a big way, but . . . I want to help people. I would never have had a family if my parents hadn't adopted me. Not every child is that lucky. So . . . maybe, someday, I can do something to help."

Automatically, I can feel a big smile spread across my face. It makes me happy to hear how naturally the words slipped out of Peter's mouth, as though they were waiting there all this time.

"What about you?" he asks.

I sigh and think for a moment, staring down at my hands. "I don't really know. Not yet, at least. I guess that's part of my problem."

"What problem?"

"Well . . . I hate change. I always have. It's kept me from knowing what I want to do with my life. My future always seemed pretty clear when I was a kid. When I was thirteen, I came up with this whole plan. I would go through high school, make tons of friends, and get a cool car. But I never thought about what would happen after that. What would I do for a career? I used to think I wanted to be a journalist . . . But I don't know—and I'm pretty sure I'm starting college this fall."

Memories swirl around in my head as I think of the countless times fear has plagued me during new seasons of life. Every scary and difficult thing that happens in the world has always affected me on an intense level. While the rest of my generation seems overly keen on just enjoying life and forgetting to worry, it's like I was born to notice all the imperfections and heartbreak in the world. Like I was always meant to carry every burden that isn't mine to bear.

"I know what you mean," says Peter quietly. "Sometimes, we make plans that . . . just don't turn out the way we'd like."

I can sense a deeper meaning to his words, and the pain that lies beneath them. Knowing that his troubles must be far greater than mine, I shrug off the memories and react nonchalantly. "Oh . . . Well, it's not worth worrying about. These things just work themselves out."

We travel in silence for a few moments. Then, just as I'm about to open my mouth to break it, Peter beats me to it.

"Why . . . why don't you want to be a journalist anymore?" he asks, looking at me from the back of the gondola. His voice is quiet, his manner hesitant–and I get the sense that he doesn't want to bring up bad memories for me any more than I do for him.

Grateful for his careful approach, I take a deep breath and muster a smile. "It's not a big deal or anything," I start. "It's just . . . Well, it's silly when I think about it. But I've just felt less confident during my high school years. It's made me doubt anything I've ever wanted for myself . . . and made it all seem so ridiculous compared to what all my classmates want. Oh–I know that my doubt is all because of them, and I've never wanted to be the person who's so deeply affected by what other people think of them. And yet . . ."

Trailing off, I wait a long moment before looking up to meet Peter's gaze. It's thoughtful, comforting, and sad at the same time. I hate seeing him sad–so much that I begin babbling nervously.

"I know, Peter," I sigh, a fresh wave of embarrassment washing over me. "I know, it sounds stupid, and I ought to stop caring about other people's opinions. I'm sure you're much more confident than me, and by all means, tell me what you would do, because–"

"Eileen," he whispers, interrupting my rambling and causing me to stop with a start.

"Y-yes?"

Peter hesitates. Then, he continues quietly, "It's not stupid. And it's perfectly human to care about what other people say. In my case, it was about three years ago when–"

He stops suddenly, and I watch worriedly as the familiar cloudy look appears on Peter's face once again. However, I'm determined not to let it put up any more walls between us–not when we've already broken down so many.

"What is it?" I ask, my voice softer and calmer now. "Please, Peter–you can tell me."

The look begins melting, and Peter steps down from the back of the gondola and reaches out to take my hand as he sits down across from me. "I know I can."

Then, he drops my hand and looks out at the glittering water that stretches out in the welcoming canal before us. "I've told you that I've always wanted to travel."

I nod, and he continues. "Well . . . There was a man I used to know. He was a childhood friend–we practically grew up together. Eventually, we went our separate ways. He . . . he joined . . . I guess you could say the military. Meanwhile, I was content to stay at home and take care of my family. This friend came back one day, trying to convince me to join him. Well, that part doesn't really matter . . . but it's the way he used my deepest desires against me."

Peter hesitates for a moment and looks over at me. I give him a soft smile of encouragement. He goes on. "Of course, I'd always wanted a family, and a place where I could belong–but to travel would be to have one of my most longed-for wishes granted. Anyway, what happened was, this man criticized the things that I was content with. My family, my home . . . he made it all seem so pathetic. Everything I loved, and everyone I cared about. I didn't believe him—not for a minute—but I couldn't help feeling . . . *confused*. As if I'd chosen wrong, even though I knew I hadn't."

So far, this is one of the deepest things that Peter has said to me—and because I relate to it so very much, it hurts me to the core. I watch as he rubs his hands together nervously and squints up at the sun. Somehow, I think this is the most he has opened his heart to anyone in a long time.

Just as I'm about to open my mouth in the hopes that I have the right words to say, I notice a look of alarm appear on Peter's face.

"What is it?" I ask. "What's wrong?"

"It's happening again," says Peter, standing up carefully.

"What is?"

Peter's eyes shift towards the canal ahead of us, and as my own gaze lands on the water, I feel a small gasp escape my lips. Instead of the water being calm and tranquil as usual, there are now chaotic, massive waves splashing as high as Peter's full height.

Fear takes over as I tighten my grip on the seat beneath me. "Peter, what's going on?"

"The flooding. It never used to be this bad, until . . . Well, I've never seen it like this," exclaims Peter, talking louder now to be heard over the crashing waves.

A flash of brown flies past my eyes, and I realize that the wind is so violent that it's whipping my hair around. "What do we do?" I yell. "There's no way we'll be able to get out of here."

I watch Peter's face closely, looking for some sort of comforting sign so that I know we'll be okay. What I see instead is a strange change of expression, from fear to surprise, then concern–and finally, to resignation.

"Eileen," he calls over his shoulder. "I'd like to show you something."

"Okay–" I start, confused, but Peter isn't finished.

"But . . . It's a bit unbelievable."

I don't reply. Instead, I wait and watch as the gondola slows in the middle of the chaotic, slightly-darker canal. I cower at the large waves that splash above us and soak us to the skin. Once the first chilly wave hits me, I let out a sudden, terrified gasp.

Before I've had a chance to catch my breath from the first wave, a second one hits. This time, I let out a cry.

To my surprise, although Peter is flinching just as much as I am, he seems almost unbothered by the waves. No–it's something else that has his attention right now. I watch as he sets down his paddle and turns back to me, stepping down from the back of the boat and sitting down across from me once more.

"When I was a boy, I was riding these very canals when I came across this one in particular."

I notice the way Peter is leaning forward, rubbing his hands together and tapping his foot. He seems anxious–the same as he was at dinner and at the opera house.

"I saw something sparkling. That's when I discovered a secret door. It's still here–it's been here all this time. And there's a whole room inside, which gives a person abilities that one can only dream of. The ability to see the past–and the future. Eileen–"

Peter utters my name as he notices the way I've begun to shrink back. "Eileen, please trust me. I would never lie to you about something like this–not for a second. It's too important."

"A secret room?" I ask hesitantly, the rest of his sentence not entirely sinking in.

"Yes." Peter leans forward even more, a few strands of wet, dark hair falling over his hopeful, pleading eyes. "I wouldn't show you this unless I trusted you, Eileen–and I do. I've never shown this to anyone before. But since I've met you, things have changed. I feel like . . . Like I have to show someone this thing that I've kept secret for so long. Do you understand?"

Instead of answering, I turn and look out at the water, searching for some sign that what Peter is saying is the truth. That's when I see it. Silver sparkling through the tall, torrential waves . . . and the outline of a large, round door, sitting at the end of the canal.

The door appears to stretch across the entire width of the canal. In fact, it's so big that it would be a simple task to fit the entire gondola through it. The handle is encrusted with diamonds, which seem to be glinting in an almost taunting way–daring me to take a chance. Daring me to come closer.

Turning back to Peter, I can feel a knot form in my stomach. I thought it would be easy to refuse. After all, what will I find in that room? What does Peter want me to know?

Whatever I decide may determine my fate–but the tie that I feel to Peter is unbreakable. Our souls are too deeply intertwined.

With this decision made, and my fear of the monstrous waves taking over, I utter two words. "Show me."

Peter nods, the look in his eyes serious. I can see him through the waves and the mist; there's a look of determination on his face as he begins paddling through the water, moving the gondola forward.

Eventually, we're so close to the door that Peter could touch it from where he's standing. Slowly, he reaches forward and takes hold of the handle.

It happens so fast that I don't even have time to scream. The force sends me flying backwards, another wave crashing into me. I fully expect my fall to be hard. Instead, a mere second after I hit the bottom of the gondola, I find myself in the strong arms of Peter, whose wet hair has been pushed out of his eyes and whose face appears fearful and hesitant. I reach for his face, desperate to know if he's real. Then, I feel my body go limp in his arms.

That's when my reality becomes a dream–except, I'm not dreaming. I'm very much awake.

Even without Peter controlling its movement, the gondola begins passing through the open door, which shuts slowly behind us. I turn my head to observe our surroundings–and my eyes widen.

We're now in a huge, cavernous room. A little less than half of it is full of water, while the rest is like a sort of island, with a cobblestone floor, small bed, and nightstand. On one side of the room, carved into the wall, is a stone archway with nothing in the center. Overall, the room is fairly normal . . . but then, I look up. The ceiling is–*sparkling* . . . and there's no logical explanation why. I feel my body convulse as I shiver. There is a strange air hanging about, and there's something magical about this place. It's all too much for me to comprehend at once, and I feel the world beginning to spin.

Carefully, Peter steps out of the gondola and carries me over to the bed, where he sets me down gently. In a state of shock, I grasp handfuls of the patchwork quilt that rests on the bed and tuck my legs underneath me. "What–what was that? What is *this*?"

"Something that even I can't understand," answers Peter. As he walks over to a nearby nightstand, I can't help but think about his words and the tone that lies beneath them. His use of the phrase 'even I' seems to imply that he understands just about everything else–and it makes me feel uneasy.

Peter takes a moment to light a few candles, illuminating the room and adding to the otherworldly feeling in the air. When he returns, he sits down beside me and hands me the dusty, ancient-looking book that now rests in his hands. Opening to the first yellowed page, he begins talking quickly as I observe. "Eileen, there are stories about this place. Ancient myths and legends that almost no one believed– because only a handful of people can access the gifts that this cavern has to offer. The gifts, and the curses."

"What kinds of curses?" I ask, my head snapping up.

"It's . . . it's difficult to understand those if you don't know about the gifts."

"Then tell me."

Peter sighs. It's not a sigh of frustration or aggravation, but one of hesitation and reluctance. "Time travel, Eileen. It's real. You may not believe me, but like I said before, I will never lie to you. I can't do that. And I'm telling you about this because I want to share it *with* you. You will never know everything about me until I explain this part."

By now, my mind has begun working again, and I turn to look at Peter with a mix of fear and confusion in my eyes. "What are you saying? That you . . . you've *traveled through time*?"

"I'm willing to tell you everything, just so you know you can trust me."

"Wait, wait, so . . . Does this mean that you're not from this time?"

Even as I say the words, it all clicks together before Peter begins to nod. His clothes, his manners, his speech–it all makes sense. And yet, it doesn't. Because either I've fallen in love with a madman, or an honest-to-goodness time-traveler. Somehow, I can't truly believe either.

"There was a portal, just over there," rambles Peter, pointing to the archway at the other side of the room. "When I found it, it took me here–and then it closed, and it never came back."

"So–so what . . . What year are you from?"

Peter stops talking. There's a long pause. Then, he answers. "1945."

The look on my face must scare him, because he starts talking at such a fast speed, I can barely register his words. "It's how I lost my family, Eileen. I told you they died–and they did. It was all because of the war. I didn't know how to tell you before, because why would you have believed me back then? But . . . I figured if you'd seen all this, you could understand."

It's exactly what I imagined he'd say–but I can't believe it. How can I? How can Peter expect me to trust him when he's just lied to me? Whatever effect he thought this little adventure would have, it's having the opposite.

"Peter, I need you to take me back."

The eager look on his face deflates immediately, and a chill seems to settle throughout the cavernous room. "What?"

"Take me back to the hotel. I need to get out of here."

This is my real test of his affection–and his madness. I wait as he tries to figure out how to reply. Finally, to my surprise, he stands up. "Alright. Let's go back."

My legs feel weak beneath me as I struggle to stand. Just as I feel them about to cave in, Peter rushes forward and catches me. Then, he helps me walk and escorts me back to the gondola. We travel through the canal where the waves have ceased, and Peter takes me all the way back to my hotel.

We don't exchange a single word on the journey back. It's not until Peter walks me up to the door that I whirl around having gained my confidence and sense of composure back.

"What's your last name again, Peter?"

Peter stares at me for a long time. There's a look of sadness in his blue eyes as he finally answers. "Chiappetta."

"Well, then," I stammer, clearing my throat and trying to look taller. I hate what I'm about to say . . . but for once in my life, I know the choice I have to make. I know that I have to step away. "Peter Chiappetta . . . I'm afraid this has to stop."

Peter cocks one eyebrow and shakes his head, taking a few cautious steps forward. "'This?' What do you mean by that?"

"I mean, this thing that I thought we had. It has to end."

"Eileen, please reconsider." The tone in his voice is so desperate that I realize he's begging. "Do whatever you need to do. Put our relationship on hold–but don't punish me for telling the truth. You're the first person I've ever told about this, and the first I've ever cared for so deeply. You opened up my heart again. I needed you to know my past, and why I'm here."

"Well, now I do," I say curtly.

"No," exclaims Peter, taking another step forward. There's a strange look in his eyes, like a fire that's been there all this time but has yet to be doused. "You don't know everything. Far from it. Please, Eileen . . . I can't go on without you knowing the truth. If you decide to listen, I'll be waiting."

With that, he's gone . . . and I'm left to wonder how in the world I let myself become entangled in this mess. With two days left in Venice, I'm not sure how I'll ever be able to fix things in time–or if I'll ever see Peter Chiappetta again.

38
PETER

VENICE, ITALY
SUMMER, 1965

It's the middle of the night now, but I'm still awake, and sitting in the one place I've ever been able to collect my thoughts: the Rialto Bridge. As my legs hang off the side of the bridge, I'm transported back to my childhood–back to when I was carefree and full of wonder.

My goodness, where did it all go? Why is it that life is full of ups and downs? Things can be perfect one minute, and the next . . .

I shiver as the cool night air drifts up from the water splashing below. Why did I ever think I would be able to convince Eileen to trust me? Sure, she did at first–until I decided to tell her that I could time travel.

Time travel. I must have sounded like a raving lunatic–*un pazzo delirante.* If our situations were reversed, I'm sure I wouldn't believe her. And yet . . . If you care about someone, don't you owe it to them to just *listen* to what they have to say?

Rubbing the back of my neck, I close my eyes and try to bring myself back to reality.

What about the night on the balcony? Sure, that kiss meant a lot to me, but what if it meant absolutely nothing to Eileen? For all I know, she's kissed plenty of guys. But no . . . That's not her. Any idiot could pick her out of a crowd as someone special–someone *different*. I'm not sure she's capable of ever doing something she didn't truly believe in.

I don't have any doubts regarding her character. Now, it's up to her to see if she trusts *me*.

I have a strange dream that night. First, I see my family, all gathered together in the back room of our bookshop. Then, I turn and see someone else–another familiar face. *Eileen.* She's smiling, and her face is absolutely glowing. She looks beautiful. I approach her, but even as I do, I begin to notice something strange, and an uneasy feeling comes over me. Everything seems to fit in this picture. Everything except Eileen. Her clothes, her voice, and everything else about her seem completely out of place. And that's when it happens.

I sort of step out of my body, looking at myself from the outside. Suddenly, my family disappears, and it's not 1943 anymore–it's 1965. Now, Eileen isn't the one who's out of place. *I* am. Still, Eileen doesn't seem to mind. She holds my hands as we stand on top of the Rialto Bridge, and the look in her eyes says that she loves me anyways. She opens her mouth, and I hear her voice call my name. "Peter."

My heart leaps as I hear her voice, but I can't seem to reply. All I can hear is my name, growing louder, and louder, and . . .

I wake up with a start, whacking my head against something hard. Checking my surroundings, I realize that I never made it back to the cavern. I must have fallen asleep before I made it there, because I'm leaning against a brick wall which rests near the water. That's when I realize that Eileen has jumped from my dreams and into reality.

She's crouching down next to me, her hands resting on her knees. Her light brown hair looks almost golden against the morning sunlight, and her green eyes are sparkling like the water that splashes quietly just a few feet away from us.

"Peter?"

I clear my throat and snap out of it. "Sorry." Then it dawns on me. "You're here?" I say it out of mere shock, but it must come out as, "You shouldn't be here," because the half smile on Eileen's face melts.

"Yes," she says quietly.

"No, no, I'm sorry. I didn't mean it like that. It's just . . . You were angry with me."

Eileen nods as I stand to face her. "I was. Maybe I still am. But . . . I've been looking for you all morning. I couldn't sleep last night. Not after . . ."

I feel my heart sink. "You should have. You don't owe me anything."

Eileen takes a deep breath. "I've never been the kind of person to rush off without giving someone else the chance to explain."

As the words come out of her mouth, I feel a wave of relief wash over me. I knew that Eileen wouldn't shut me out that easily. It's not in her character.

"Really?" I say, a slight bit of disbelief creeping into my tone.

Eileen nods slowly. Every movement of her eyes alerts me to the fact that she's examining my every thought–sizing me up to see if she can truly trust me. "Sure. I just . . . I hate it when people are too quick to judge. And . . . and maybe it's crazy, but I just want to hear the whole story. I mean–you know what I think about all this, right?"

She's babbling–something she seems to do whenever she's anxious. I can tell that she's extra nervous right now, but no more so than I am. I nod and feel a familiar energy begin surging to my feet. Bouncing slightly, I swallow and realize that my mouth is completely dry. "Yes. I know."

"I mean, it's like something out of Star Trek . . . or Doctor Who. Or my brother's science-fiction comics. It's not the kind of stuff that just *happens*. It can't be real. But I'm trying hard to understand. So . . . I just need an explanation–and answers."

I smooth my hair back with my hands and try not to appear too eager. "Alright." I lead her to a nearby bench. Slowly, hesitantly, the two of us sit down next to each other. Luckily, the bench is long enough to allow for some space in between us.

The feeling that settles in the air is the complete opposite to the one that surrounded us the other night. Still, although my gut is now tied into knots in a strange mix of shame, sadness, and anger, I accept it. It's what I deserve.

"So . . . Where do I start?" I ask.

Eileen turns her head slightly to look over at me. "The beginning."

The beginning. The very place I *don't* want to start. I've always hated talking about my past. Sure, my childhood turned out alright–but there was too much pain laced within it all. My past has defined me all my life. How can I explain it to the best person I've ever met? There's nothing wrong with her–no shame, no secrets.

Still . . . As I look into Eileen's eyes, I can suddenly read so much more there. I can see pain and suffering. Maybe it's not the same as mine, but hopefully it's given her the capacity to understand what I'm about to tell her–and that helps ease my mind a bit.

As soon as my mouth opens, there's no going back. I tell her almost everything, carefully leaving out my entire plan to find Matteo. Everything about my childhood that I've left out or glossed over, I present for her to do with what she likes.

Before I know it, I've reached the end of the less-than-believable tale. I haven't made eye contact with Eileen once during this whole time.

Hesitantly, I turn my head to look at her. She's facing the water in front of us, her green eyes slightly narrowed from the bright sun. Her hands are pressed down against the cool bench, holding her upright, and there's a thoughtful look on her face.

"You're a writer, Peter," she says, her tone a mix of tenderness and disbelief. "So how am I supposed to know that everything you just told me isn't a story?"

Even as she says these words, I catch a certain look in her eyes–and I realize something. Eileen has seen the door and the cavern that I told her about in the story. The fact that these exist is undeniable. She's also felt my pain as I revealed the truth about my family. Whatever she says, she can't truly believe that everything I just told her is a lie.

"Sometimes, during the war," I begin quietly, "I'd find men sick, or injured, or close to death–and some would beg me for relief. Yes, I'd killed people in battle . . . but it was different. It's one thing when you're fighting for a cause you believe in or fighting for your life. It's another to sit in front of a man who you know might have a chance, and to hear him beg you to end it all."

My words falter here, and I take a deep breath, trying to regain my composure. "So, I got desperate. I started telling the men stories from memory. I told them about Venice. Even better, books I'd read when I was a boy came flooding back to me, and they started to help. I was glad about that. I kept telling those stories . . . but the one thing I could never do was tell my own. Sure, I could describe the sights of Venice, or talk about the weather–simple things–but I was never able to get into the events of my past. I was never able to relive that. Even now, it hurts. But I'm telling you all this because . . . because I love you, Eileen. And I need you to believe me."

She turns her head away, and I can see the wheels turning in her brain.

"Eileen," I say softly–and just like that, she knows. I can see it in her eyes as soon as her name escapes my lips. Whether she wants to or not, she knows exactly what I'm trying to express. So, she moves on to the next matter at hand.

"What I can't get past," she says slowly, "is the reason that you're here."

I sigh. I should have known that she'd bring that up. A girl as thoughtful and kind-hearted as her would never want to hear that the boy she kissed just a couple days ago was actually in the midst of a plot for revenge. Still, it's not as though I gave her all the details about this. What I did say was that I wanted justice for my family, and to make things right. I suppose I should have been more clear.

Quickly, I begin talking. "The reason why I'm here is to fix the past. I need to do something for my family–and if it doesn't mean saving them from death, then I'll just have to find something else . . . and I can't stop until I do."

Eileen stares at me, long and hard. I know that she's just trying to read my thoughts and figure things out for herself, but I begin to break under her gaze. It's like she's not even here, and I'm just talking to myself. Just replaying the events of my past over and over again in my mind.

"I should have been with them." The words come pouring involuntarily out of my mouth, like strange unspoken sentences that were written on my heart years ago. "I should have died–not them. God got it wrong when he made them Jewish instead of me. And now that it's too late for me to change the past, all I can do is change the present."

Out of the corner of my eye, I can see Eileen move slightly closer to me. It's a kind gesture, and it also brings me back to the present. Looking over at her, I feel my jaw clenching as a sinister desire begins burning within me once again. It's the first time that I've had this feeling in a long while. In fact, I haven't felt it since before Eileen arrived. She brought out the good in me–and now, she's about to see the bad.

"Do you want to know what I *really* want, Eileen? I want war and hatred to stop snuffing out the light and wonder in the eyes of children. And I want justice for those who never got that light back."

Eileen slips her hand close to mine, and she takes it gently, barely touching it. "I want that, too."

I look over at her, almost surprised to hear her speak after the emotional outpouring of my heart. Encouraged by this, I continue.

"After I lost my family, I promised myself that I would change; that I would become a different person. Someone unrecognizable. Someone who could never get hurt. But . . . Everything about you makes me want to become the person I used to be."

Eileen looks at me for a moment, and although I've been avoiding her gaze, I can feel her deep, wise eyes staring through a window into my soul.

"I'm sorry," I say. The second the words come out of my mouth, the two of us realize something. I'm apologizing for everything–every bad deed I've ever committed or *wanted* to commit. Because I want to be perfect for her. And when she reaches out to take my hand, I see the smile on her face, and I can read a look in her eyes that says, "You don't have to be."

39
EILEEN

VENICE, ITALY
SUMMER, 1965

Peter and I talk for a little while longer, and although I act casual, I am in disbelief the entire time. A war is waging inside me. I'm struggling to understand which part of myself is the real me: this carefree, reckless half who follows her heart, or the logical, smart half who follows her head? I used to think I was wiser than this . . . but if I was only logical, then there is simply no way I would believe any part of Peter's story. I'm truly starting to wonder if this world is more magical than I ever realized.

Peter walks me back to the hotel, leading me down cluttered, cobblestone streets. When we reach the door, the two of us simply stop and look at one another for a moment. The sun is warming my skin, and the smell of water and flowers is drifting through the air. It's all so perfect . . . but that's my heart talking. It's time to return to reality.

"I have to go," I say quietly, glancing warily at the door out of the corner of my eye. The last thing I want to do right now is to leave him, just to spend more time with my classmates. But I have to. Lies and excuses can't get me much further.

"I know," he replies, his voice soft and his blue eyes smiling.

I give his hand a squeeze before turning and walking inside.

By the time I've reached the balcony outside my hotel room, Peter is just about to turn around the corner of the street. Leaning over the railing, I wait until he's disappeared from view. Then, I retire into my hotel room, full of questions and emotions that I can't identify.

I've been in my room for less than ten minutes when there's a knock on the door. Reluctantly, I stand up from my bed and walk over to answer it, brushing off my rumpled skirt before letting the door swing open. However, instead of seeing Sandy on the other side, I see . . . two people I've never seen before in my life.

Surprised, I find myself taking a step back and shutting the door slightly. "Hello?"

The couple is composed of one man and one woman, both appearing to be middle-aged. The man is wearing a smart-looking charcoal gray suit, while the woman is wearing a white blouse and long black skirt. Her blonde hair is piled up on top of her head in an elegant twist.

The woman, whose tall form gives off an intimidating air, gives me a sympathetic half smile. "Hello, dear," she says in an Italian accent, staring at me with icy blue eyes. "You don't know us, so I'll make this brief. We're looking for a young man by the name of Peter Chiappetta. We have reason to believe you know of his whereabouts. Could you tell us anything about him?"

I feel my breath catch in my chest. Instinct kicks in, and I find myself dodging the question. "I don't . . . know."

The man, who's so tall that he must bend to see me through the doorway, gives me a disapproving, impatient look. "Miss," he says in an Italian accent similar to the woman's, "you must know that we only require this information for your benefit. Mr. Chiappetta has proven to be less than capable of handling the gifts entrusted to him."

"I don't know what you mean," I say, my voice barely above a whisper.

The two exchange a glance before turning back to me. "We believe you do," says the woman, her eyes narrowed suspiciously. "We have reason to believe that you're well aware of what he can do, and the powers he has abused."

I shake my head fervently. "No, I'm not. Now, please–I don't know who you're talking about, and I'm feeling very tired. I'm sorry."

"I wouldn't lie, if I were you," interrupts the man. "Mr. Chiappetta has broken the barrier between time and space for unforgivable reasons. Whether he has succeeded yet, we do not know–but he must be stopped, no matter the cost. If he is not . . . Well, let's just say that many people will suffer."

The gravity in both the man's words and his tone makes me shudder. All I want is to learn more from these people, and figure out what exactly they're trying to tell me–but I can't. I'm afraid for myself, and I'm afraid for Peter.

"Again, I'm sorry," I whisper, preparing to retreat. "I don't think I can help you."

With that, I quickly step back into my bedroom and shut the door, locking it behind me. Pressing my ear to the door, I listen over the pounding of my heart for the pair's footsteps to begin, and then die out. After this, I rush to my balcony and watch the couple disappear.

Without hesitation, I go running out the door and through the hotel, past my classmates sitting in the lobby, past everything familiar and certain. The one person who matters here is Peter–and if I'm not mistaken, he's in deep trouble. I can only hope I'll be able to reach him with the news before it's too late.

40
PETER

VENICE, ITALY
SUMMER, 1965

I'm sitting in the cavern, listening to the menacing roaring of the waves outside. Although I know they can't bother me here, the sound is unnerving.

My love for Eileen kept me from revealing the fear that I truly feel when it comes to the waves. As far as she knows, there's been some irregularity in the normal weather patterns. After all, she doesn't live here, and doesn't know how to tell the difference between what's simply odd and what's just plain dangerous. But I do. I know that there has to be a reason for the waves–and somehow, I've got the feeling that they have something to do with me.

Venezia has been sinking for years, and has never quite succumbed to nature. It's held on with all the strength it has, and so far, nothing has disturbed it but the natural progression of life. But now . . . I don't really know anymore.

Frustrated by my inability to think of answers, I grab my worn journal from the bedside table and sit down on my bed. It's the same journal that I found the cryptic diary entry in—and now, it's the place where I keep all my evidence. Everything that I need to find Matteo and ensure his ruin lies between these yellowed pages. However, that's not all.

As I open the book, my eyes land on the flower that I've slid inside it. It's the pink flower that Eileen gave me on her balcony. Gently, I run my thumb and pointer finger over the soft petals and imagine Eileen's face before me: innocent, curious, and beautiful.

That all took place mere days ago—and yet, I feel as if an entire lifetime has passed since then. I've not just learned about Eileen, but about *myself*, as well. She's reminded me of the parts of myself that I've buried deep within for so long. She's given me a new appreciation for the traits that I had begun to see as weak. My love for her has allowed me to remember the way I used to love everyone around me, without hesitation or fear of losing them.

With a deep breath, I set the flower back down and resolve to stop sitting here, wasting my time. Every moment I have should be spent with Eileen. The fact that she's leaving soon isn't lost on me. I don't know what I'll do without her—but if a life without her feels like the way I'm feeling now, then I know I can't go on.

Determined to see her again and make the most of our remaining time together, I rush to my gondola and exit through the door, entering the canal. The waves have calmed momentarily, and a new sense of peace seems to wash over me. Without thinking, I begin softly humming a cheery tune. That's when I hear it.

"Peter!"

My head whirls around towards the direction of the sound. My eyes land on Eileen, and my heart rate quickens. She's standing on dry land near the water, and I make my way over to her.

"*Ciao*," I say, a grin on my face as I help her into the gondola. I expect her face to be as happy and tranquil as mine; however, once I get a good look at it, I realize that it's quite the opposite. Beads of sweat are running down Eileen's forehead, and her light brown hair is wild and wind-blown. Most importantly, her eyes are wide with worry, and her mouth is curved downwards.

I feel my own smile disappear. "What's wrong?"

Eileen shakes her head quickly, and I notice the way her eyes are shifting back and forth. "We can't talk here."

Without asking questions, I move to the back of the gondola and begin paddling again, back to where I came from. Neither of us say anything until we've entered the cavern, and the large door has shut firmly behind us.

Leaping from the gondola, I rush to help Eileen out. "Listen," I begin babbling nervously, "did that guy do something to you again? Because, if he did, I swear I'll–"

"Peter!" exclaims Eileen, causing me to stop and look at her. "I'm alright. I promise. Listen, I need to talk to you. I don't know what's going on, but these people came to my hotel, and they were looking for you."

I feel my heart begin racing wildly. "What? Who were they?"

"I don't know. They didn't give me their names. All I know is, they're angry—and they seem to know that you can travel through time."

I feel my stomach lurch and my head begin spinning. "How is that possible? I've never told anyone but you. This must be a mistake—"

"But it isn't!" cries Eileen. She takes a step closer to me and stares into my eyes, her green ones shining with fearful tears. "They knew your name, and they knew to come to me. Peter, I can tell they're dangerous."

As I look at Eileen, I realize that the panic in her expression is overwhelming. She's truly afraid for me.

Hesitantly, I reach forward and take her hands, hoping that the gesture will calm her. I open my mouth to speak, but no words come out. I know what I have to say—what I have to tell her—but if I do, I may lose her forever . . .

And even for a time traveler, that's a long, long while.

My despair must be written on my face, because Eileen drops my hands and takes a wary step backwards. "What is it?"

I open my mouth again. Still, nothing.

"Peter . . . What's wrong?"

I try to utter her name but end up choking on it. Clearing my throat, I begin hoarsely. "Eileen. I haven't . . . told you everything."

Distrust flickers in Eileen's eyes. I expect her to back away some more, but she doesn't. Instead, she stands a little taller and crosses her arms, as if she's daring me. Daring me to do something wrong. Daring me to break her heart. Of course, this is the last thing I want to do—but I've been left with no choice. If there really are people looking for me, and I really am in trouble, then the least I can do is tell Eileen the whole truth before things get worse.

"You know just about everything," I croak, my voice barely above a whisper. "Except . . . When my family died, Eileen . . . It destroyed me. I wanted nothing more than to avenge their deaths. I wanted–no, I *needed*–justice. Since no one was keen on helping me find out who killed them, it took me years. I had to fight in a war to win my own freedom, and then I had to continue fighting my own battle to win justice for my family. Eventually, I discovered who killed them."

I take a deep breath. I don't want to utter his name. It feels filthy as it rests on my tongue, like a curse. Swallowing hard, I continue. "It was my old friend–a boy who I'd grown up with, named Matteo Bianchi. He was the one who I told you about. The one who joined the National Fascist Party. He tried to convince me to join him, Eileen. When I was eighteen. He tried to tempt me with the idea of travel, on the terms that I began fighting on his side. And to think that I considered it. To think of how many lives I could have taken . . . just like Matteo did . . ."

I take a moment to breathe deeply. I avoid eye contact with Eileen, knowing that the only thing her face will bring me right now is pain, and confusion.

"Once I knew he killed them, I vowed I'd do everything in my power to . . . to make things right again. I knew that I couldn't bring my family back, but–I wanted him to *suffer*, the way I did. The way my family did. And that's when I discovered time travel."

I feel my hands beginning to shake nervously, and I clasp them together in the hopes that they'll stop. "I thought I'd found the answer. With time travel, I could spare my family from death, and I could bring Matteo back to his senses. Well . . . I never got the chance. I was sent forward in time instead of backwards. But I couldn't just let fate intervene. So, I tried to find as much information as I could while I was here. It's taken me a long time, but I finally have a lead–an important one. I have to use it. While he's alive, I'll never have closure. I'll never have the justice that my family deserves."

Without stopping to look at Eileen's face, I continue talking quickly. "Eileen, if we don't take our lives by the reins, nothing happens in our favor. Nothing *right* happens. So, I made my choice."

Instead of outlining what this choice is, exactly, I finally summon enough courage to slowly look Eileen in the eye. Unfortunately, I see just what I expected: disappointment, confusion, and heartbreak, all wrapped up into one. And on top of all this is fear. Fear, because now, she knows that the man she put her trust in has plans to exact revenge on someone else. No, not just revenge . . . murder.

I can feel myself beginning to lose my nerve–so I talk faster and louder, trying to justify my words. "No justice comes about in this world without a little prodding. We can't sit around all our lives and wait for someone else to decide our destinies."

Eileen stares at me for what seems like forever. Then, she replies. "But have you ever stopped to think that maybe, it's not up to us? Maybe there's a purpose for everything?"

I can't help myself; I scoff and shake my head, turning away. However, Eileen rushes towards me and pulls me back.

"Peter, stop. I know that's not what you want to hear. It's not what I would want to hear, either. If I knew that all my life, I could've stopped myself from being hurt . . . Well, it would have made things a whole lot easier. But it's not up to me."

"Eileen," I whisper, words tumbling out of my mouth before I can stop them. "I must avenge them. I don't have any other choice. Not if I'm going to do what's right, for my family. Maybe this isn't the way most people think I should be going about it, but . . . the world is changing. We can't be left behind."

"The world *is* changing–but we don't have to."

Her words are earnest and so full of determination that I'm struck by the deeper meaning behind them. The meaning that she isn't aware of.

"So that's it, then?" she asks suddenly, her voice shaking but louder than mine. "You've told me everything?"

"Yes. Except . . ."

I hesitate for a moment, knowing that once I say this, there's no turning back. But I must. I love Eileen Madison. If I don't ask her to continue being a part of my life, then I'm not sure I have much of a reason to go on living at all.

"If I'm correct, the portal will open very soon, Eileen. In fact . . . I'm not positive, but . . . it could be tonight. I can't stay in this time anymore, and I don't know what time the portal will send me to, but it doesn't matter–so long as you might consider coming with me."

As soon as the words are out of my mouth, I know that it was a mistake to say them after all. I watch Eileen's shoulders tense up, and she moves away, shaking her head. Even from ten feet away, I can see her tears beginning to spill over.

"I can't."

I always knew that she would say that—but for some reason, there was an inkling of hope left inside me. Something that made me believe that she was so in love with me, she would be willing to follow me anywhere. Still—that's where love has always gotten me. That's what happens whenever I care about someone. I always lose them in the end.

So, I don't beg her to stay. I don't grasp at straws for the right words. Instead, in a hoarse voice laced with resignation and regret, I whisper, "I know."

"Peter," she breathes, staring at me through her tears, "you are . . . so different . . . from anyone I've met before. And you don't know how hard this is for me. But I'm logical, Peter. I can't just give up my whole life to run off with you. There's my family . . ."

At this declaration, she falters a bit—but only for a moment. "My life might be difficult sometimes, but it's *mine*. And I love my family. They've all suffered in different ways, and so have I. My parents were never there for me—not really—so I don't think I ever learned how to be there for them. But I *have* to be, if only for my siblings' sakes. What would Tommy and Julie do if I disappeared? I would only be making their lives worse. I would only be giving them more pain, rather than helping them heal from what they've already been through."

Every word she says makes perfect sense. Still, the more she says, the more my heart feels prone to break.

Suddenly, I see something flash in Eileen's eyes. It's something like hesitation–and for a moment, I wonder if it's enough to keep her here, with me. However, this time, I decide to act before she can ask. I feel as though there is lead in my shoes, weighing me down–but I can't let it stop me from doing what's right. What's right for her.

The next few minutes are a blur as I lead Eileen to the gondola and escort her out of the cavern, dropping her off at the canal nearest to her hotel.

She doesn't seem to be angry this time. Now, she just looks . . . scared. And lost. And it's all because of me.

I refuse to let this be goodbye. I will see Eileen again before I leave. Still, I have a feeling that she needs some time to think. So, I don't say goodbye. I don't say anything at all. Instead, as I stand in my gondola and she stands on dry land, I take her hand and kiss it. So much is unspoken between us, but I can see it all in her green eyes which are so full of confusion and heartache. Most of all . . . they're full of pity.

This, I cannot stand. I release her hand and begin floating away down the watery streets, leaving the girl I love behind.

41
EILEEN

VENICE, ITALY
SUMMER, 1965

Only moments remain in this beautiful, floating city. Of course, all good things must come to an end, and this trip is no different. Besides—concealed within every wonderful thing, there is something fleeting. Just like this city that is so alluring on the outside, there is something crumbling inside.

There was so much beauty in mine and Peter's relationship, but it's gone now, swept away in the waves of time. Swept away in revealed secrets that will keep us parted forever. Secrets that I wish I'd never known.

Every day that I got to know Peter, I felt us drawing nearer together. I felt honesty and communication grow between us in a way that I've never experienced with anyone else before. However, I'm now sure that this was all a facade.

Sitting on my balcony, I watch the water sparkle as the light hits it, and I think back to when Peter and I first met. He came like a knight in shining armor, although less brash and more reserved. After my initial shock, I began to see something in him that was so much deeper than any fairytale hero. He *cared* about me. We had just met, and already, he trusted me enough to divulge his past to me.

Well, people have always told me that I'm a good listener. I'm used to hearing that. What I'm not used to is that courtesy being reciprocated.

Whenever I was with Peter, he did just that. I could tell him anything, and I knew that he wasn't going to run off and share my deepest thoughts with the rest of the world. The love he showed me through his words and actions was like the music that drifts peacefully above the waters of Venice, lulling the city gently to sleep at night. That was what made me hesitate before leaving him. That was what made me wonder what I was going to lose.

I almost turned around. I knew that if I just went back, I could leap into his arms and tell him that I love him. The best part is, I know that he would tell me the same, and truly mean it.

It's too late, though. I made my choice, and I know that it is the right one. I'll be heading back home tomorrow, and I'll most likely never see Peter Chiappetta again for as long as I live. The events of the last few days have left me feeling numb, and I'm not sure I can handle any more surprises.

The sound of the balcony door brings me back to reality, and I twist around in my chair to see Sandy. "Hi," I say, forcing a smile.

"Hey–someone's here for you."

At the sound of these words, I can feel my heart stop for a brief moment. The only person who would come to see me right now is Peter. Although he seemed to accept my decision fairly well, I wouldn't put it past him to come see me one last time before I leave. I don't think I can bring myself to face him again.

"Thanks," I reply, standing up and heading inside with Sandy.

"He's downstairs."

We've taken barely ten steps down the creaking, old hallway when I stop and turn to face my friend. "Sandy, tell me now. Is it Peter?"

Sandy's eyebrows raise in confusion, and I remind her, surprised that she's forgotten. "The boy I met."

"Oh . . . No, it isn't. Are you expecting him?"

I feel my body relax, and I shake my head. "No. I don't think so."

Sandy stares at me for a moment, her blue eyes obviously searching for more information–but I can't bring myself to tell her anything right now, even if she is my best friend. This experience has gone beyond words. To try and explain it all to Sandy could be disastrous. She might think I was crazy, or hallucinating. I've been called many names by judgmental classmates before, but crazy has never been one of them.

Once we reach the bottom of the staircase, I immediately begin scanning the lobby for any sign of Peter–but he's nowhere to be seen. "Sandy," I begin, looking back at my friend, "there's no one–"

"Eileen May!"

I whirl back around and stare wide-eyed at the one person who calls me by my first and middle name: my father.

He's just stood up from a high-backed armchair, which had hidden him from view until now. Wearing a suit and a genuine smile, he looks so at home here, and his dark features seem accentuated.

"Dad?" I ask incredulously, too shocked to say anything else.

"Told you it wasn't Peter," says Sandy, just quiet enough so that my father doesn't seem to hear.

"Are you going to stand up there all day, or come say hello?" laughs my dad.

Still in shock, I make my way numbly down the remaining steps and give my dad a hug, hoping that my smile isn't wavering. When I step back, he's still there—smiling in an almost clueless way.

"Dad," I start, trying to act casually but feeling as though Peter will come bursting through the hotel door at any moment, "why are you here?"

An almost dumbfounded expression appears on my father's face. "Eileen . . . Do you realize what day it is?"

"Wednesday. Why?"

"No, not that . . . It's your last day in Venice before leaving tomorrow."

"And?"

My father looks less confused and more frustrated at this point. "Eileen, you didn't contact us once throughout the trip. Not a single time. No letters, no calls . . . We were afraid something had happened."

I shake my head in bewilderment and watch as Sandy moves away behind a nearby green, leafy potted plant to let us talk in private. "I . . . I suppose I've just been busy. I'm really sorry, Dad. I don't know what happened–there's just been all these activities, and they've kept us so . . . so . . . ."

"Busy."

My mouth feels dry. I nod slowly. "Yeah."

My dad rubs his hand over his face–and I realize that my lack of communication was not the only reason for my father flying across the ocean to see me. "Dad. What's wrong." It isn't a question.

The look in my dad's eyes seems to reflect every thought running through my mind. "The war . . . it's getting worse."

"In Vietnam?"

My father nods. "There are rumors. People are saying that President Johnson will be sending more troops soon. Your mother and I . . . we were worried . . . ."

My dad pauses, and I find myself filling in the blanks in my own mind. My parents lived through a world war, and their parents lived in another before that. Life is uncertain; unexpected. So, how is anyone supposed to know that the war in Vietnam won't catch like wildfire? How could my parents, or any of my classmates' parents, for that matter, know that their children would be safe in another part of the world?

I look my dad straight in the eyes–and all I see in them is fear. Fear mixed with relief. Suddenly, I feel very foolish. "I'm sorry, Dad," I say, my voice full of remorse. "I didn't know."

My dad steps forward and wraps me in another hug. "I know you didn't," he says, his voice soft and soothing. "I'm sorry if my worry seems . . . overdramatic. I just don't know what I would do if . . . if something happened."

"I understand."

"I know it's unexpected," continues my dad quietly, releasing me, "and you probably want to spend the rest of the trip with your friends. Don't worry about me. I haven't been here in over twenty years, and I'd like to look around."

"Okay."

I watch my father's chest heave slightly, as though he's letting out a long breath, and he smiles at me. "Alright. Well, I'll be staying here for the night, and we'll leave tomorrow. Nothing in your plans has to change."

Nodding, I give my dad one more smile before he heads upstairs. I wait until he's disappeared, up the stairs and past the twinkling chandelier; then, I rush over to Sandy, who's still hovering behind the plant. She's busying herself with brushing off her pink skirt when I walk over. When her eyes land on me, she gives me a look of anticipation.

"What's going on, Eileen?"

I shrug and try to act casual. I'm at a loss for words. "I, uh . . . don't really know."

"But . . . Why is your dad here?"

The two of us walk together through the lobby and out the front door, and I breathe in deeply, letting the smell of water and sunshine pour into my nose and lungs. "He says the war's gotten worse, and my family was worried about me. I don't know how it happened, but . . . somehow, I forgot to contact them throughout the trip. I said I would, and I didn't."

"That's not hard to figure out," comments Sandy. "You've been a little distracted with Peter."

I feel my heart sink to my shoes at the mention of his name. Now, I'm wishing that I hadn't spent so much time with him. I should have known it would all end in disappointment. Worst of all, I neglected my friends.

"Have you minded?" I ask quietly, my tone ashamed.

"Of course not!" exclaims Sandy, her eyes wide. "Whatever's happening with you and him . . . it's special. Something everyone wants to experience someday. Just because it's happening here and now doesn't mean that you should forget about it."

I give her a short nod and a half-smile. Odd that 'forgetting' is next on my mental to-do list. "Um . . . We're all going out to dinner soon, aren't we?" I ask, changing the subject and trying not to think about the cruel twist of fate that's come to haunt me.

"I think Mr. and Mrs. Nelson are already at the restaurant. Do you want to head there right now?"

I nod and force a smile, and the two of us continue walking. All the way to the restaurant, I find myself looking over my shoulder, wondering if Peter will appear–but he never does.

Inside the restaurant, I try to soak in the clinking of silverware and the pools of light that the candles cast over the white tablecloths. I try to enjoy my food; I laugh when one of my friends makes a funny comment, and I nod intently when they talk about other things. I try to act normally, as though my heart hasn't been broken. But it's no use pretending.

I finally let someone in, after years of living in constant fear of disappointment. For the first time in a long time, I felt that another human being was able to break through to my soul. Someone loved me for me, without expecting anything in return. Peter was that someone. I loved everything about him. From the moment I met him, I found that he was a gentle, caring, no-strings-attached person. But that was just an illusion; a fantasy. To know what he's been planning all this time, and the secrets he's been carrying . . . It's too much for me to bear.

I watch as my friends and classmates eat and talk cheerfully with one another. It's strange to think that just hours ago, I didn't want to leave this city, because Peter was here. Now, all I want is to go home and move on with my life.

42
PETER

VENICE, ITALY
SUMMER, 1965

"Excuse me," I say in Italian, my voice quiet and almost reverent as I stand in the darkening hotel lobby. "Can you tell *Signorina* Eileen Madison that Peter Chiappetta is here to see her?"

The large, dark-haired man at the counter opens a thick, leather-bound book and glances over it briefly. Then, he looks back up and says, "*Mi dispiace*, but I believe she is out for the night."

I feel my heart sink in disappointment, but I simply nod. "Thank you anyways. Will you let her know that I came by?"

"Well, yes, sir–but she'll be leaving tomorrow."

A strange, sickening feeling comes over me as these words slowly sink in. "Yes . . . I remember. At what time?"

"Around eight in the morning. Her entire party is checking out then. If you're looking to talk with her one last time, I'd suggest finding her sooner rather than later. I assume she's having dinner now, although I don't know where."

Frustrated rather than gratified by this man's advice, I nod again and rush out of the hotel. I knew that Eileen wouldn't stay forever, but it never really hit me that she'd be leaving so soon. I thought that perhaps I might be able to reassure her of my love. And even if she didn't want it, or refused it . . . well, at least she could be sure that I meant it. Now, though, I don't know how I'm going to find her in time.

Walking through the quickly-darkening city streets, I feel the cobblestones under my shoes and the warm summer breeze against my face–and for a brief moment, I'm transported back to my childhood. Back to 1938. Back when all may not have been right in the world, but it was with me. Because, even though the world was falling apart, I didn't have to. I had people who loved me.

Convinced that Eileen is having dinner at this moment, I decide to take a shortcut through St. Mark's Square and check those restaurants first. My pace speeds up a bit as I near the square, and by the time I get there, the sun has disappeared almost entirely. Only a few strands of golden sunlight remain, slipping quickly into the swirling, purple darkness and making way for a few twinkling stars.

Stepping into the middle of the square, I spot a nearby restaurant and resolve to check it for Eileen. However, just as I'm about to walk over, a chilling feeling comes over me, and I shiver. There's something wrong here. Something . . . *familiar*.

I turn around in a circle, scanning my surroundings for whatever is making me feel uneasy. There's barely anyone in the square tonight, and although that would usually comfort me, it makes me feel uncertain and nervous.

Worried, I retreat back into the shadows and out of sight, not wanting to be in the middle of the square anymore. I begin walking towards the basilica–and that's when I see him.

Dark hair, olive skin, and a muscular jawline. Those are three things that haven't changed–but even without them, I would still recognize him.

My first reaction is denial, and I stand rooted to the spot for a moment, trying to figure out whether I'm dreaming. One look around St. Mark's Square tells me that I'm not. I am most definitely awake–but I still can't quite believe that this is happening. My entire being has always expected my encounter with Matteo Bianchi to take place after a mad chase around the world, traveling and searching for years. To be faced with him right now, of all places . . . It's the last thing I would expect. And I don't feel prepared for it in the slightest.

I continue staring at him from afar, unable to recover from my shock. Even though he seems a shadow of his former self, I recognize him beyond his hunched, nervous exterior. He can't hide from me any longer. Not when I lost my old life trying to take his.

Just like that, I feel myself come alive. I turn on my heels and run like the wind. A thousand thoughts are flying through my mind at once, but I don't take heed to any of them–not even how to reach the cavern. My feet know where to go. They've always been able to take me home without me having to think.

I jump into my gondola and make my way into the cavern, clambering onto dry land before the boat has even stopped moving. That's where I retrieve the weapon. Lying down on my stomach with the cool stone ground beneath me, I reach under my bed, feeling around for my gun.

Dust has gathered and settled over the smooth gun, which has been waiting for me for almost a year–but no 'mental' dust has gathered on my original goal. Even with the many setbacks I've faced in this past year, I've never strayed far from keeping the promise I made to myself. The promise to avenge my family.

As soon as I've taken the gun up in my hands, I feel something change inside me. The warmth and light that has recently been rekindled within me has been immediately snuffed out. I have, and always have had, other business to attend to. Important matters. Matters like avenging my family, and finally getting justice for them.

With this new, darker mindset, I head back to the square, where all is quiet, peaceful, and cloaked in the moonless cover of night.

Quickly, as I approach the shadow that was once my friend, I glance around to make sure that we're alone. My palms begin sweating, and I wipe them quickly on the knees of my pants. *This is it. This will be for you, Papa. For you, Mama. For my sisters. For anyone who has ever suffered at the hands of someone who did not know their worth.*

"Matteo!"

My cry isn't loud at all, yet it pierces the silence and causes the man to freeze in his tracks. Slowly, he turns around–and I finally get a chance to see his face fully. His eyes are haunting . . . but the strangest thing about them is that there is a quality in them that I recognize. A quality I've seen in my own eyes. There's a deep hurt within them that I can only find in those who lived through the war. People like us. Except, he and I are not similar at all. He killed everyone I loved, while I had no idea that my old friend was betraying me.

On Matteo's face, I see confusion, and then shock—but most of all, fear. He's afraid of me. *Me.*

He was the man who killed.

He was the man who destroyed lives.

I always feared him, and it was never the other way around. Now, though . . .

We stand about ten feet away from each other, simply staring. I've finally reached this moment, and I don't quite know what to say. I never did know what to say around Matteo as we got older. When we were kids, I was the one who was certain, and sure of myself. I was the one with freedom, who could do whatever he wanted. But then, we grew up—and we both changed.

"Matteo," I say again, determined to be in control.

His eyes widen to the point where I wonder if they'll pop out of his head. He takes half a step towards me, the sound echoing eerily, and I feel my heart begin pounding in anticipation. My gun is hidden in my jacket. All he has to do is come a little closer, and it will all be over. Finally, I'll have done what I should have two—or twenty—years ago.

"P-Peter?" he stammers.

At the sound of his voice, I flinch in surprise. It's entirely different now, and practically unrecognizable. His Italian accent is still present, but he sounds more American than anything.

Recovering quickly, I answer, "Yes."

"Are–" his voice trembles, "are you a ghost?"

"No."

"But," whispers Matteo, his voice cracking, "you . . . you died."

I stare darkly at my old friend. "According to who?"

"To . . . to everyone. They said you disappeared in 1945, leaving everything behind–including the bookshop."

"That's true," I say, my voice strangely unfamiliar in my ears. "But as you can see, I didn't die."

"No . . . you didn't," murmurs Matteo, rubbing his wrinkled forehead. "And . . . you look the same. It's . . . It's as if you haven't aged at all."

"Perhaps I haven't," I reply, tiring of this back-and-forth. It's time for me to end this, once and for all. "Matteo–I've been looking for you for a long time, and I'd just like to know a few things."

I stop for a moment, allowing the two of us to stand in chilling silence. The summer air that was so hot mere hours ago now hangs around us like an icy curtain, separating us from the rest of the world. Matteo appears to be uncomfortable, but he nods slightly in agreement.

"What I want to know," I whisper, feeling my fists clench and unclench, "is why you killed my family. And I want to know what you were thinking when you, their old friend, betrayed them."

Matteo's face freezes, and for a split second, I can see all the ghosts of the past hovering near us. They want me to do this. They *need* me to do this. I can hear their voices–their screams. Their pain. And just like that, I'm eighteen again, sitting inside the bookshop, reeling from that telegram. Dying inside from the news that I had lost everyone I loved.

Slowly, I retrieve my gun from inside my jacket.

"Peter," begins Matteo, his voice shaking, "it was the *worst*, most unforgivable thing I have ever done and will ever do in my life. I want you to know that I suffered for it. I swear to you, I still do! Not a day has gone by that I haven't lived in total agony as I think back to those days."

"You?" I cry, my voice growing louder. As I speak, I feel myself mentally traveling even further backwards in time, and I feel just like a boy again. The fragile casing over my heart begins to crack as I feel all the agony of those years come rushing back, just as if time had never passed. "*You* have lived in agony? What about me, Matteo? What about the person whose life you utterly destroyed?"

"I wanted to find you, Peter," whispers Matteo, rubbing his hands together nervously. "I wanted to repent for my unforgivable sins. I knew it might not do any good, but I wanted you to know how I felt. Then, I thought you had died and . . ."

"So you left? You ran away?" I seethe, all the hurt and anger I've ever felt seeping into my tone.

"I moved to America. I needed help. That's where I restarted my life."

"Oh, I see," I exclaim, my voice laced with mockery. "So, you thought you could just leave everyone else to clean up the messes that you made. You thought you could escape all this. You thought you could forget who you were–who you *are*."

"No one can do that, Peter. I didn't understand at the time, but I was young and foolish. I regretted fighting for the other side, and I always will. What I did to your family . . . It was the last thing I ever did in the war. Even then, I wasn't the only one who aided in their deaths–but I may as well have been. I should have stopped them . . . But I wasn't brave enough. I didn't know how to refuse. I made so many mistakes . . . Many of which I've tried to atone for these past twenty years."

"How could you atone for the deaths of innocent people?" I whisper, gritting my teeth.

"I wanted to try, Peter," replies Matteo. His worn face is so full of remorse–but I know that it's all a lie. None of his pathetic excuses will keep me from doing what I must.

I'm so angry, I'm shaking. I can hardly think straight. But I once again repeat the most important question of all.

"Matteo . . . Just tell me why you did it?"

For a moment, I can see a sort of battle being waged in Matteo's eyes, as if he isn't quite sure how much to reveal to me. However, when his eyes land on my gun once more, it seems that he's made his decision.

"Peter," he says, lowering his voice so that I can barely hear him, "there is so much you don't know."

I feel my mouth go dry at these words. This isn't what I was expecting to hear. "What don't I know?"

Matteo's dark eyes dart back and forth. "When I was sixteen, my parents gave me a mission. It's true that they wanted me to be a soldier, and to follow in my father's footsteps . . . but it was so much more than that."

I stare blankly at Matteo as he continues. "My parents wanted something. Something they could only get through pain and devastation–and stealing from someone else. At first, I didn't see a future like that for myself . . . But I cared about my parents, Peter. I wanted to make them proud. So I agreed. And that was when they told me that the person who I would be stealing from was you."

My heart rate seems to speed up dramatically as these words sink in. If I'm right, Matteo is telling me that he had an alternative reason for killing my family all those years ago. If I'm right, then this is much more personal than I thought.

"I know, Peter." Each word is like a punch to the stomach. "I know your secrets. In fact, I probably have more of them that you aren't even aware of. But . . . I'm not that person anymore. I couldn't carry out my parents' wishes. I failed. And now, I must live knowing how much pain I caused you. For that, I am truly sorry."

I've heard enough. Now, all of my suspicions from the past many years have been confirmed. Matteo Bianchi is weak–but he is also a murderer.

"Perhaps, in another case, you would be forgiven," I say suddenly, finally revealing my gun and cocking it. "Not with me."

Even as I say these words, and I go to raise my gun higher, a strange thing happens. A sudden movement causes my eyes to shift away from Matteo, and to land on–

Eileen.

She's standing not far from Matteo, partly hidden behind a nearby column. Our eyes lock, and a thousand thoughts hit me at once.

First, I feel ice coursing through my veins as I realize that the girl I love is about to watch me murder someone in cold blood. Then, I see the past week flash before my eyes as I come to terms with the fact that, with this act, I will most definitely lose her.

Finally, as the two of us stare at one another, and I look from her to Matteo, an indescribable sense of dread fills me as I suddenly understand. An ache begins to form in my stomach, and I feel my legs begin to give out underneath me. This is the last thing I could have expected–and yet, even though neither of them have admitted it, I know the truth.

Eileen Madison is not who I thought she was–and neither is Matteo Bianchi.

Turning back to Matteo, I fight hard against the nausea that's quickly taking over and resolve to finish what I started.

Matteo's face goes white, and I'm just about to pull the trigger when a voice draws me out of my feverish stupor.

"PETER!"

Eileen comes running from behind the column and stands beside Matteo, her face just as pale as his. "What are you doing?" she shrieks.

Still unable to entirely comprehend the scene playing out before me, I watch dumbfounded as Eileen rushes to step in front of Matteo.

"Please, Peter," she begs, her voice full of utter horror. "Don't do this."

I feel my outstretched gun beginning to shake, and I steady it with my other hand. "Eileen, you don't understand," I say, my voice icier than the water in the canals.

"Yes, I do," she cries in a way that makes me truly believe her. She takes a few steps towards me, and Matteo yells her name, but she doesn't stop.

"Eileen, I have to do this," I whisper as she comes closer. "This is what I've been waiting for. Finally, my family will be proud of me for doing what's right."

"Peter, he's my father."

The words hit me like a ton of bricks, and I feel my grip on the gun beginning to falter. Her father . . . Some part of me already knew . . . but I so deeply wanted to believe otherwise that I wasn't able to accept it until now. Until the words came straight out of Eileen's mouth.

Even as reality begins to sink in, I shake my head furiously. "Your . . . no. *No.*"

"Yes, Peter," says Eileen. She's standing directly in front of me now, so close that I can look through her green eyes and into her soul. There's something inside her, and something inside me as well, whispering, *You don't have to do this.* That voice has always been there, but I could never bring myself to listen to it. Not until now.

"Eileen . . . My family . . ." I croak, trying to get her to understand the gravity of the situation.

"I know," she whispers, her tone gentle. Within those two words, I can sense every emotion that Eileen is currently feeling. There's pity, sadness, fear, guilt–and love. "But, Peter . . . in your mind, that event is fresh. For my dad, it's been twenty years–and it's haunted him every day of his life. Surely, you can see that."

As the two of us stare into one another's eyes, an unspoken conversation seems to take place between us. Eileen knows my heart, and she knows what's right. My love for her is greater than the hate I have for Matteo, despite me coming so close to ending his life.

I didn't think Matteo and I were similar at all, and I never wanted to be like him. By killing him, I would become just like him. I would let my hate win over my love. I can't do that to Eileen . . . and most of all, I can't do that to myself.

I can hear my heart thumping in my ears, and as I try to decide what to do, the world seems to begin moving in slow motion. It's as if I'm on the outside, looking in, and all I can do is watch as the one goal that I've had for all these years goes slipping right between my fingers. No matter how great a loss this is, though, I'm confident in my choice–because I'm confident in my love for Eileen. For as long as I've known her, she's brought out the best in me. She's the most important person to me in the world, and she is a thousand times more important than any ill-fated plan of revenge. Now, as I look into Eileen's green eyes which are so full of love, I know that I'm doing the right thing.

Feeling as if I'm in a dream, I slowly lower my arms and let my gun fall to the cobblestones. The sound of it hitting the ground is deafening to me.

As soon as I've done this, Matteo steps forward, his eyes fixed on me. "Eileen, come here."

Eileen obeys and rushes over to her father, letting him wrap his arms around her and hide her from me. From the man who was about to ruin the lives of an entire family.

"I'm . . ." I whisper, my mouth dry. "I'm . . ."

"Peter Chiappetta!"

At the sound of my name, I whirl around and find myself face-to-face with two people. There's one man and one woman, both well-dressed. However, it's not their appearance I care about. It's what they're holding.

Both have guns in their hands, both aimed at me. Immediately, I realize that these are the people who Eileen described. The ones who were looking for me.

"Peter Chiappetta," begins the man, reaching into his jacket for a pair of handcuffs, "you are under arrest for the fatal misuse of time."

On instinct, I take a few steps backwards and practically run into the brick wall behind me. I put my hands up in the air. "*Signore*, I don't know what you're talking–"

"Your misuse of time travel has left the citizens of this city in jeopardy. By interacting with others and trying to change the natural course of time, you alone have been the cause of Venice's rapid descent into the water."

I stare at the two people for half a second, dumbfounded. I knew it. In my case, it seems that most gifts come with curses–and when it comes to the gift of time travel, I should have known it wouldn't have been that easy.

Slowly, I begin backing away. Then, in a flash, I turn and bolt.

"Peter!" yells Eileen.

I keep running, faster than my legs have ever carried me before. I've already turned around the corner when I realize that I'm not alone. I throw a glance over my shoulder and realize that, instead of being chased by the man and the woman, I'm being followed by Eileen.

Shocked, I wait a moment and let her catch up to me. Then, holding hands, we make our way to where my gondola is waiting and jump in.

43
EILEEN

VENICE, ITALY
SUMMER, 1965

"Oh," breathes Peter as he leaps out of the gondola. Confused, I watch as he runs over to the other side of the cavern and motions to something that's never been there before: an archway with a swirling, sparkling portal.

"It's happening, Eileen," he says, his tone a mix of excitement and fear. "Tonight."

I stare at the portal for a moment, numb. Then, I finally do what I thought I would a long time ago: I break.

"I can't do this," I sob. I feel my legs give out from under me, and I fall against the cool stone wall, letting my head drop into my hands. I'm shaking. I can't stop shaking.

I feel a strong hand grab my arm and pull me to my feet. Its touch both comforts and frightens me, and I let out another sob.

"Stop, stop, stop," whispers Peter lovingly, the word echoing over and over again in my mind. As I draw in deep, shaky breaths, he rubs my arms with his hands–a surprisingly soothing gesture for someone who seems just as distressed as I am.

He doesn't release his grip on me until my breathing has slowed. Then, he lets go of my arms and staggers backwards.

His forehead is covered in sweat, and his eyes–those blue eyes that I fell in love with–are haunted. In a panic, he turns towards the wall and throws his hand against it in a move of utter confusion and despair.

He stands there for a moment, breathing hard. I stay where I am, rooted to the spot. I can't move. I don't know whether I should run away from him or run towards him.

As if he can read my thoughts, Peter turns around and wipes his arm against his forehead. His white sleeves are rolled to the elbow, and suspenders are attached to pants which are rolled up just enough to reveal his long, dark brown socks. Everything about him suggests that he is from another time. How could I not have known? How could I have doubted him for so long? If only I'd believed him, then maybe none of this would have happened. Maybe I could have stopped it.

I try to steady my breathing and wipe my sweaty palms onto my dress. I've never seen him like this before, and I wish I never had. He looks tortured inside, and his lips are moving slightly, as if he's trying desperately to come up with some master plan to get out of this horrible situation.

Abruptly, the expression on his face changes. It's as if a lightbulb has gone off in his mind. He turns and rushes to the bedside table, which he begins filing through madly. I watch as papers and books go flying, each hitting the ground with an echoing *thud*.

"Peter," I say in a voice barely above a whisper.

He doesn't hear me, so I say it again, a little louder. "Peter."

He turns around wildly. "Yes?"

"What are you doing?"

Peter shakes his head quickly, his untamed dark hair falling over his manic, guilty eyes. "I . . ."

"You can't just leave!" I exclaim, darting forward. "They'll find you. They'll come after you. They'll never stop looking, and you know–"

"I'm not just *leaving*, Eileen," whispers Peter. There's a look in his eyes that I can't comprehend–a look I don't understand. That is, until his gaze shifts to the other side of the room, where the circular archway awaits.

The portal. The archway has sat there for so long–but never once did I actually believe that it could transport Peter to another time. Now that I know the truth, though, it means that Peter truly can leave–and the idea scares me more than anything.

"Peter, no."

Peter rises to his feet and walks over to me. For some reason, I take a step backwards, causing him to flinch. Ashamed of myself, I glance down and begin playing with my hands.

"Eileen, you're afraid of me. I've broken your trust. Your love is the most precious thing to me in the world, but I can't have it if I know that you don't love me back."

"But I–"

Peter shakes his head. Then, hesitantly, he holds out his hand. Determined to prove that I'm not afraid, I take it immediately and stare at our two hands, intertwined–just like our hearts.

"I'm lost without you." His words come in a broken whisper, and I look up to see a single tear rolling down Peter's face. "I've known it since the first time we met." He reaches forward and twirls a loose strand of my wet, brown hair around his finger. Then, he releases it and lets his hand rest on my cheek. "But I can't hurt you. And if not hurting you means that I can't have you, then . . . so be it."

"No," I whisper. I'm sobbing again. "I don't care whether you've made mistakes. You're a good man. Anything you've ever done, or were going to do, you've repented for–I know that." I take a deep breath, trying to collect myself, and continue. "You're the brightest spot in my life. I've always needed you, even when I didn't know it. And I still need you."

Desperately, I find myself babbling, hoping my words will convince him of my love. "Peter . . . You changed me. No, no . . . It's not how you changed me. It's how you changed the way I see myself. I'm lost without you, too, Peter. So–let me go with you."

Peter slowly shakes his head and gives me a sad smile. He looks . . . *defeated*. His eyes are brimming with tears, and his wet, dark hair is matted against his forehead. For one last time, I can see the man that I fell in love with–and the shadow of the boy he used to be. The boy I never got to know.

Then, he presses his forehead against mine. "I love you, *il mio unico*. Never forget me." He takes a deep breath, and then he kisses me.

It's a painful kiss. It hurts because it's so final. It hurts because I know it's the last time I'll ever feel his touch–the touch of the other half of my soul.

The moment we break away, he runs. He grabs his suitcase and heads directly for the circular archway. There, he stands in front of the portal: silver, swirling, and ready to take away my heart.

He's just about to step inside when my voice breaks the silence. It's strained and panicked. "Where will you go?"

Peter sighs and turns to face me. "There's nothing for me in the past, now that I know that I can't change it. So, I'll go forward–or, at least, I'll try."

"The future?" I ask, furrowing my brow. "But, if you have the chance to save your family–"

"Eileen, I can't." His tone is urgent, and his sapphire-blue eyes are fixed on my green. "If I were to change the past, it would change the present–I mean, *this* present. Anything I did could alter the life of Matteo–I mean–your father. And if his life were changed . . . then I could change your life, too."

My heart drops to my shoes as I realize what Peter is saying. If he were to go back in time, saving his family could mean erasing my existence. It could mean a trade between his family . . . and me.

I shake my head firmly, reaching out and taking his hands in mine. "I refuse to be the person standing between you and your happiness."

"Eileen . . . *You* are my happiness. Without time travel, I would just be a regular person who had to move on with his life after tragedy, like everyone else did after the war. And life gave you to me. I can't go back to what was. And I can't lose you."

I hate myself for being an obstacle to Peter's happiness, and I love him at the same time for refusing to sacrifice me for his gain. I feel a thousand emotions at once . . . and I know I'm not thinking straight enough to make sense of them all. So, I take a deep breath and try to ask the next logical question.

"How far will you go?"

"I don't know. I'm not sure if that's something I can control. But I swear, I'll find you. I swear I won't stop looking until we're together again. And I don't know how long that will be for you—but we *will* see each other again."

The look in Peter's eyes betrays him. It's a look of hopelessness—and a look that tells me his only wish is to rush towards me and embrace me, just one more time. But instead, he simply gazes at me through his watery eyes and whispers, "I'll see you soon." And with that, he's gone.

I don't know how long I cry after Peter leaves. All I know is, I never want to leave here. I want to stay here forever, curled up in a ball in a cool, wet corner of this enchanting, horrible room. That's all I have left. It's the only place I can ever feel like Peter is still with me.

I'm still aware of the place on my cheek where his hand touched for the last time, and I reach up to feel it, tracing the paths that my tears have made on my face.

As if in a dream, I stand up slowly, leaning against the wall for support. I walk to the other side of the room and sit down on Peter's bed, rubbing my hand over the covers. And that's when I notice it: the pink flower that I gave Peter, that night that we met on my balcony. He kept it all this time, sitting on top of his pillow.

"I'll see you soon," I whisper, picking the flower up gingerly and pressing it against my lips. "I'll see you soon."

EPILOGUE
EILEEN

CHICAGO, ILLINOIS
SPRING, 1967

Time is a mystery. It's unpredictable. It has a way of blurring some memories, but it can't always remove the pain they leave behind.

In some ways, many things are the same. The war in Vietnam is still raging. The Beatles are as much of a hit as ever. The world keeps on moving, and the sun keeps on rising and setting. And yet . . . It's strange how much can change in just a couple of years.

I'm twenty now, nearing the end of my sophomore year of college. These past two years have been an odd mix of excitement and confusion. Excitement, because I am doing what I've always wanted: I'm training to become a journalist. Confusion, because no matter how much I've gone through in the past couple years, I've never gotten used to change. But that's alright. It's alright, because I'm learning how to cope. The one thing I regret is the fact that I've had to do it on my own.

Once Peter left, the people who were trying to capture him disappeared–along with my dad's memory. Something made him forget everything that had happened with Peter on that fateful night. After I discovered this, I never mentioned it– and yet, somehow, he still seemed different when we returned home. He seemed . . . *whole*. That was when I realized that, although I had been wrong not to call home during my trip, my father coming to Venice was truly the best thing that could have happened for him.

While no one had been able to anticipate the unusual events that would take place when my dad arrived in Venice, it seems that everything worked out in the end. For the first time, it was like he could change, and heal. With this healing came peace for the rest of my family, as well. My childhood was full of whispers and secret glances, and talks with my mother about my father's past. "We won't talk about it," she told me when I was just eight years old. "Talking about it will make him sad."

I don't know if she ever found out the truth of my dad's past. Maybe she never will–but she knows how to love him, anyway. Amidst all his pain, she was able to show him that, even though there is darkness inside all of us, there is also the potential of light. In our lives, we are all faced with a choice: Do we accept the way things are, or do we allow that light to defeat the darkness? That was how my father was able to change. I think he's still learning, but he is finally finding peace in the knowledge that he can be forgiven.

What happened in Venice changed me, too. Amidst all the turmoil of the world, I found myself starting college without all the childish worries I used to have–and I know that it was all because of Peter. He gave me confidence, and he helped me see the beauty in every simple thing. Just when I had begun to doubt the existence of love, he proved that it was real. Our love was a unique thing. It was not merely a fleeting passion; it was two halves of one soul wondering why it had taken so long for them to become whole.

Since then, I haven't expected love to come back into my life the way it did before–but I haven't stopped hoping that maybe, one day, Peter will find me again. Peter, with his wonderful old soul and tremendous love. Peter, who is somewhere out there in time and space, looking for me.

Until that happens, I've kept busy with school, and the changes that life has brought. It's true that I look a little different on the outside; I'm two years older, and I've grown out my hair like most of my friends. The biggest changes, though, have taken place within.

I'm walking through the courtyard of my college now. Spring is in the air, the scent of freshly-cut grass and fragrant flowers traveling on the wind. Everything is blossoming, showing the usual signs of rebirth. I breathe in deeply and turn in a slow circle, my brown hair flying behind me as I take in my surroundings.

It hasn't been easy without Peter. I miss him every day. Sometimes, I try to convince myself that I'll be okay without him. After all, I don't want to lose him again. I don't want to get hurt. But, what's life without a little risk? What's life without loving someone?

Slowly, I resume walking through the courtyard, knowing that I'll be late for class. Still, something keeps me outside. Something is calling to me from another place–and another time.

I let my imagination run wild as a scene takes place before me. In my mind, I'm sitting beneath a nearby magnolia tree when Peter appears. He's dressed the same as always, sticking out like a sore thumb in this year and place, but belonging at the same time. His blue eyes are full of more love and peace than I've ever seen them before, and that's how I know that he's here for me. The best version of himself–the adventurous, carefree version that I've been able to picture from the stories of his childhood–is here. The other half of my soul is here. I will never be alone again.

Without any more hesitation, I leap into his arms, holding him tighter than I ever have before and wondering if he's real. As we stand there in total bliss, the spring breeze picks up stray magnolia petals and lets them swirl around us, creating a beautiful picture. It's perfect. And it's not mine.

With a pang in my heart, I turn and begin walking again, the illusion melting away. However, as I walk, I realize something. Peter may not be here, and maybe he never will–but it's like he told me that summer. Even when a person is gone, your memories of them never leave you, and neither do the things they did for you. That couldn't be more true with me. Although Peter isn't here, I will never be the same person because of him. Even with all the pain that a person may go through in their lives, there is always a way to deal with that pain, and to move past it. All you have to do is find the people who truly matter, and find your way *with* them, rather than alone.

As these thoughts run through my mind, I realize that finally, I've found what I've been looking for since I was a little girl. I've learned how to move past the change and hardship in my life and turn it into something . . . *beautiful.* Something *bellissimo.*

ACKNOWLEDGMENTS

The story which you have just read could never have been completed without the help and support of many incredible people. Although they are not always front and center, their work behind-the-scenes is what has made this dream of mine come true. I would be amiss without thanking each of them— so here it goes!

To Mom and Dad: I still remember those days when I was younger, and you would read my favorite stories out-loud to me. It is not lost on me how much you two have influenced my love for reading and writing. Furthermore, you have gone above and beyond to support me in everything I do! You two are the best editors and cheerleaders a person could ask for, and I love you so much.

To my sister, Ivy: I truly believe storytelling is what you and I do best, and the greatest part is that we've done it together. Thank you for being with me every step of the way and for always being my first reader. I love you forever!

To my family: You all mean more to me than you may ever know. I cherish every word of encouragement and advice. I love you so much and am so grateful for you!

To all of my beta readers/friends (Shirley Freeman, Caitlin Harstead, Mary Henderson, Ivy Henkle, Elena Perigo, Annie Stoner, and Maren Wingard): Dedicating quite a bit of your summer last year to help me polish up this book means so much to me. Peter and Eileen's story would not be where it is today without the essential feedback you gave me each week. Thank you so much for your love and encouragement!

To my friends not already mentioned: You all are the best! Thank you for being there for me and cheering me on throughout this process. I don't know what I would do without amazing friends like you!

To my street team: Thank you so much for taking the time to make this book launch memorable! I have no idea how it might've gone without your support and hours spent advertising *Everywhere I've Never Been*. You are all incredible!

To you, dear reader: Thank you for taking a chance on my story. I hope it has blessed you and taken you on an adventure that is just getting started.

Finally, to my Lord and Savior: You have taught me that there is a time and purpose for everything. Thank you for helping me to understand your will and to see your goodness in all things.

ABOUT THE AUTHOR

Daisy Henkle writes stories that shine light in a dark world. Having fallen in love with reading as a young girl, she now enjoys stories set in another time—often with a sprinkle of magic in them. When she's not writing, Daisy might be found listening to her favorite oldies, performing onstage, or spending time with family and friends. Daisy is the author of *Therefore I Have Hope*, a YA coming-of-age novel set in the 1980s. She is passionate about spreading the love of Jesus through her writing. You can visit Daisy online on her website, Instagram, Facebook, or by subscribing to her newsletter.

 www.daisyhenkleauthor.com

 @daisyhenkle

 @daisyhenkleauthor

 Subscribe to my newsletter (https://tinyurl.com/DaisyHenkle)